T0095071

Jaleen

Jaleen

D'Sarah Daniel

authorHOUSE®

AuthorHouse™
1663 Liberty Drive
Bloomington, IN 47403
www.authorhouse.com
Phone: 1-800-839-8640

© 2013 by D'Sarah Daniel. All rights reserved.

No part of this book may be reproduced, stored in a retrieval system, or transmitted by any means without the written permission of the author.

Published by AuthorHouse   03/05/2013

ISBN: 978-1-4817-0535-6 (sc)
ISBN: 978-1-4817-0534-9 (hc)
ISBN: 978-1-4817-0533-2 (e)

Library of Congress Control Number: 2013900393

Any people depicted in stock imagery provided by Thinkstock are models, and such images are being used for illustrative purposes only.
Certain stock imagery © Thinkstock.

This book is printed on acid-free paper.

Because of the dynamic nature of the Internet, any web addresses or links contained in this book may have changed since publication and may no longer be valid. The views expressed in this work are solely those of the author and do not necessarily reflect the views of the publisher, and the publisher hereby disclaims any responsibility for them.

❀ Acknowledgement ❀

Jaleen is dedicated to all the single women who, for one reason or another, are afraid to take a chance on love. Pain is a part of life. Love is also a part of life. Sometimes we have to search long, hard and carefully to find someone special. Don't give up. He's out there and he's hoping you would notice him, too.

To my husband, I love you. You have made living worthwhile. Thanks for everything you've done and continue to do to let me know how much you love and care about me.

To our son and his family, you are the love of our lives and we pray that you and your family enjoy many years of happiness as you travel the road many have walked before you and will traverse after you. Let love be your guide. Let love be your healer. Let love motivate your actions. Communicate with and in love always. When the answers are hard to find or the choices too clouded, look to the Creator. He is always there ready to listen, help, heal, guide and protect you as you move forward. Remember, you can do all things through Christ who strengthens you.

To my mother, you have raised some very strong, independent children. I love you. We love you. Sorry Daddy isn't here to celebrate all of our successes with us. But we have you and we will continue to celebrate together and remember him as we do. We love and miss you, Daddy.

To my in-laws, and other family members, friends, and faithful readers, I love you. Thanks, always, for your continued support and encouragement. ❀❀❀

❀❀ *Chapter One* ❀❀

Jaleen Cole lived alone in a medium sized, three hundred unit condominium complex. She was seldom at home long enough to know who her neighbors were. She was unaware of the new couple that moved in two doors down from Jasmine or that the couple upstairs had retired and was moving to sunny Florida. There was a big Pan Handle Party for the couple and she knew nothing about it. That's because the only thing Jaleen knew and paid attention to was work.

The few neighbors she knew gave up on keeping her up to date on the happenings. If she attended two Floaters for the year, she attended a lot of them. At the Floaters, everyone got a chance to meet the new residents, learn what they did and in turn widened their networks to include them. There were no age restrictions to the condo complex. The only restriction was no children. So the experience level among the residents was vast. Most of them in her building simply knew her as Jaleen in three twelve. They knew she worked and she came home to rest. She was polite, friendly enough and worked long hours. That's it.

Her closest neighbors, Aaron Michael Hammond, in three eleven and Jasmine Lé Anna Murphy in three thirteen simply kept an eye on her apartment to make sure everyone knew it was occupied. They slipped notes under her door informing and sometimes reminding her of upcoming events and hoped she found the time to attend.

Door watching, as Aaron called it, kept him busy. He was not interested in whether or not she brought anyone home with her.

He was more interested in the fact that she came home and that she was okay. Most of the time, her arms were either bundled with groceries or filled with folders and her briefcase signaling work. He had long concluded that she was either working for a powerhouse attorney or she was a paralegal in a small firm that did not want to hire adequate help. When she did come home at a reasonable hour, he heard light sounds of jazz or classical music. So he assumed she was probably working. Conversations were non-existent and she was just a quiet person.

Her lights came on after seven and they didn't turn off until the next morning. That meant she, most likely, fell asleep with them on. His concern had gotten him no where and he had decided to have a talk with her to make sure she was not burning herself out. The holidays, he felt was the right time. But when he approached her door the second day of Christmas to wish her well and share some of his homemade eggnog with her, to his disappointment, she was not home.

Jasmine and Aaron kept an eye on her but neither of them knew where she was or when she would be back. Because her vehicle was in the parking lot, they assumed she took a cab and that meant she was possibly out of town for the holidays. As they marked the time on their calendars, they commented, "We need a life." Watching Jaleen wasn't it. "She doesn't even know we keep an eye on her or her apartment," Aaron commented. Jasmine used the opportunity to rib Aaron a bit. She suspected that he had a crush on Jaleen. But wasn't sure. He often went out with friends and they all shared movies, dinners and other festive gatherings together. He seldom attended alone. But, again, she wasn't sure.

"Are you sure you are watching her apartment or watching her?" Jasmine asked. Feeling trapped, Aaron refused to answer directly. "Well, as her neighbor, what are you watching? Her apartment or her?" he asked coyly. Jasmine had to admit, they were both keeping an eye on her *and* her apartment. It was obvious she had no family in the city. No one visited her. She never introduced them to anyone of significance. In fact, she never introduced them to anyone at all.

Both confided among themselves that she must be an only child until they saw evidence of a sister and two brothers in the form of pictures in her living room, on her glass wall unit and matching end tables. Her living room ensemble was very homey, chic and comfortable. On a few but rare occasions when Jaleen hosted their little get-togethers, they were given a glimpse into her life. Though she never spoke about them too much, it became evident that she and her younger brother were very close. So then their theory shifted to: she's the middle child who enjoys her freedom and independence. Hence, she lives far away from her immediate family and siblings.

Aaron admired her. He secretly wished he could get to know her. She was focused on one thing though: work. So he didn't know how to approach her. She kept her apartment neat and clean. Immaculate was a better description. Whenever they got together they always had a good time. Occasionally Jasmine brought along a girlfriend or two but for the most part, they dined together—the three of them—alone. "An oxymoron if there ever was one," he mused to himself over his own thoughts.

The few times when Aaron got her to dine in with them, he would prepare something new and special which instantly became their favorite. He loved to cook. So invitations to dine were seldom rejected. Around his apartment, there were pictures of his parents, his aunts and an uncle, three sisters and two brothers. Though his dad passed before he moved to the city, he still kept a picture of him on his wall. He was a very strong and energetic person and Aaron admired everything about his father. Deep down, he was a family man. Jasmine kept photos of everyone. She had pictures of the three of them together, pictures of her co-workers as well as members of her family. She even had pictures of the places she had visited on vacations taken from time to time.

Jaleen's walls were decorated with beautifully framed art work. Pictures of some of her favorite places she'd seen and places she would like to visit someday were also on her bookshelf and walls. She had pictures of her grandparents on the wall, too. But that was all. No pictures of her parents were ever seen.

Now, as far as they could tell, she was missing. They had not seen her in almost a week and were beginning to worry. She usually indicated to one or both that she'd be away for a few days. But, again, she didn't always tell them. Aaron said he hadn't heard her phone ringing so obviously her job knows she's not at home, too. They decided to give her one more day to appear. If she didn't, they were going to report her missing. There were no sounds or signs of life in her apartment, day or night; early dawn or late night. So they were certain she was not at home.

Together, Aaron and Jasmine rang in the New Year with the other residents and vowed to work harder on keeping better tabs on Jaleen. Though they doubted she would have joined them. They knew they would have insisted on her not opening

4

❀❀ *Chapter Two* ❀❀

Aaron worked at a landscaping firm. He was not a partner and had no desire to become one. He was an artist who enjoyed decorating new buildings, home sites and parks with plants that had the potential to make people stop and take notice. He loved the colors that plants and shrubs brought to the site. The brightness of the flowers and their ability to sleep during off season amazed him. They had no fashion coordinator or season monitor who told them what to do. They just did it. They showed up on time as the seasons go and left on time.

The company owned a greenhouse and laboratory. It grew all types of flowering plants, shrubs, low lying foliage, tall plants and other attractive greenery. Some trees were stunted so they did not exceed a specified height. That was left to the horticulturalists. Their work produced some amazing results. The cross breeding of some plants yielded flowers and shrubbery that simply added to the beauty of the buildings, homes, parks and other areas they were allowed to decorate, illuminate and thrive in.

Aaron enjoyed working the hospital contract. The topiary garden on that property had been featured in the local gardening and home decorating magazines and on several national broadcasts dealing with the power of healing and nature. Many people had indicated how much better they felt when they were able to sit in the sun room and admire the flower garden the hospital had invested in for the peace and tranquility of its staff and the family members of those who were convalescing as well as those who were terminally ill.

Whether it was true or not, he just loved tending that garden. The plants, flowers and grass made the garden a surreal place to be. The aromas from the flowers were neither too strong nor pungent. They gave the garden a fresh scented fragrance almost like the essence of life itself. Pure. Clean. Fresh.

To him, it was the perfect place for lovers. He wished the city would invest in similar displays downtown and in more residential areas. They gave a sense of hope, life and beauty to anyone who took the time to appreciate them. The aroma was something else, especially in the evenings. He recalled coming by on occasion when he was feeling down and just sitting and enjoying the place. The flood lights hidden behind the undergrowth made the garden feel safe and romantic.

The fact that it was being used to calm the hearts and souls of those who were terminally ill or involved in close calls with death, spoke to the wondrous healing power of plants and their harmonic balance in nature. Their beauty transcended all boundaries between sickness and health, life and death, beauty and tragedy. Yes, Aaron loved his work and especially nurturing this garden.

His second favorite place to maintain is the garden in the commercial complex on Lake Shore Drive. That was twice the size of this one and it was used to house special gatherings for clients and the companies' staff members. Whenever he returned to do the maintenance work, he was always amazed at how much respect was given to the plants in that garden. The benches, canopies and other additions for the functions were in place days in advance and the day following the function, everyone was there to remove their rented property and he would take care of replenishing any damaged shrubs or foliage surrounding the fountains. The dance area was outlined and covered with a temporary wooden floor designed to keep the grass breathing though patrons above were using it for dancing. The platform was raised above the grass and slatted flooring allowed the air to continue to circulate and support the growth of the grass below without crushing the entire length and width the dance platform took up.

Everything was as expected, despite the amount of equipment and people who traversed the grounds during the afterhours function. That, too, was featured along with the hospital's garden and rightly so. They were designed and maintained by the company he worked for and they took great pride in the quality of work that was done; from caring for the plants, to transporting and transplanting them in their new surroundings, to pruning and enriching the soil with special fertilizers that promoted their growth. Care was evident and it was definitely required if the plants were to survive.

As he reflected on the kind of work he did, he was drawn to include Jaleen in his care circle. She was sweet, though cautious. She was very private yet somewhat friendly in her own kind of way. She didn't visit unless invited and you had to catch up with her to get that invitation in place. She greeted whoever was out and about as she went about her own business. She never seemed to pry or appear overly interested in the day to day life of the people in the complex. She just worked.

"It's funny," he thought, "how his mind ran to her whenever he was not thinking about what he was doing." She occupied those secret places in his mind and his heart. He often wondered

9

what it would take to actually go on a date with her. But, she never gave the opening and he never pushed it.

"This year would be different," he pledged. If she shot him down, then so be it. But he wanted to give himself a chance. Maybe she liked the high-powered type. Maybe she was working hard, trying to make an impression on one of them. Well, whoever he was, he wasn't worth it, Aaron concluded. He was sure she was thoughtful, considerate, kind and caring. She obviously cared about what she did to earn a living, even if she allowed it to consume her. Again, his mind was on Jaleen. "This was sick," he thought. "I'm the one who's sick," he chided himself once again as he moved his mind back to the pruning and off of Jaleen.

As he walked and trimmed, pruned and removed browning and fallen leaves and flower petals, he was moved by the number of persons sitting in the garden this second day of the New Year. He hoped they were here simply to enjoy the foliage and the fragrances and not because they were losing someone they loved. The garden was alive in a bright green, despite the chill in the air and some of the flowers were out in full bloom greeting and wishing everyone the best for the New Year. He loved this job! He loved the plants and he loved the way they made him feel as he worked around them.

One day there will be someone in his life who appreciates the simple things in nature such as the flowers, the shrubs and other types of foliage which makes breathing and feeling content in this world possible. "One day," Aaron sighed. ❀

❀❀ *Chapter Three* ❀❀

Jaleen was excited about her brother and his wife's new business. She was also glad she had taken the trip. It had been a while since she had visited her grandparents and the wedding notice was too short notice for her job. She was working on a project and its deadline was on her like the Christmas celebrations. She had to get it done. But, she was glad she had taken the little trip and gotten reacquainted with her brother, his wife, their lovely daughter and of course her grandparents. "Selecia's family was nice too," she concluded to herself. It was also obvious that her mother and sisters, Selecia's aunts, were very close as well.

She could only envision the terror that Selecia had felt when she learned she was pregnant. She could also imagine the hurt and disappointment her mother and aunts had also experienced as a result of her pregnancy. Despite that, she reflected, things are working out for them both. Brad's finishing up this year, she's preparing to open her own business and both families were behind her one hundred percent. Jaleen knew that Selecia's mother and aunts loved her dearly. To include a store front as a part of the Handles' home spoke volumes about their respect for her talent and love for Selecia. It must have been difficult accepting her pregnancy, especially since it happened in her last year of high school. "I don't think I would've gotten over that at all," she surmised softly to herself.

"Life and love often called for some ugly sacrifices," she continued mentally. Their acceptance of Brad could not have been easy. Brother or not, I would not have gotten over that pregnancy at all," she stated resignedly. It takes a lot to raise a child and to watch your child make such a mistake must have been heartbreaking. I guess that is the biggest part of love: forgiving and moving forward.

Jaleen enjoyed her visit and getting to know her niece. She was cute as could be and just adorable. She knew her mom, her dad, her great grandparents—Grandfather and Grandmother, her grandmother and her two great aunts. She even knew the Samuels. She was definitely one to place inside your heart to love and protect always. Most importantly, she had an opportunity to see young love in its purest phase.

As young as they are, her brother and Selecia loved and respected each other. The sacrifices they've made thus far can only strengthen their relationship. If they continue along this path, they would certainly have the stuff good marriages are made of: communication, commitment and love, openly and freely expressed. She really wished them all the best.

"Imagine, her baby brother is a dad before she is even a wife or mother," she mused. Still, she was happy for him and hoped that his marriage lasted. They both knew the tragedies associated with a broken home. Their parents' divorce had left her scarred for life. She used to think she and Brad were scarred. Now she can see that she is the one still nursing the scar and delaying it from healing. She was certain he did not want that for his daughter or any other children they may have.

But this New Year, she promised herself she was going to take some time out for love. Not because her brother was married and settled down but because it was possible for her, too, if she gave it a chance. She really didn't think so sometimes. However, she was becoming a little more accepting of the notion that love was possible as long as you're not afraid to make it work, together.

Opening the door to her apartment, she realized that she did not let her two neighbors know she had planned to be gone over the holidays. She quickly wrote a few thank you notes to her brother and his family and her grandparents for having her over the holidays. She also wrote her two neighbors a note of apology and slipped it under their doors. She even added a bonus by inviting them to dinner that weekend. They may be able to help her with her special project, too. But most importantly, she was going to begin by spending some time with friends. The few she had needed to be appreciated. That's also a part of life: having friends who are there for you. That's the start of building relationships: trusting people. Friendships require trust and a whole lot of room for growing and forgiving. It's time to grow the friendships she had if she intended to get involved in a more serious relationship by the end of the year.

Returning to her apartment, Jaleen took out the 'To Do' list she had made. Some were places visited when purchasing furnishings for her home or office space. A few were stores she knew that supplied what she wanted to contribute to her brother and his wife's new business. She wanted to get straight to work on her end of the project. With the wrapping tissue paper nailed down the personalized boxes and bags would be a breeze.

After a few phone calls, she had the tissue paper, shopping bags and gift boxes nailed. She had to visit a few stores, make some selections and they would have her samples ready by the end of the week. Without a moment's hesitation, she was out the door in her car and out the complex.

Jasmine was the first to notice the car was gone when she arrived home. Aaron would be arriving around six thirty and would probably notice it too. She decided to wait and check his reaction. She was almost certain he was in love with Jaleen and didn't know how to let her know.

She was involved in a few relationships enough to know when someone was silently in love. She wished it were her. But admittedly, she was not in love with Aaron. "What am I mooning about?" she asked herself. "I may be barking up the wrong tree for all I know. Aaron may be concerned about her the way a big brother is concerned about a little sister. She is single, lives alone, works hard and basically stays to herself when it comes to men. Maybe she was in a bad relationship and is avoiding men all together. That must be it," Jasmine said sounding all sure. "That must be it." she declared. "Maybe Aaron knew that and is not pushing to give her some time. He's about two years older than Jaleen. But then," Jasmine interjected in her mental ramblings, "Aaron had never done or said anything in particular that indicated he was in-love with her." However, Jasmine felt it in her bones. There was love there—somewhere. Love was around them.

As she opened the note that was slipped under her door, she was relieved. Jaleen had apologized for leaving and not letting them know she was going to be out of town. She even invited them to dinner that weekend. "Now this just adds another twist to my already neatly figured out scenario," Jasmine decided. "That could have been a secret tryst she went on. Wow!" She exclaimed excitedly. "That's it. She's in-love with a married man and has to see him when he's available. The relationship exists on his terms because he is legally unavailable. So, there's a man somewhere in this picture and he's married. Isn't that some stuff?" Jasmine queried contritely. "Here I am trying to get a mental hook up with Aaron and she is already hooked up. Well, Aaron, sorry. Looks like you need to move on" and she placed the note in her desk calendar.

Upon arriving in the complex Aaron noticed that Jaleen's car was missing. He went to his apartment, stepped on the note and grabbed his phone. He immediately called Jasmine and asked if she had seen or spoken to Jaleen. "No," she answered. "But she did leave a note under the door apologizing and with that she's given an invitation to dinner." Aaron immediately turned around and saw the paper on the floor. He told Jasmine he'd call her right back. Picking up the note, he read through the lines quickly. It was as Jasmine said. She apologized for not letting them know she would be gone for at least a week and she invited them to dinner that weekend.

Though he was annoyed that she forgot to let them know, he was immensely relieved that she was alive and alright. The invitation would be accepted, of course. But he was going to give her a little piece of his mind, too. He had every intention of notifying the police if she hadn't returned today. That was on his mind all day. However, her return negated that action and he was glad about that. "But how could she have forgotten about letting us know. Didn't she think we would have been concerned?" he asked himself out loud. Annoyance began climbing up in his spirit once again. Sighing deeply, he tried his best to relax and allow the anger and annoyance to seep out of him.

Nevertheless, she was home and that's really all that mattered. He would slip her a note letting her know her invitation was accepted. She wasn't big on small talk—the gossip around the complex. He liked that. In fact, she never knew the gossip around the complex until Jasmine brought it up and even then, Jaleen appeared disinterested. She never did any of the follow up checks on any of the stories shared. She didn't spend her time in other people's affairs. That was something that attracted him to her instantly. Believing what you heard always had the potential for trouble and trouble was something he tried to avoid at all cost.

He had three sisters and he knew from their experiences where gossip began and ended: at the tip of one tongue and off the palate of another. Their shenanigans were hard lessons learned by him. As he watched them maneuver the maze known as friendship, he was mindful of the many situations and end results. They always talked things over and he always listened. They were older and he was among the last of the siblings. He had nothing to offer and everything to gain from their encounters.

They never pitted friends against each other and they never played bring, come, carry, go. In other words, what they heard they never repeated, except at home to each other. But they never repeated it beyond that. Bringing and carrying gossip created more confusion and negative discourse than it helped. They did not participate in actions of disloyalty and they tried to discourage their friends from engaging in the same. Bringing and carrying information, however juicy at the time is never repeated as first delivered. Therein laid the chafe, the pain of being misaligned and spoken about out of character, sometimes deliberately so, due to jealousy, most often. So Aaron knew that friendship had boundaries and rules. The lessons he learned from his siblings reinforced that for him and the rules were especially true when it came to matters of the heart.

Lesson One—Keep your love interests to yourself. Someone else may ruin it for you before it gets off the ground. Jealousy oftentimes lives in the heart of friends and has ruined many friendships. Lesson Two—Keep your friends and potential love interests out of each other's paths. Trust is easily broken when love is new and the relationship is still very fragile. Friends again, will mess you up, sometimes unintentionally and sometimes intentionally. Lesson Three—Keep your heart hidden until the interest of your heart has expressed an equal amount of faith, trust, and desire for the relationship to develop and go forward. This lets you know you're off to a good start and together you're ready to face friends and adversaries alike, having established the ground rules of trust, sharing and communicating with each other.

All of his sisters were married. If they were not living by the lessons learned then the only student present at the time the lessons were being taught was him. He has tried to keep his interests away from his friends, except in this instance. They shared the same neighbor—Jasmine. She has been trying to feel him out for a while now. He has been trying to keep his smoke screens intact. But he's not sure he will be able to keep the smoke going up much longer. She is as persistent as a mosquito and annoying in that way, too. She is going to keep stinging him until she draws enough blood or he simply claps her mouth shut . . . outing her interests in his love interests.

However, he had to add in her defense, she had never said or done anything to cause him to doubt her loyalty as a friend. She was helpful, resourceful and kindhearted. She just liked to stick her nose where it's not invited sometimes. That's all. Aaron doubted that Jasmine would do anything to sabotage his relationship or chances of a relationship with Jaleen. However, he knew he wasn't willing to take any chances. When love is new, it is very fragile. The simplest things can become the biggest things between two people who are uncertain of themselves and the boundaries of their relationship. The getting-to-know-you stage of a relationship, especially one that is a love interest, is the shakiest part of all. Each is a little nervous about relaying just how they are feeling for fear of being used, rejected or simply taken for granted. Nevertheless, he intended to pursue a relationship with Jaleen and he intended to thread lightly but assertively while doing so. No Jasmine as the monkey in the middle for him, he concluded. This may not be school days, but one nosy neighbor prank from her could set him back faster than he wanted to even consider. ✿

❀❀ *Chapter Four* ❀❀

Jaleen completed her orders at the last stop. Paper World should have been her first stop, she decided, when she got into her car. It had everything and the prices were incredible. The tissue paper was available in several sizes and the cost per sheets of one thousand was unbelievable. She placed the order for five sets for a total of five thousand sheets altogether. She ordered one thousand peach, mint green, white, baby blue and pink, complete with embossing, the total cost was two hundred seventy five dollars and that included shipping and handling charges for the order to be delivered to her. The peach paper was being embossed in mint green; mint green tissue paper was being embossed in peach; the white paper was being embossed in silver; the baby blue and pink were being embossed in silver and white ink, respectively. The words "Handle-Cole" were alternating with the H-C letters in script. She thought it was rather cool and upscale looking. "Just what Lecia deserved," she smiled to herself. The clothes she had seen her niece wearing were of excellent quality and she didn't think the ones to be sold would be any less.

The boxes were available in four sizes and she selected the last two sizes and all three sizes of the shopping bags. She ordered two hundred of each sized box and three hundred of each of the shopping bags. These came up to six hundred plus dollars and she used her credit card to pay for them. All the items would be ready within three weeks and shipped to her mailing address.

Jaleen felt a special tingle all over as she reflected on her role in the new business. She was excited and happy for her brother and his wife. They were starting not just a lifetime commitment to each other but they were also venturing out and starting their own business. In her heart, she felt it was going to be wonderful for them. They had the support and assistance of family members who really and truly cared about them and wished them well.

When she thought of her niece, her heart just melted and flipped flopped in her chest. She missed her adorable, cute little angel self. She promised to go home more often and not wait for tragedy to strike. She wanted her niece and sister in law to get to know her and she wanted to remain close to her brother. They always shared everything, especially after their parents divorced.

As she maneuvered the car into a parking space in the supermarket, she mentally listed the items she would need to get her through the next week or so. She had emptied her fridge in time for the little trip and now she had to replenish it. She also had to pick up some of the items she needed for the dinner invitation she extended to her two neighbors.

"They're going to tear me up," she muttered to herself as she entered the supermarket's sliding doors. "But they will forgive me, too. I just got caught up trying to get everything done for work before leaving and didn't remember to let them know." With a heavy sigh, she wished she could take that back. She made a mental note to herself not to let that happen again. Friendships must be valued.

As she walked down the aisles, reading labels, comparing prices and selecting what she wanted, Jaleen wondered if this was the year and the place she would meet that special person who was meant for her. Love is where you find it and it dawned on her that perhaps she was passing her Mr. Right and not even realizing it. Looking around, she realized there were several men, women and a few children in the aisle with her. Most appeared absorbed in what they were doing: shopping. As she tried to scout out the men in the aisle, she resignedly sighed when she didn't experience a nibble or magical pull in the direction of any of them. One simply walked by her without even a side glance. Probably married, she thought. "Enough of this," she scolded herself. "I'm not that desperate yet."

With all items carefully selected, she headed towards the check out area, looking for the shortest line. As the cashier greeted her, she responded in kind and added, "Happy New Year!" She was still feeling good about her brother, his wife, their daughter and her visit with her grandparents. She was also happy about the new business they were all working on bringing to fruition. Prosperity was in the air and she was hoping that love would also be in the air for her this year, as well. True love: a love that's real and meant to last.

Heading home, her mind wondered on the two individuals she had tried to share her life. As she pulled into her parking spot in the complex, she paused for a minute to figure out why the relationships had failed. Clay always treated her with respect. But somehow she felt he was hiding something from her. He was dabbling in drugs and that wasn't a part of her life. That relationship was over without getting a second chance or visit to rehab.

As she took the first two bags from the trunk, she began to replay that relationship in her mind. Clay was sweet; he always treated her like she was the most important thing in his life. But somehow, she just felt that things were too perfect to be real; moving along too smoothly to be happening. He always picked her up, took her to some of the best restaurants, movie premiers and sporting events. They spoke regularly on the phone and made jokes about everything in their lives. He wasn't one who was easily angered or annoyed. Her co-workers adored him, the few who had met him while they were at one function or another and she was beginning to feel certain he might be the right person for her to entertain thoughts about a future together. One afternoon, she was in the area of his job and it was a few minutes past quitting time. She was going to surprise him and they could leave together. With the receptionist gone, Jaleen entered his office unannounced and found him snorting a line of cocaine. When he tried to explain, she just walked out and never looked back.

As she entered the apartment and placed the bags on the counter, she realized she was crying. The tightness in her chest that gripped her that day had suddenly returned. She hadn't thought of him in two years. She had cried for days and days. Her heart felt trampled, crushed. She felt as though when he had snorted the line of coke, he had snorted the love out of her heart. On the way home, she wished she hadn't gone in. She wished she had arrived earlier. Maybe he would not have even done it. Then all her rationalizations came to an end when she realized that if he hadn't snorted it then, he would have snorted it sometime later. He had it. He had the coke. She wondered why he felt he needed to use drugs. Why? Every message he left on her answering machine was deleted without being listened to it in its entirety. She didn't want anything to do with him just like she never wanted anything to do with drugs.

The light knocking on the front door brought her out of the bathroom with the wash towel blotting her eyes and drying her hands. As she opened the door, she saw Aaron with the remaining two bags of groceries in his hands. She had intended to place the first two in the door and go back and bring up the last two bags she had left sitting on the trunk of her car. When she didn't return, he went down stairs, retrieved them and brought them upstairs for her.

"Thank you." Jaleen said. "I was coming back for them. But thanks. I appreciate this." she offered. Aaron noticed her eyes and asked if she was okay. Jaleen didn't want to talk about it and so she told him she was. As she reached for the bags, Aaron ignored her and he entered the apartment and placed the bags on her kitchen counter next to the other two.

Hugging him, Jaleen wished him a Happy New Year and thanked him again for his help. Not wanting to seem pushy, he accepted her expressions of gratitude, kissed her on the cheek and wished her a Happy New Year, too, before turning to leave.

"May I ask you something?" she asked rather timidly. "Sure," Aaron said, not wanting to leave just yet. It was obvious that she had been crying. He was hoping it wasn't the kind of vacation where the break up happens, leaving you nothing else but to return home, feeling lost, sad and aching all over.

"Have you ever used drugs?" she asked him bluntly. Taken aback by this question, he quickly assured her that he hadn't. "Not even marijuana?" Jaleen asked. "Not even marijuana." Aaron repeated. "Is there a reason men or women, for that matter, use drugs?" she asked him. "Different strokes for different folks," he responded. "Some people used drugs to impress friends; some to give them courage to face a bad situation and some because they have nothing to live for. I'm sure there are other reasons, but that's all I can come up with," he said as he shrugged his shoulders.

As she motioned for Aaron to sit down, she began to share her story. "Two years ago I broke up with someone I thought I was in love with and who was in love with me," she started softly. "We had a good time together. He was kind, considerate, thoughtful, hard working and funny," she said. "I thought he was the one I was going to spend the rest of my life with until I . . ." Jaleen began crying as though her heart had just been broken—all over again.

Aaron moved to sit beside her and embracing her around the shoulders he hugged her to him and allowed her to cry until she had basically worn herself out. When the tears finally subsided, she was making the little shivering, hiccup sounds of a child who had just been woefully disappointed by having her favorite toy promised and not delivered on her birthday.

Leaning her gently against the sofa, he went in search of another face towel. After wetting it with cold water and squeezing out the excess, he returned and placed it on her forehead. Quietly, they sat together, Jaleen with the cold towel across her head and eyes and Aaron with his arms holding her against his chest. As her breathing returned to normal, he began to rock them ever so gently.

This comforted her so much so that she drifted off to sleep. Aaron sat with her in his arms. The slowed rhythm of her breathing confirmed that she was, indeed, asleep. He was content to hold her for as long as she needed him to do so. He wanted her to need him for the rest of her life.

Softly, he sighed at his own thoughts. "Now is not the time. She is in need of a friend not a companion right now. Besides," he chided himself, "I need to know what this drug head did to upset her and make her cry on this the second day of the New Year."

Quietly, he continued to cradle her in his arms, rocking them both as he looked out into the distance. If this is all he can give at this time, then it's what he will give, for now. "Hopefully, hopefully," he contrived, "She would permit him to share his love for her with her and she would give him a chance to love her as she deserved to be loved." ❀

❀❀ *Chapter Five* ❀❀

When Jaleen awakened, she was surprised to find Aaron sitting quietly, looking out in the darkness. Feeling embarrassed, she quickly collected herself and apologized for monopolizing his time and thanked him for what he had done for her. "Are you okay now?" he asked. "Yes, y-yes," she stuttered. "Are you sure?" He pressed her. "I am here as long as you need someone to listen. I am here for you," he assured her.

As she collected her thoughts, she realized that she had begun to tell him about Clay and how she had broken up with him. Feeling somewhat embarrassed, she decided to finish what she had started as a means of thanking him for sharing his time with her and giving her the opportunity to purge this affair from her conscience and her mind once and for all. "I left him and I never looked back, until this afternoon," she concluded, looking out into the night after stealing a glance at him. "I began this year, wondering and hoping that this would be the year I meet someone special; someone who was willing to love me as much as I was willing to love him. I'm not sure what caused me to think about Clay. It's been two years and I've kept busy just to avoid thinking about him and feeling sorry for myself. I know I did the right thing. But it hurt so much at that time. I guess it still hurts now, too. To know how close I came to loving him and also how close I came to living a nightmare that I would not have been able to awaken from as easily if the relationship developed and gone on for much longer also bothered me."

"I'm sure you made a good decision call for yourself," Aaron added. "If you're not willing to use drugs then why should you be willing to settle for a relationship with someone who is already in a relationship with drugs?" Aaron asked her pointedly. Jaleen looked at him shyly and replied, "As for him already being in a relationship, I hadn't even thought of it like that. You're right about that. He already was in a relationship," she concluded. "But what I don't understand and I guess I will never understand is, why? Why does anyone think it is the answer for them? What is gained from using drugs? The problems we face do not disappear because of the substance. They're right there when you come back to being yourself," she stated matter of factly. Aaron nodded in agreement.

She exhaled deeply. "Would you like something to drink?" she offered. I have some water and a few cold sodas from last year," she said jokingly. "Some water would be fine," Aaron said. Then he got up, motioned for her to sit, went to her refrigerator and retrieved a bottle of water for himself and one for her. As they sat and sipped the water, Aaron reflected on what he had learned about her and Jaleen reflected on what she had revealed about herself.

"Would you like something to eat?" Aaron asked concerned. "We can call for pizza, Chinese food or delivery of some hot, juicy wings," he offered raising his eyebrows. He tried to entice her with the wings. They always brought out the best in company. He loved them. They were smoked, barbecued and the sauce was sweet and hickory scented with a slight sting of cayenne. "The wings would be nice," Jaleen said. "Are you sure you don't mind sitting here with me? I know I wasn't part of your evening plans," she reminded him, offering him the opportunity to leave if he wanted to.

Shifting slightly to get to his cell phone, Aaron smiled and indicated he was fine keeping her company, unless she was trying to kick him out. "No, no, no," she defended. "I just know I've taken up a great deal of your time and for all I know you were probably on your way out when you decided to stop and bring up the bags for me. So, I don't want to keep you from your previous plans," she finished.

"I'm fine," Aaron reminded her with a smile. "Besides, you're good company, even when you are a little blue." They smiled and Jaleen began to relax a little bit more. He called in the order and they made selections for the kind of sauce they wanted over their wings. Cajun fries were selected as the side order and they were ready to spend some quality time together as friends.

They had been friends since she moved into the complex and that was the week she had broken up with Clay. She had been downtown to sign the lease and because she had gotten through with the signings, she was going to invite him over to check it out and arrange for him to help her move. They had talked about it and when she had decided on a place, she was determined to show it to him and solicit his assistance in packing and preparing to move. A moving company was going to move all of her heavy items and she was going to take care of her personal, smaller pieces. That included her clothes, shoes, favorite books and other family items that made her feel comfortable and safe.

Instead, she ended up spending that weekend crying, packing and moving in. All the while she was trying to rid herself of the memories associated with that heartbreaking relationship in her old apartment. When she finally finished arranging the furniture and other furnishings to her satisfaction, she was about to go out in search of something to eat when she ran, literally ran into Aaron on the balcony. He was sweaty, dirty from doing God knew what as she hurriedly exited the apartment and slammed right into him.

After many apologies, she asked him about the nearest place to grab something hot to eat like a plate of food or something simple for takeout. He then invited her into his apartment where he gave her several numbers for takeout restaurants and recommended the wings. That's how they became acquainted and their neighborly friendship began.

With another deep sigh, Jaleen sat back and placed her head against the couch. Aaron settled in and decided to wait for her next topic. This was her night. He was here for her. "Aaron, do you remember how we first met?" Jaleen asked. "You almost knocked me down," Aaron recalled with a little chuckle. "I almost did, indeed," she agreed with a smile. "Well, that was the weekend I pledged to avoid men, relationships and the heart aches they caused. That was a little over two years ago." "So, are you changing your mind about men, relationships or both?" Aaron inquired lightly. "I am," she admitted. "I have a niece whom I just met for the first time this Christmas. She stole my heart away. Her parents, my brother and his wife, are doing a terrific job trying to make their relationship work. Watching them just made me more aware of what I am missing out on," Jaleen surmised. "How long have they been together?" Aaron asked. "About a year and a half," Jaleen replied. "They met last summer and fell in love. Then he returned to college and noticed that she wasn't writing him as frequently as he wanted her to or that her letters were not as detailed as he expected them to be—I'm not sure. But something drove him home for Christmas break and that's when he found out she was pregnant. If it weren't for that, he would have spent Christmas here, with me." Aaron wondered if the baby was his. But decided to wait to hear what she wanted to share. "They got married last Christmas and they have been trying to make it work ever since."

"He loves her. It's written all over his face that she is the center of his world. Whenever she enters the room, his eyes follow her and they have a very special and bright light in them. When you look at her, you can see the same thing. She loves him. He is her world, too." At that point she got up and retrieved one of the pictures on her wall unit. "This is my niece, my brother and his wife," she said as she pointed them out.

"They are in a relationship that has the potential to last. I want something like that," Jaleen admitted. "I want to feel the power of that love circling me, surrounding me no matter where I am. Home, work, church, out and about I want to feel loved like I've seen with them and like I've known with my grandparents. So, do you think that's possible? Do you think people, especially our age, can still fall in love and enjoy a love that makes them feel whole and safe and secure?" Aaron was ready this time but he didn't want to send the wrong message or signal. He realized she was feeling vulnerable so he decided to play it safe. He would express his true feelings for her another time.

"People can still have that kind of love today. But," and he paused, "they also have to be able and willing to recognize it when they see it, too. In life we each want different things. This puts us in different places and situations and in the company of people in search of similar or different things in life all the time. It's rare but it happens. Two people can be at the right place at the right time and meet, discover that the chemistry between them is strong, powerful but not overpowering and they decide to explore the boundaries of that friendship, those feelings, that chemistry. Through their explorations, the boundary lines are developed, expanded, and love becomes a part of the emotions they feel. A lifetime of happiness can then become a reality. But we have to be patient enough to see and hear with our hearts what our eyes and ears are not always attuned to capture," he concluded.

"I opened this new year with hope. I'm going to continue to hope and pray that I meet someone this year who is willing to love, honor and cherish me as much as I am willing to love, honor and cherish him. I want us to have a lifetime of happiness that we pass onto our children and their children and their children's children. I want that love to be the legacy that keeps my family and relatives together through good times and bad. I want my children to feel the love that my little niece feels each day when she looks into the eyes of her parents and when she sees them looking at each other. I want that for me and mine. For her sake, I also hope her parents' relationship lasts as long as they both live and even beyond," Jaleen said.

"Then that's what you're going to have," Aaron stated firmly. "This is the year you are going to meet someone who will captivate your heart, soul and mind. This is the year you are going to be swept off your feet and still remain standing. You are going to be loved and you are going to wonder if it's really happening to you. This is the year," he repeated softly. "I hope so," Jaleen responded, "I really hope so." Their conversation continued along the same pathway and they both expressed some of the challenges that relationships faced today which hindered many from staying in love and remaining married and sincerely committed to each other.

The ringing of the doorbell signaled the arrival of dinner. As they ate their fries and wings, they shared the sauces, dipping their wings and licking their fingers as they looked at the remaining holiday lights that were lit up around the complex and the skyline beyond.

Aaron shared some of his favorite childhood memories with Jaleen and she listened and laughed heartily at his follies. He was surprised to learn about some of the antics of her siblings. Two were older than her and lived further north. When she shared the news about her parents' divorce, she was able to smile, even when she felt like crying. Remembering some of the funny things that happened became easier since the veil of silence had been lifted. She had openly admitted that her parents were divorced and she was able to move forward and have a discussion around the little things that once made her smile, feel happy and safe as a little girl surrounded by both parents and her siblings. He also shared with her what he did for a living and even invited her to join him at his favorite site one day.

When they finished eating, they cleaned up the mess they'd made with the sauce and bones and Aaron helped her pack away her groceries. He even volunteered to come home early and help her prepare the dishes she was planning for her dinner date with him and Jasmine. When she accepted his offer, he felt like the kid with the long awaited and wished for birthday puppy. There was nothing else that could be said or done to topple his world. His foot was in the door and he was going to slowly but surely make his way to her heart. One step at a time; one day at a time. That was his New Year's resolution and he was on his way to making it happen. As much as he wanted to share with her how he felt, he knew that his time to do so would come. Pouring his heart and soul at her feet right now was not a good thing. She was dealing with some very private memories of her own and as soon as she buried them, once and for all, then she would be more receptive to him and his subtle advances toward her heart and forever land. With another hug and quick kiss on her cheek, Aaron bid the love of his life goodnight. ❀

❀❀ *Chapter Six* ❀❀

Jasmine observed Aaron leaving Jaleen's apartment around midnight that night. Returning home from a little outing, she wondered if Jasmine was okay. Why hadn't she been invited to sit and talk? "I knew it," she declared. "He is in love with her and she must be in love with him, too. Let's see how long this game of charades will last," she pouted to herself. "If they think they're fooling me, they have another think coming."

As she entered her apartment, she thought of going back out and knocking on Jaleen's door, then dismissed it. "I've always had a vivid imagination," she muttered "and it always, always got me into trouble. This time, I'm going to let go. Jaleen and Aaron are adults. Knowing Aaron," she thought out loud, "he was probably helping her bring something in." She locked her door and went inside her bedroom. It was late and she had to get ready for work the next day. "Still, why was he leaving her apartment at this hour?" Jasmine persisted. "Was Jaleen okay?" There was no noise or sounds of other guests. "He really was a nice guy and if he loved her, there was nothing wrong with that. Jaleen is a nice person. She works hard and minds her own business. So if they hooked up that's great. It sure beats feeling alone when you don't want to be alone," she exhaled. "Then again," she continued, "Aaron is too much of a gentleman to just fool around with Jaleen. He really looks out for her and he treats her with respect." So she couldn't see them just having sex and saying goodnight. That was not like the Aaron she knew.

Jasmine's mind would not let go. She decided to needle it out of Aaron if she could. He was coy, but she would persist until he told her what was up. She liked knowing and being in the know. If they are having an affair, great! If not, well she would continue to watch Aaron squirm under the closeness of their friendship with Jaleen and not take the first step to get the ball rolling in the direction he obviously craved. "Again," she had to remind herself, "You are the one who believes he's in love with her. Maybe he isn't. He is the last of his siblings and maybe he just likes having someone to keep an eye on for a change. But," she persisted again, "she was almost certain that he loved her. She would stake her reputation on it and she believed strongly that she was right." Then she would be able to rib him with pleasure. "Sick," she chided herself with a smile. "You need to leave that man alone and get a life."

Aaron was in high spirits. It was the happiest night of the New Year for him. She's single! She's hardworking! That he already knew and she wants to find someone nice to love and be loved in return. "I can be that guy," he smiled. "If she's willing to take a chance on me, I can be that guy. I can make her happy. I know I can!" Aaron repeated to himself.

As he prepared to go to bed, he folded up his tee shirt and placed it under his head. He wanted to smell her. It was the closest she would be to him for now and he was content to accept that. She was in his arms and she fell asleep in the comfort of his arms. The beating of his heart comforted her and she forgot about her pain, even if it was for two hours and twenty minutes, as she slept in his arms.

He had the answers and he now knew he had a chance. She wasn't having a fling with some married jerk. She was working hard and trying to forget one: a dope head jerk. He was glad she had the sense she was born with. He was glad to hear her say she walked away and never looked back. There was nothing to look back for. If you have someone as beautiful as she in your life and you're still messing with drugs, then you don't know what you have and you don't know how lucky you are to have that special someone like her to share your life with. "You don't know yourself period," he enunciated aloud. You'll never find yourself in drugs either. If anything, you will continue to be lost and will continue seeking that which isn't real or healthy for you or anyone associated with you.

"He had a chance" he smiled, thinking to himself. He had an opening and he was going to make every opportunity count. He wasn't going to rush her. He wasn't going to overpower her with requests to go here and there. He was going to simply be her friend and ask her out every now and then as smoothly as he knew how. He would wait until she felt comfortable; ready to have someone else share her personal space.

An occasional movie followed by dinner and a walk in the park every now and then—his favorite park— should be a good start, he thought. He would find out what some of her personal interests are. She mentioned things *they* did but what is it that *she* liked to do? He had to find out. His mind was racing. He was so excited. He was simply overjoyed. He had a chance! He had a good chance of winning Jaleen's love and making her a special part of his life, too.

She was in his arms tonight! The second night of the New Year and he had the one he loved in his arms. It wasn't as he would have liked it to be but he was willing to accept what he had received. It was a safe start. She was single and looking for someone she could feel happy and comfortable loving. "You said that already," he scolded himself happily. He was going to do all he could to be that guy who made her feel happy, loved, comfortable, safe and secure.

When Aaron left, Jaleen looked around the apartment, decided that nothing really needed her attention and decided to go to bed. She took a long shower as she reflected on her evening with Aaron. As she toweled down her body, she began to realize that so many things could have gone wrong and that despite her disappointment with Clay, so many things had gone right for her, too. She had immersed herself in her job, had endured some of the new changes and had done quite well, as far as her job performance and level of productivity was concerned. As she finished applying some body cream to her skin, Jaleen closed down her rambling mind, took a few minutes to pray and went to bed. She was returning to work the next day and wasn't looking forward to it that much. The little break did her some good. Her mind and body were in full relaxation mode and now she wasn't ready to return. Another week was probably what she should have taken to fully relax her body and mind until it began to crave going back to work.

She worked hard to make sure the specifications for the various contracts were in order. The furniture company she worked for had in and out of state clients who special ordered home and office furnishings. While it was a challenge, she was able to review the requests, notify the manufacturer, secure the services and prices needed and communicate that to the clients. It was a job with lots of benefits and she was able to take care of herself. This made her happy. She was capable of taking care of herself and she was able to assist her brother. She provided him with financial assistance each semester, to supplement whatever he had earned during the summer and to help him get through the spring term. He usually spent Christmas on the mainland to save on the cost of airfare. But, with a wife and daughter, he now returned home. He had a family waiting for him. That was special and very important to him.

She had a decent savings and kept her checking account at a five hundred dollar balance, in the event of an unforeseen circumstance she would be able to respond without delay. When her brother wanted to go home, she knew she would have been able to assist him because of the emergency threshold she maintained in that account. Now, she was able to cut it in half with the order of tissue papers and she would be able to pay off the balance by the time the shopping bags and boxes came in. The payment of bills made her feel independent and self sufficient. She did not need assistance from her parents and she was grateful for that. She took care of herself and was saving to be able to make a down payment on a home in an area that was zoned for families. If nothing else, her niece would be able to visit her when she's older. But she really hoped she would be able to settle down with someone special and raise a family of her own. Her niece would have someone to play with and share her joys, her concerns and her ups and downs with as she traveled through life. With her niece on her mind, she slowly drifted off to sleep.

Morning came quickly. Jaleen was up and out before seven fifteen the next day. Her mind was racing with the various assignments and tasks she anticipated would be waiting for her. She had been with the firm for four years and had moved up slowly but steadily in her department. She worked diligently and conscientiously to ensure that all requests were met as specified to the letter and honored in a timely manner. Some days she worked longer than usual to keep clients in the various time zones satisfied. She had received several commendation letters for her customer service skills and her willingness to go the extra mile to ensure that the customer received what they desired.

When invoices were provided for review, prior to being approved for payment, Jaleen patiently reviewed the order specifications, the work order and the deliverables invoices which detailed what was being shipped to the customer. This way the company was sure to receive payments due and the customer received what was requested.

But today, the third day of the New Year, she felt anxious and a little rest less. She wanted to be a part of something new and invigorating, but she wasn't sure what it was. So for now, she was on her way to work and would make the best of it. She knew the routine and would do her best to ensure that the company and the customers were happy with the level of service and the quality of the merchandise they provided.

Despite the restlessness in her spirit, her soul felt light and carefree. She was glad she had spoken with Aaron. Sometimes the only male perspective she had was Brad's. She and Maurice were not especially close as he and Claudia were. She seldom shared any of her male-related concerns with him nor did she share too many of her female worries with Claudia. Just like how their parents had separated, so did the siblings. She hadn't realized it until now. She and Brad were close and Claudia and Maurice were close. "Isn't that something?" she pondered. The parents and the children separated. But despite the separation, they were connected. Her parents, though divorced, were still their parents. They just weren't living together or married. Her siblings were still her siblings though they all lived in separate dwellings and grew close to one sibling or another, after the divorce. They were still related.

Claudia was in a relationship. She and Willard Taylor had been seeing each other for a little over two years. They were thinking and talking about getting married. They worked together, but at different branches, for the same bank. They met at one of the company's annual charity events and they began seeing each other ever since. Maurice was in and out of relationships. He was very serious at times and he wasn't hung up on anyone just yet, at least not at the time of their last conversation some time ago. She didn't think he was skittish. He just enjoyed being a roamer, as he called it. Sometimes she wondered if his inability to remain in a relationship was a direct result of their parents' divorce. "You can't blame everything on the divorce," she reminded herself. "Some people take a while to settle down. It takes time and energy," she wailed, "to find the right person. Look at me," she groaned inwardly.

As she pulled into the parking lot for her job, she said a quick prayer for her siblings. She also prayed for their parents. That's who they were and will always be, even though they had divorced. They were still their parents. She prayed for her grandparents and her niece and her niece's parents. She hoped they would be as happy for as long, if not longer than her grandparents' were in their marriage. She also prayed for someone loving, thoughtful and healthy in mind, body and spirit to enter her life and make her as happy as she could ever be. Mostly, she, too, wanted what her grandparents had: a long, loving relationship.

Aaron crossed her mind. She wondered if he had someone special in his life. He was thoughtful, he was kind, he was a good friend and he was an excellent listener. She could only imagine what a wet noodle she must have looked like as she shared her two year old heartache with him. Still, she felt better, having dumped the load in a tiny little box labeled 'no regrets' and allowed her friend, Aaron, to absorb it, absolve her and disperse it into the air; gone for good.

As she took note of how she felt after reviewing the details of last night's conversation, she realized she did not feel the need to pick up that emotional baggage and walk around with it anymore. She was free of the memories. She had cleansed herself and did not have to walk around with those memories anymore.

Jaleen took a deep breath, opened the door and entered the building. As she greeted her colleagues, she wished them a Happy New Year and hoped that they had the kind of Christmas all good 'children' enjoyed. They enjoyed the fit of laughter and began to share the tidbits about their holiday celebrations before they settled down to begin working for the day.

As they began they assumed their roles and responsibilities, Jaleen smiled to herself. Yes, she was back to work. Her vacation was officially over and it was time for business, as usual. ❀

❀❀ *Chapter Seven* ❀❀

Friday's dinner party was what the doctor ordered. Jasmine shared the latest news around the complex and Aaron and Jaleen listened and laughed at the funny parts. As they reminisced about the Christmas holidays, Jaleen shared with them the details surrounding her sister-in-law's new store.

"You didn't tell us he was married," Jasmine responded immediately. "I was looking forward to meeting him after his graduation from college," she added. "Well," Jaleen said, "You could still meet him and his wife and their daughter," she replied with a smile. "Maybe they could stop over for a brief visit before heading home."

As they ate and talked, Aaron paid close attention to the details Jaleen was sharing. He wanted to learn more about her and at the same time, he wanted her to learn about him. "What's Christmas like in the islands?" he asked. She was too happy to share some of the old traditions she had experienced when they visited during the holidays. "Based on memory," she began, "There is a Christmas Eve service held in many of the churches. When that is finished, various groups get together and they go caroling." Jaleen talked about the homemade brews that were offered as the carolers went from house to house singing. "They sang from town to country and country to town, enjoying the fellowship and warmth of the Christmas Season," she continued.

"At the end of the caroling, it was time for the Christmas morning service and this gave the carolers an opportunity to snooze during the service and be taken home when it was finished. They were usually all tired from the singing and drinking they did from after the Christmas Eve Service. Their families collected them for the Christmas morning service and from there, they took them home. Those who were in no condition to be in church were simply taken home. "You mean some of them really get drunk enough to miss church?" Jasmine asked laughing. "They did," Jaleen confirmed smiling. "Family members arrived early at the main park in town to hear the carolers square off and when it was finished or their relatives were finished, whichever came first, they simply took them home. Many got ready for the morning's church service before relaxing and enjoying the day with family and friends."

"So even though they sang all night long, they still come together for a big sing off before church?" Aaron asked. "Yes," Jaleen answered. "They sing all the old time favorites and the crowd enjoys the tradition. When we spent Christmas on the island that's the way it was. Since I went home on Christmas second day, I'm not sure if it happened this year, given the level of damage and rebuilding that is still needed to get the residents as close to normal as possible," she concluded.

Jasmine shared some of her childhood memories and compared them to the types of celebrations she had participated in. She acknowledged that "the grownups had more fun. However, as a kid, waiting for the day to open the presents was the best part of Christmas," she concluded. "You know what your present is when you are a grownup and treat yourself to something special. Still," she lamented, "I wouldn't trade any part of it for anything in the world."

44

Aaron shared some of his funniest moments. He made them laugh until they were breathless. As they moved to the living room for coffee and dessert, they were still laughing and repeating some of the things he had shared with them. He specifically shared stories involving his older siblings and what they had done to either make Christmas more exciting or special. Having a houseful of brothers and sisters sounded like a world of fun. Their parents were pranksters, too.

They made them believe that Santa Claus came early on Christmas morning and he required them to have at least eight hours of sleep. The amount of sleep they got in was counted by Santa Claus and he made sure they had the same number of presents. "What my parents had done," he shared, "was they bought presents throughout the year. If someone indicated an interest in something special, they waited for it to go on sale and purchased it. Then they had fun hiding these items around the house. One year, dad had all the girls and mom had the boys," he said. "Another year, dad had all the boys and mom had all the girls. So they made lists and they checked things off the list as they purchased them. As we got older," he continued, "they placed our stuff on layaway." "Why?" Jasmine asked. "Mom said we were getting older and nosier as the years went by and she didn't like lies and didn't want to lie to us if we stumbled upon some of the things they had purchased prior to the start of the season. So they placed them on layaway and took their time paying them off and hiding them until they could be gift wrapped." "They gift wrapped the presents early?" Jasmine asked.

"Yes." Aaron answered her. "There was a rule about gift wrapping. If it was wrapped, then you couldn't open it. If you did, you would have to give it away when it was opened. So everything stayed as neatly as it was wrapped with your name on it. But you only saw the gift wrapped items as it got close to December." That's when we knew how many things were bought and we had to get that many hours of sleep in order to be able to open them on Christmas Day."

"That's different," Jaleen said. "It sounds like the kind of thing that would make Christmas extra special, especially for kids. After all, Christmas is about kids and seeing the look on their faces as they open their presents, hoping it's what they really, really wanted," she said. "When you have a family of your own, how much of what you experienced will you make a part of them?" Jaleen asked.

Jasmine jumped in quickly and responded, "I'd like all of it. As kids we had to wait until we ate our breakfast before we were allowed to open one gift. They all went under the tree by Christmas Eve and then you had to eat first then open your presents. Now that I'm talking about it," she confessed, "it was really practical to make sure we ate breakfast first. Sometimes we didn't eat again until Christmas dinner. We were all too busy with the presents. It's really the most wonderful time of the year. The memories are more cheerful and they make you feel warm all over. At Christmas time, you tend to miss and love everyone all at the same time," Jasmine noted. "When and if I have a family of my own, I want them to enjoy Christmas the way I did. So, I guess I won't change anything!" she concluded.

Aaron took a while to respond and Jaleen prompted him for his answer. She really wanted to know what he would keep if and when he had a family of his own. "Well," he said slowly. "I think

I would keep it all too. When you look back at our Christmas, the number of gifts included some from family members and close relatives. It wasn't just from our parents. But the ones from our parents were the ones that really counted. I think the number of hours to sleep just gave them some down time together. They had a chance to finish wrapping the left over treats, they hung stockings for each other and placed their tokens in that. Looking back, they focused on us and left themselves out of it. Dad gave mom things like brooches, costume jewelry that had the earrings and necklace as a set. Mom gave him things like cuff links, handkerchief sets, a watch and things like that. Practical presents were what they exchanged. We were just too busy to notice it because we were all excited about what they'd given us," he said.

"I guess I wouldn't change much either," he restated again. I would use the number of gifts to ensure that my children went to bed early and gave me an opportunity to enjoy my wife's company. It would be a time to let her know how much she meant to me as we each braced ourselves for the onslaught of squeals and laughter associated with children on Christmas morning."

"Christmas time is too important not to have something handed down to your children from your parents and even their parents," Aaron stated. "That's what makes and keeps it special. It also lets you remember those who are gone and still treasure them through the memories you have of them while they were with you, especially at Christmas."

"Jaleen, you're not in the islands so what would you keep?" Jasmine asked. Laughing together, Jaleen shared what she would keep. "I know the caroling is out. But the ability to share the time with each other, especially attending the Christmas Eve and Christmas morning services is what I'd keep and make a part of my family. That quiet time allows you to reflect on the real reason for the season. It also gives you an opportunity to reflect on the year you've had thus far and to be appreciative that you are with the ones you love. Opening the presents after breakfast sounds great! But, we were allowed to open them right away, one at a time every few hours. That way you only opened another one if you were bored with the first or previous gift item. So I might let them open them all or open a few at a time every couple of hours, just to spread out the joy and anticipation," Jaleen finished.

"Let's toast," Aaron said. As they held up their glasses of their own personal preference, Aaron began, "To family traditions, Christmas and good friendships: may they last forever." "Cheers!" They said together. As they lifted the glasses to their lips they said it again, to family. But it was said in their hearts. It was a new year, and they were all looking forward to more out of life and nothing less, especially this year.

They talked about their wishes, hopes and dreams until they were ready to call it a night. Aaron began to collect the glasses and the snack dishes. He entered the little kitchen, set up the water to wash the dinner utensils and dishes and began the task in earnest. Jaleen told him he didn't need to do that. But he insisted and asked Jasmine to help her straighten up the couch and dining area. Jasmine assisted Jaleen with tidying up the living room and dinner area. With that finished, together, they stood on the little porch and talked and teased each other about their plans for the future.

Jasmine seized the opportunity to uncover any details that could help her understand Aaron's late departure the other night. All she learned was that there was no one in her life at the moment and then she teased Jaleen about the amount of time she spent working. Jaleen told her it kept her from missing someone she broke up a little over two years ago. Again, she was surprised at the lack of pain she felt when she mentioned the brief affair. "It's really over," she told herself. "It's really over."

When Aaron was through, he thanked Jaleen for the wonderful dinner and evening and he bid his hostess goodnight. With a platonic hug for her neighbor, but one that meant the world to him, Jaleen thanked him for coming over, helping her with the preparation of the meal, and for saving her the clean up chores in the kitchen and then she bid him good night. Jasmine also made her exit, thanking Jaleen for the invitation and letting them both know that the next get-together would be on her. They hadn't done this in a while and it was just what they needed: some down time together. ❀

❀❀ *Chapter Eight* ❀❀

Jaleen spent the weekend going over some of the new proposals and getting ready for the responses. She usually stayed focused and outlined her tasks and responsibilities prior to arriving to work each day. This weekend was no different. The first meeting of the year was also coming up and that's when the announcements were made as to the profits of the previous year. All of her accounts were closed. All payments were received on them. She had taken care of that prior to leaving on her one week furlough with her family.

Once the numbers looked good she knew she would be able to receive a raise, even a bonus. With this in mind, she had made plans. She wanted to send fabric home to Selecia. She also wanted to send the trimmings that would elevate the styles and appearances of the outfits. When she thought of her niece's clothes, she had no doubt as to the quality of work Selecia was capable of.

Jaleen knew several craft and sewing stores. She planned on sending samples to Selecia so she could select the pieces she wanted and indicate the yardage that would be necessary. She also intended to give her an operating budget. That way, she would have some capital for additional purchases, such as a contribution to her mother's electric bill. As she allowed her mind to roam to the little store, she couldn't help but see the possibilities.

The original creations could and quite possibly would be worn by family members, friends of family members, island residents and visitors alike. The visitors would bring the most exposure. The outfits would leave the island, bringing additional free advertising.

Suddenly, a light bulb moment occurred. There were no labels in Alaine's outfits. Selecia needed labels in her clothes to identify with her store. Receipts get lost and tossed. Bags and boxes get recycled and eventually they are no longer around. But the labels or tags in the outfits would be there as a reminder of where the clothes came from or who made them.

Within minutes, Jaleen was through the door. "Two birds will be killed with one stone, today," she thought. She was going to look for the fabric samples and invest in the labels for the back of the clothes. She was certain that Selecia would begin sewing when Brad left and she needed to have the labels to sew in the outfits prior to completing them. She also had to let Selecia know that the labels were being made. Jaleen hoped it wouldn't create any setbacks. But the labels had to be sewn in prior to the completion of the outfit. This order would need to be expedited to ensure no delays in her ability to complete her inventory for the opening date.

A business was really an adventure. It required thought, planning, keen attention to details, execution, resources, reasonable timelines, and a product worthy of consideration, not just by the business owner but also the prospective consumers. A business also required support, patience and sustainability throughout its initial or inaugural period. Silently, she prayed for all business owners. The risks, planning and other angles they had to consider must have been great. But to be able to last beyond the expectations of the owner must have been the greatest reward of all. As she entered the snail paced movement of the traffic Jaleen compared her sister-in-law's new business venture to the company she was working for. Someone had to come up with the major as well as the minor details in order to put a working plan together that had the potential for success. The items Selecia needed right now were the major details to make her product line successful. Originally, they were the minor details until the store was actually finished. But now, they are the main details that must be addressed in a timely manner in order to ensure some measure of success when the business is launched. She likened her performance on her job to the success of the company. With everyone doing their part, the company has the opportunity to make a profit. The product line must be deliverable; the customers must be satisfied to return and make additional purchases and they must also be satisfied and comfortable with the product to recommend it to others. Their recommendations generated additional sales that were not factored in when the advertising budgets were created and ads launched. The product had to deliver or the ability to turn a profit would be severely impacted.

This is where the labels come in, she reasoned. If parents and customers are satisfied with the way the clothes fit and look on their children, they will return and purchase additional outfits. They will also recommend it to others. Jaleen decided that while the labels were being made, she would go ahead and send the fabric samples to Selecia. By the time the labels arrived, the new fabric would also be delivered and she would be well on her way towards building up her inventory.

As she made her way to the first plaza, the parking was horrific. "I guess it's the early bird specials for next Christmas," she muttered. "Well, this is one time a special will help me," she concluded as she made her way to the parking spot four lanes away from her destination. As she got out of her car, she began to hum one of the island's carols. She was also wondering if she would be able to return home twice in one year. "Home!" Jaleen chided herself. "You are home right now!" But she knew in her heart that her grandparents' homeland was really her homeland, too. The memories and feeling of safety and security could never be matched anywhere else. Where she currently lived simply represented independence.

"Besides," she continued, "living here, affords the opportunity to help maintain a healthy inventory. I could provide yarn for Grandmother's projects, threads, trimmings, needles and a wider selection of fabric for Selecia, her mother and aunts to use to build up her store's inventory throughout the year. So this was definitely home. Her second home anyway," she agreed.

Walking into Michael's she wished she had continued down to Hancock's. The crowd is probably just as thick there, too, she moaned exasperatedly. She hated crowds. "But a good sale is worth a crowd any day," she reasoned. As she pushed open the door, the cool air inside helped to simmer her down. The baskets of sewing notions near the door refocused her attention and she was back on track.

Jaleen never considered sewing or sewing notions to be a part of her life. Grandmother crocheted for them and she never paid particular attention. She could do the basic chain stitch to get the project going but couldn't take it any further. The actual cutting and sewing of clothes never really sparked her interest. Now, here she was examining notions, scissors, trimmings, fabrics, even laces. She remembered wearing dresses with lace collars and lace hems that added an extra dimension to the appearance of the dresses.

Two hours later, Jaleen was still looking at various fabrics and notions. The arts and crafts area became her focus as she looked at crochet needles, yarns and books featuring the how to behind some of this year's holiday wear. Confident that Grandmother would love some of the mixed colored yarns, she filled her basket with several sets of varying colors and sizes. She also selected a few new needles for Grandmother.

Another hour later, she was at the register with more than fifteen fabric samples, thread for the serger, threads for some of the fabric samples that she especially liked large and medium sized brightly colored buttons that were as captivating as the personalities of toddlers. She was certain there were fabrics that could carry them off quite well, and given the talents of her sister-in-law, she was certain Selecia would make them look magical when the outfits were completed. She also threw in three separate pieces of fabric that were dedicated to her niece. Whatever her mom made out of them was up to her. She just wanted her niece to have something new and pretty to wear, like the ones she had observed her wearing during her visit.

When the items totaling less than two hundred dollars, Jaleen decided that a sale was worth the effort and money saved every time. Throughout her time in the store, the crowds thinned out and thickened back up and she barely noticed it. As she traversed the aisles looking and trying to decide what to select, she realized she had become engrossed in her own world and their presence was of no consequence to her. The other shoppers browsed, made selections, chatted with their friends or significant others, discussed and made their purchases and left. Now, she, too, was leaving. She had four bags and they were loaded. She also had the order form that was required to select and order the special labels. She would fill it out and mail it in. With much satisfaction, she placed the items in the trunk of her car and headed home.

Mentally, she reviewed what she had purchased. There were several styles of buttons for boys' as well as girls' clothes. She selected samples of various lacey trims and ribbons. She also chose threads for the sewing machine and serger, sewing needles for the sewing machine in various sizes, crochet needles, crochet yarns in various colors and sizes and a few caps and hats that she felt could be trimmed and tied into a couple of outfits. A few small boxes, tape, magic marker and brown wrapping paper were also among her purchases.

Jaleen wanted to pack the boxes and mail them out along with the order for the labels. With not much time to play with, she hoped they would arrive before Selecia had completed her first round of outfits. She decided to put a note in the box concerning the labels so that she would be able to make adjustments in her sewing to insert them when they arrived. The best surprise with the labels was that she planned to have the name of the business, Handle-Cole, on the labels. Selecia won't be expecting that.

She especially loved the three pieces of fabric she'd selected for Alaine's outfits. With three yards of each fabric, she believed she'd bought enough to have a dress, complete with a pinafore, a bonnet, pair of shorts and even long pants with a short sleeved top made for her niece. She also included three yards of white and peach eyelet ruffled trimming for her little outfits to be adorned with. She could almost picture Alaine in her new togs.

Jaleen smiled as she remembered her times with Alaine. She was just bubbly, happy and sweet. It was easy to love her. She wasn't fussy; at least not on this visit she wasn't, Jaleen thought. She opened her arms and allowed you to lift her just as easily as she had opened her heart to love you in return.

A soft tug at her heart made her realize that she really wanted to settle down. She wanted to have someone to love and to have that love returned. She did not want children without their father present and involved. That she was certain. Still, she longed to have someone special to share her life with. "A little girl and boy would be just right," she added. She had long ago analyzed that a boy and a girl were not a pair as everyone kept saying. They were simply one of each. A pair of girls and a pair of boys is what she was a part of. Her parents had a pair of each. Pairs were two of the same thing. A pair of shoes looked alike. A pair of gloves looked alike. A pair of salt and pepper shakers meant both shakers looked the same. A boy and girl was simply not a pair. However, she would settle for one of each. If a third one came along, that would be fine. Be it a girl or boy, she was sure she and her husband would love it just the same.

But first, she had to find a husband who was ready to settle down and raise a family. "Not all in one year, now," she reminded herself smiling. But ready to settle down, spending their early years getting to know each other before adding others—their children, into the inner circle of their relationship. ✽

❀❀ *Chapter Nine* ❀❀

Aaron was relaxing in his living room when Jaleen pulled in. He had positioned himself to see when she'd returned. "She'd been gone for the past three hours and forty minutes, but who was counting?" he reminded himself as he rose from his favorite chair and opened the door.

Armed with his keys, he made his exit and swiftly descended the stairs to meet her in the parking lot. Her arms were filled with the bags and he was able to offer a helping hand. Pocketing his keys, he retrieved several bags from her arms and they proceeded to walk up the stairs. He was surprised she had opted for the stairs and not the elevator.

"Starting a new project?" Aaron inquired. "Not really." Jaleen said with a smile. "These are to send to my sister-in-law. They are my contribution to the new business." "Sounds like you're getting these little details out of the way," Aaron said. "Trying to," Jaleen agreed. "My brother will be leaving soon and I know she will begin sewing her heart out to build up the inventory for the store. So I have some pieces I want to contribute. I was busy getting ready for work tomorrow when the labels came to me." "Labels?" Aaron repeated. "Yes, labels," she continued. "You know the tags that appear in the backs of garments? Well, it came to me that the clothes should have labels in the back to identify whose they are. I got the order form and I plan to fill it out and mail it in the morning," she stated excitedly. "So while I was there, I decided I would kill two birds with one stone—get the fabric samples for her to choose from and take care of the order for the labels."

"That's good," Aaron said. They'd arrived at her door and Jaleen unlocked the door for them to enter with the bags. Aaron placed the bags on the first chair and said, "Take it easy and have a good day tomorrow, too." "Thanks," she said as she closed the door.

Jaleen began the business of packing up the materials and notions. As she filled the boxes, she made a note of what each box contained and she wrote the note to Selecia about the labels. She also explained the fabric samples and that she wanted her to select the pieces she liked. They were Jaleen's gift to the store. There were more than fifteen samples and they were purchased in quarter inch blocks to give her an idea of what the design and pattern layouts were.

With the items neatly arranged in the boxes, Jaleen wrapped and labeled the boxes and left them near the door for easy pick up and mail out the next day. She then worked on the order form and when that was finished, she placed a check in the envelope and placed it on the top box near the door. Her assignments were completed for now.

The last detail to be taken care of was the balloons. She decided she would work with Brad on those. She was also going to look into being able to take some time off for her brother's graduation and to get home in time for the opening of the store. She didn't want to miss either event. That said, she prepared the check that she usually sent to her brother to help him with his expenses. This being his final year, she knew that the store would also be on his mind and he would cut back on some things to ensure that he, too, was able to add to the inventory. She added a little extra to the check and smiled. In the note, she indicated that she wanted him to take care of everything for school and the extra was to help him with the store. She ended her note with a smiling face in a heart and placed it in the envelope and sealed it. That, too, was also placed with the first envelope on the boxes near the door.

Jaleen ate her dinner in silence. She had finished packing up the work she had been working on prior to her little shopping excursion and decided that she would complete it and be prepared for the meeting and announcements the next day. Reviewing her actions for tomorrow, mentally, she felt she had a basic idea of what approach she was going to take and dismissed everything else.

The request for additional leave to attend her brother's commencement exercises and the opening of the store were uppermost on her mind, now. Both would be happening within weeks of each other. How could she arrange for the time off? That was her concern right now. What if she could attend only one event, which would it be? She decided to wait until Brad returned to the mainland and called her. She would get the dates from him and finalize her plans.

Tomorrow, however, she would inform her supervisor that she needed some time off in May and June and that the dates would be provided by the end of January when her family was sure about their own plans. Both events were important. Both warranted her presence. She wanted her brother and Selecia to know that she was behind them one hundred percent. She wanted her brother to know that she was especially proud of him and his willingness to stick things out, after learning Selecia was pregnant and more so after the storm.

Life really has its ups and downs. It has its ins and outs. But the relationships that were formed along the way helped to strengthen resolves or weaken barriers that hinder progress and promises made. Looking back, she realized that she invented barriers to keep from feeling the pain associated with loving. She loved and looked out for her brother. She believed that they were all they had. Their other two siblings, Claudia and Maurice, had each other and she and Brad had each other as well. They often got together on their mother's birthday. Brad seldom came because he was in school. "Perhaps that will change," she said to herself. Once he is working and their business is off the ground, they would be able to plan vacations that would allow their mother to get together with Brad, Selecia and Alaine. "Imagine," she realized, "I'm the first member of the family to meet Selecia and Alaine in person. We have really splintered apart as a family," Jaleen acknowledged.

Though her mother worked and recently began dating, neither she nor their father had returned home since the devastation. They had sent money. She had actually taken the time to visit and learn what conditions her grandparents, her brother and his family were experiencing. She made a note to give them a call later. She wasn't up to the two or three questions everyone would have regarding their grandparents' living conditions or that of the residents. She just wanted to feel whole and be involved in a loving relationship by the time the year came to an end.

With the passing of time, along with her observations and interactions with others, she was beginning to realize that the divorce did not end her relationship with the other two siblings or her parents. It simply ended her parents' relationship with each other. "Still," she reasoned quietly, "it made me feel torn in half." As she walked slowly back in time, she remembered her first boyfriend. She remembered the excitement of feeling in love. She also remembered their first kiss. He had walked her home from one of the games and they were just talking about this and that. When they got to the corner before her home, Lyle held her hand and stepped towards her in one motion and gave her a kiss on the mouth. She was so amazed at the feel of his mouth on hers but the slight invasion of his tongue caused her to pull away. He was a senior and she was a junior in high school. Then the turmoil began. Her parents were splitting up. She got lost in their drama and didn't know how to cope or share it with Lyle. Eventually, they, too, drifted apart and then they'd broken up. She was too busy grieving the loss of her parents to officially grieve the loss of her first boyfriend.

Lyle Washington moved on to college on the east coast and she saw him occasionally until they had moved. That was one time she felt connected. They had a church they attended, friends they had known and who had known them through each other's siblings and they had a routine that had been dismantled once her mother moved to be able to afford the expenses associated with raising children alone. Though they were allowed to visit their dad, he did not go out of his way to keep up with them. That had hurt her most of all.

With a gentle sigh, she laid those thoughts to rest, again. She had come a long, long way, alone, and she was determined to go further in life. She just hoped it would be with someone loving, pleasant, enjoyable, respectful, committed, responsible and witty but not overly protective or filled with anger or drug use issues. She knew she didn't want someone with obsessions, addictions or compulsions in her life. No one's perfect. "I'm not perfect," she surmised. "But I am not willing to settle for much less."

"I do want to meet someone who is down to earth, honest, hard working, willing to commit to a relationship and respect me as an equal partner in life," she declared inwardly. She really wanted someone who was willing to love her with the totality of his being as well as she was willing to love him completely. She wanted a partner for life; a best friend; a special confidante that made her warm and tingly yet young and dizzy with the spontaneity of their love. She wanted someone who would respect her opinions and whose opinions she also respected. She wanted someone who was willing to raise a family and be a part of the day to day experiences raising children entailed.

Sitting and staring out into the night sky, Jaleen allowed herself to dream. She sat there envisioning her life a few years down the road. She saw someone who was happy; someone who was in-love. She even saw children. Two boys and she looked closely to see whom they resembled. It was difficult. Her imagination did not allow her to make out the facial features of her boys. The boys appeared to be under the age of ten, possibly seven years old. There was a babyish look about their faces. As she tried to figure out their facial images, the movement of her plate on her lap brought her out of her reverie. Walking towards the kitchen, she tried to determine if they were twins. She also became alarmed that she remembered that moment, though it seemed more like a dream. She had actually drifted off to sleep. If only it was that simple.

After cleaning up in the kitchen, Jaleen took a long shower and went to bed. The work week was waiting and she needed to be well rested to tackle the challenges it brought. She was hoping that her night's rest would include the continuation of her latest delusion. ✿

❀❀ *Chapter Ten* ❀❀

Jasmine was busy working on her romantic theories when Aaron emerged from his apartment for work. She noted that he had exited his own residence and was on his way to work. Of course, Jaleen had left earlier. She was an early mover. Aaron left around the same time each day and so did she. Seven thirty was a slow but efficient time for both of them. They worked about forty-five minutes away in the opposite direction to each other. The traffic usually pooled around the downtown area much later and they were able to make the trek sometimes in a shorter period of time.

Jasmine worked for a job placement agency. They assisted in matching clients to working situations that were considered ideal based on the information on their résumés. Jasmine enjoyed the conversations. She liked feeling that she made a difference in someone's life. She also knew there was a thin line between being employed and being unemployed. Therefore, she was extremely careful with what she repeated. She did not want to seem like one with no integrity or professionalism.

Often times, she shared the goofs and mix-ups that clients experienced and shared with her. The transposing of a number can lead you down a very unproductive street and corner. What was experienced often lead to the most hilarious conversations, especially when the clients returned seeking clarification on what they had written down. The things they had seen or witnessed often left the office staff in stitches.

The supervisors would sometimes listen to the re-enactments and then scold them in meetings. They were reminded time and time again to make sure the correct addresses and numbers were written down. Many of them had begun having it typed and ready for dissemination. Still, there were those, who were with the company from its inception who felt that employment meant being responsible and one must be responsible enough to get there on time and at the right address. Even with that attitude, the errors still occurred.

As a result, they now provided their clients with computerized directions that were guaranteed not to cause mix ups. If they were catching the bus, the address and telephone numbers were provided along with the name of the contact person. If they were driving, then the instructions were provided in writing and the client simply had to follow the directions and arrive to their destinations with less drama and hassles.

There were always clients waiting for employment assistance. Some wanted work for six months. Others wanted to work evenings only. There were some who wanted to work part time; that was mostly college students and then those who were just looking for something to occupy their minds and they were retired individuals who wanted to work for someone willing to make their day and their blood pressure increase. She met all kinds. Every day was different!

A new representative was joining the staff today. She was excited about that. They heard it was going to be a man. There were no other specific details provided. Everyone wanted to know if he was cute, available and young. A few wondered if he was retired, had any eligible grandsons and whether he would be able to fit in with them. Either way, today they would all find out. They worked from eight thirty to five thirty and they had a full hour for lunch. Their breaks rotated depending on who was on leave, but for the most part, they all managed to make switches among themselves whenever they needed to take care of personal business or attend the function of their children. So the big test would be how well he would fit in when it was crunch time for sure.

Jasmine had been with this company for five years. She was good at placement opportunities. She had learned to listen keenly and seek out those details that made it possible for the clients to successfully fit into their new assignment. Many of her clients were grateful for the selections she had made on their behalf. They communicated about being well matched and that they had enjoyed the environment they worked in, even if it was a temporary assignment.

Some remembered them with flowers for Valentine's Day. Others provided them with fruit baskets for Thanksgiving. The company helped to sponsor the annual Labor Day picnic and many of the clients attended and brought their families. This extended the agency's family base as well. They were number one in the temp industry in the county and employees, like Jasmine, were a major factor.

"Good morning!" Jasmine said as she greeted her co-workers enthusiastically. "Is he here yet?" she asked with bright shining eyes. "You're up to no good already," Beth Ann chided her. "I hope he's married, settled down, has three children with another one on the way and a task master," Beth Ann concluded. Meredith joined them in the laughter. "Beth Ann, are you on your crusade again about someone having a family? Not everyone is in a hurry to populate the earth," she reminded her jokingly. With a few minutes to spare, the girls settled into their stations and began their preparations for the first round of clients they would be seeing.

Helen, the receptionist, usually did an excellent job of scheduling clients and Mondays was their toughest days to get through. They often had clients waiting to see them, some with their temp assignment coming to an end and trying to line up another one so they could keep going. With the end of the holiday season, many of the temporary positions came to an end and the task of matching to the available openings became a daunting one. The temporary positions involved gift wrapping, assisting in customer service, restocking shelves and warehouse type jobs. Hotels often requested additional help to ensure their ability to satisfy the holiday travelers. So this January would be no different.

They worked until noon when they had the first real break of the morning. Jasmine realized that no one had taken the time to notice or say when the new guy arrived. They were all hopping, trying to situate clients and upload new requests. The uploaded requests were quite a challenge. They had to read, more like scan the work orders, and then see if they had anyone who could be assigned to the new requests. They were quite busy and now, it was time to seek out the new member of the staff.

Meredith was the first to say, "He's cute and he's quietly working over there," pointing in the far corner near Beth Ann. Jasmine groaned outwardly. "Why?" she lamented, "Why was he sitting over there? Why is he near Beth?" "Why?" she groaned. Meredith was laughing loudly. She knew Jasmine was overreacting and she enjoyed it when she mocked Beth Ann.

Beth believed that everyone was to be settled down by twenty-five, with at least three children and a scout troop to lead. She was happily married and she and her husband Ken had two girls, Melissa and Audrey. They were five and seven and the light of her eyes. Everyone was waiting for the announcement that Ken Jr. was on the way. It was the longest time she had gone without being pregnant. Her station was decorated with their pictures at various stages of their development. The girls were involved in karate and dance lessons. She believed this would help them to be graceful and still able to defend themselves.

As they made plans to eat in the diner next door, the new guy emerged from behind his station. "He was good looking," Jasmine agreed. Boldly, she invited him to lunch with them. Graciously, he turned them down. He had made other plans. "It's on," Jasmine thought to herself. The chase was definitely on. Who makes arrangements for lunch on the first day when you could spend it getting to know your new colleagues? Feeling miffed, she decided to keep her feelings to herself as she joined her friends in laughter out the door.

The load was hectic throughout the afternoon. The morning had its predicaments and the afternoon was no better. The streams of clients appeared endless, all the way until quitting time. There was no time for prolonged water breaks or ribbing each other. The jokes that they usually shared were on hold as they worked throughout the afternoon to match clients, update applications, and review new listings to assist those currently in their midst.

When she got in her car and started the engine, she was glad the day had ended. Mentally, she was pooped. Emotionally, she was annoyed. She did not expect the new guy to not want to eat with them. She would ask again tomorrow and see what happened. She wasn't trying to make a play for him. She was just trying to be friendly. But if he didn't want her hospitality, then so be it.

As she made her way home, she decided to stop by one of her old hang outs for a few minutes. She wanted to unwind and didn't feel like being alone just yet. As she entered CJ's Ribs and Beer she felt at ease instantly. She remembered the good times she had when she was with her college friends. They hung out here every weekend, watching the games that were played out of town and simply clowning around.

Jasmine sat at the bar and ordered her usual, a soft drink with a twist of lemon and ice. After sipping on the first one, she decided to go home. It was quiet for a Monday and she wanted some noise. As she began to leave, Max the bartender, pinched her about her friend, Amber. She had lost her job and was believed to be working for an escort service. He even had her number from an out of town client.

This news greatly disturbed Jasmine. Amber was a high strung sorority sister. She always felt she needed to prove herself. Well, she may have proven herself out of a job. She was competitive and a hard worker. Sometimes she was a bit extreme but, she always knew the bottom line: to be successful. She was an only child and her parents pampered her and gave her whatever she wanted. They, too, expected her to be successful.

She wondered if they knew and she decided to get in touch with her. Jasmine thanked Max and left the Ribs and Beer. Now she was really depressed. Her concern for the new guy paled in comparison to what she had just learned about one of her friends. As she made her way home, she felt compelled to call Amber and find out if what she had heard was true.

"I work at an employment agency, for Christ sake", Jasmine stated aloud. "Being unemployed is a state of being but it wasn't permanent nor is it the end of the world," she argued aloud to herself. "Many people lose their jobs for various reasons. The reason for their unemployed status wasn't the issue at the agency. The results were." Jasmine felt she had let her friend down. Though she did not know that she was unemployed, she knew now and it hurt. It hurt because had they stayed in touch, she could have provided her with assistance in getting another job. Getting people connected to the employment scene was a priority at the agency and they did it with more success than most.

As she entered the complex, she hurriedly got into her parking space and rushed upstairs. She had an important phone call to make. ❁

❀❀ *Chapter Eleven* ❀❀

Aaron worked hard that day on the three assignments he had. He loaded his truck, unloaded it at the sites and began immediately to prune, hedge and remove any debris associated with the tasks. If fertilizer was needed to invigorate some of the greenery, he added it and moistened it before moving on to the next section. He was focused on his work at the last site, a small area in the city park when he saw an old associate. She had been sitting alone, staring out into the distance. As he came upon her, he called her name. K'Leah Greaves was an old school mate he had a secret crush on.

He had admired her secretly for months and when he did muster up the courage to say something to her, she had politely dismissed him and walked away. He was crushed. He couldn't believe that after he had gotten the courage to say something to her, she had simply dismissed him in such a rude manner. He went to great lengths to avoid her from that day. That was his ninth grade year in high school. They graduated together and she had left home to pursue a degree in business management. She wanted to operate her own modeling firm. She felt she had the right stuff to make success stories of other young girls. He'd never heard about her since. Now, here they were many, many miles away from home and she was simply sitting and staring out into space.

As she looked at him she knew she had no idea who he was but she tried to be polite in her response. "What are you doing here?" Aaron asked. "Where have we met before?" K'Leah asked in a very soft spoken voice. In a flash, Aaron decided to admit he'd made a mistake and move on. But something kept him from saying it. Something was wrong. He knew it. Taking a deep breath, he told her they had attended the same high school and graduated together. When he gave her his name, she did not remember him. "Is something wrong?" Aaron asked. "Are you okay? Is there someone I can call if you're not okay?" he continued.

K'Leah simply looked at him and then pretended to look right through him. She wasn't about to explain anything to a perfect stranger. They may have graduated together but she did not remember him and didn't feel like doing so right now. "I am fine." K'Leah responded. "I am fine," she repeated.

Aaron looked at her one more time and decided to move on. Her business was her own and if she didn't want his help, then so be it. As he walked away, he bid her a good day and hoped everything worked out as she desired. K'Leah watched him walk away. His stride did look familiar. His face did not and his physique wasn't what she had remembered with the stride. Still, she simply watched and allowed him to move on with his day and his work. Her troubles were her own and of her own making and she didn't feel like talking right now.

Her husband of nine years had asked for a divorce. She thought she had done everything to make him happy. She gave him a son. She kept his home clean. She even entertained his clients whenever he needed her to. The evening socials required a caterer; to save money she did the work herself. As he climbed the ladder in his office, she apparently moved further back on his list of priorities. Now, he wanted a divorce. As she sat quietly, she was contemplating her options.

She did not want a divorce. But if he insisted, she had no choice but to give in to him. He also wanted her to move out the house. There was no way he was going to maintain the payments on the house and maintain the lifestyle he wanted. Their son would live with her and he would have visitation rights. He wanted his son to be a part of him and his new family. One of the clients she entertained in her own house had been secretly sleeping with her husband. Of all the thoughts that ran through her head, murdering her rival was the only one that kept reverberating through her mind.

K'Leah had never felt so hopeless; so powerless. He was the catch at college. She remembered the day she had broken up with Jamaal. They had been a couple from eleventh grade. They had even attended the same college. Jamaal Haille Williams was the light of her world. They did everything together. The only thing that separated them was their majors. She was business management and he was civil engineering. Jamaal was her world until she met Keven. Keven Ahmad Baxter was smooth, popular and appeared to be going places. He was a junior when he met K'Leah a sophomore. They had a class together and were partners on a group project. When he decided K'Leah was the one he wanted to share his life with, he was relentless in his pursuit of her personal time and space.

Without thinking twice, she broke up with Jamaal. He did not see it coming and it was the last thing he expected. When she told him she wanted to share her life with someone else, it sounded shallow but it was true. Keven had made her his and she was willing to take her chances with him. Eleven years later, he wanted her out of his life. She had been his for eleven years and now she had to move on. He did not want her in his life anymore. She was no longer needed.

Tears slowly streamed down her face. She was being discarded like an old pair of shoes. Her son was like a pawn on a chess board and he had no idea what was in store for him or his family as he knew it. "How do you tell an eight year old that his father had decided to move them to another income bracket? How do you explain that life as he knew it, with both parents sharing in his day to day experiences, was going to change?" K'Leah cried as though her heart had been ripped from her chest and stomped on. And again she wanted to murder the woman who had caused her this pain. Everyone knew Keven was married. She was never that far removed from his life and his business socials.

The more she cried, the freer she felt. The freer she felt, the more she wept openly. She needed to release the anger and energy associated with this grief. She needed to feel free and whole right now. She needed to feel that she mattered even if only to herself. K'Leah cried as though her world had come to an end. She cried because all that mattered had been removed from her daily existence and she couldn't do anything about it.

As he worked from a safe distance away, Aaron continued to keep an eye on K'Leah. When she started crying, he wanted to find out what was causing her so much pain, but decided to keep his distance. She was trying to work some things out and she did not want to talk it out with anyone right now, not even someone she may have perceived as a total stranger. He knew nothing of her current life and he didn't really want to know. She

was a part of his past and he was no longer interested in her like that. But, he did not want to know she needed help and he did not offer assistance. They were from the same hometown. They were classmates and their families knew each other.

Aaron decided to get in touch with her parents through one of his sisters. Someone needed to know that she appeared to be in need of a friend or family member. This is where family came in. Whatever was troubling her, she needed her family to support her right now. She did not need to be alone. As he continued on with his work, he sincerely hoped that things would be okay for her soon. Despite her poor treatment of him in the past, he wished her no ill will.

If it were one of his sisters in this same situation, he continued inwardly, he would like someone to feel a sense of responsibility and duty to try and contact someone in his family to let them know what they had observed or more specifically what was going on. When in distress, people oftentimes made very, very dreadful decisions. Thoughts of suicide and other random acts of violence often begin in the minds of those who are depressed, sad or simply overloaded with anger, disappointment and other feelings of rejection.

Though he never felt like killing her or any similar actions, he felt badly enough not to want to be around her or anyone else for a long time. He was extremely grateful for his sister and her willingness to step up and be his friend as he got over K'Leah and her rejection of him. She brought a semblance of balance back to his shattered world and he hoped that someone would be able to do the same for her now.

Moving on, he once again focused on his current love interest, though the interest was one-sided. He hoped that her little meltdown regarding thoughts of her ex will be a thing of the past. He also hoped that with their blooming friendship, she would eventually find in him, not just a friend but someone she could count on through thick and thin. Jaleen was independent, thoughtful and she appeared focused on making something of herself as she assisted her family. Getting to know her better was something he was looking forward to doing. There were a couple of good pictures playing in the theater this week and he was considering asking her out on a date.

They are already used to spending some time together and he would slowly increase that alone time so that they could give themselves the time to get to know each other better, without Jasmine as a buffer or screen between them. Of course he was certain she would be annoyed at being left out, but when you are trying to establish a relationship, three is always a crowd. ✿

❀ ❀ *Chapter Twelve* ❀ ❀

Jaleen's day was organized frenzy. But it kept her and the members of the staff busy during the first full week of work for the New Year. When the meeting was finally over, it was revealed that the company had turned a profit and that bonuses would be made available during the first month of the first quarter of this year. Everyone was ecstatic. They were especially proud of that report.

They had reassembled teams, invested in a lot of managerial training, which focused on team building skills, working collaboratively, communicating effectively and making the decisions collectively while working to reach the established goals as a team. This was the litmus test for this effort and it had paid off. The five teams celebrated and the HR department was asked to organize a celebratory dinner at the end of the month. That's when the bonus checks would be made available.

During the morning and afternoon breaks the conversations centered on the same things. The news made everyone's day. The hard work, the extra hours spent preparing and reviewing orders had paid off. The extra effort made to familiarize each team with the types of requests; the level of customer service and the time line needed to actualize the deliveries were worth it. Everyone had made it happen and, most importantly, it had happened because of team work.

As they left for the day, the buzz throughout the building made its way to the parking lot. The new way of operating had paid off. The margin of profit was wide enough to ensure that this method of operating would be continued and modified as needed. The Board was pleased that the suggestions from the upper level management team had indeed paid off. The trainings were expensive. Many times they occurred on weekends and once per month during the working hours.

Jaleen and Crystal Addison left the office together. Crystal was excited about the news. She was expecting her first child and she and her fiancé', Jeffrey, were looking for a bigger place to live and raise their family. The bonus would be in time for her Valentine's Day wedding that was coming up. She was almost two months pregnant and didn't want to be showing under her gown. Jaleen was especially happy for her. She was new to the firm and she had worked hard. Whenever she had a question or concern she shared it with Jaleen who gave her the assistance that she needed to help her learn and be successful. They were on the same team. Crystal learned to pay attention to the fine details and to review her work thoroughly prior to submission for approval, processing and payment. That's the kind of action that yielded success.

Jaleen was also the only person Crystal had told she was pregnant. She and Jeff began planning their wedding from the time they learned about her pregnancy. They had been dating each other for the past three years and a summer wedding was the original plan. But, with the pronouncement of the baby, Jeff decided to move the date up.

"Thanks for the patience and assistance you gave me throughout this process," Crystal said. "Thanks also for encouraging me whenever I felt discouraged. You made me stronger by supporting my efforts. Whenever you reviewed my invoices, I cringed but at the same time I learned. Whenever you reminded me to call a client, I felt you were being pushy and I resented it. At night I would share how I felt with Jeffrey and he always took your side. He kept reminding me that you were trying to strengthen me so I would not be the weak link on the team. After today's announcement, you can push me and remind me anytime. Thank you for all you did to make today's announcement a positive one for all of us." Crystal stated apologetically. "I really appreciated everything you did," she said once more smiling.

Jaleen was happy for her. She thanked Crystal for her honesty and told her that the notes she had taken, the reminders she had received would no longer be necessary. "Once you've learned what to do and you do it consistently, reminders become obsolete." Jaleen reminded her smiling. They laughed together as Jaleen mimicked the words of Frank, one of the trainers. Then, licking their thumb, they removed the invisible note from the pad, just the way Frank did.

As other groups exited the building, the smiles, laughter and celebratory cheers were heard reverberating throughout the lot. Teams were extremely proud of what they were able to accomplish in such a short time. It was not the first time they had turned a profit. Last year, the profit margin existed but it was very small. So it was the first time they had turned such a large profit margin, given the investments that had been made to restructure the company's operations and managerial teams. The news of restructuring had made everyone nervous. Rumors of firings and transfers spread through the building like a wild fire in a national park. When the managers called the restructuring meeting, everyone was nervous. The plan was outlined. Individuals were placed on teams and team leaders were required to attend specified trainings and so were team members. The atmosphere was intense and the new learning curve was in place. Everyone became each other's keeper. So though they had been teamed up, they were teamed up within the teams as well. Hence Jaleen and Crystal's close working relationship emerged. Whatever was done to make one member successful had to be duplicated to make their partner successful, too. Though Jaleen did not expect Crystal to take work home, she did set goals for her and they met and reviewed them weekly to keep Crystal focused. Whenever she completed her work orders for clients, Jaleen reviewed them and gave her feedback to strengthen her performance and the anticipated outcome. If she did not show any communication between herself and a client, Jaleen reminded her to get in touch. Staying in touch kept errors to a minimum. It also positively impacted their sales.

After the first performance reviews, which occurred at the end of the third quarter last year, teams knew their strengths and weaknesses and additional training was provided to address those. These sessions occurred on weekends and many of them attended, eager and willing to learn. There were a few resentful attendees but they were in the minority and now, they were in the majority, sharing in the great news. This was a terrific way to start the New Year!

On the way home, Jaleen said a prayer of thanks. She remembered as a child when her parents would encourage them to think of one thing they were thankful for and to give thanks each night for it. It had been a long time since she had done a prayer of thankfulness. Though she has always remained humble and appreciative of her life and what's she's been able to accomplish, she had not continued with the evening prayer of thankfulness as they were encouraged to do growing up. The drive home was relaxing and quiet. She had not turned on her music and the silence was not deafening at all. It was the welcomed silence she needed to reflect on what they had heard and, at the same time, give thanks.

She was grateful for the opportunity to learn and to be able to take care of own responsibilities. She was also happy about the news they'd received. The bonus would allow everyone to do something personal and special as a reward for the effort and sacrifices made during the past year to meet the goals established under the reorganization and alignment teams approached implemented last year. They had given up many personal hours being trained and it had paid off. There were numerous meetings that lasted well into the night as they reviewed team goals and the actions that were being utilized to accomplish them.

It was an exhausting year, but it paid off. She was relieved to hear how Crystal felt. She knew she had stayed on her and was unwilling to let her fall. She really had a tough assignment. Crystal was new to the company, barely there four months when the changes began. She was trying to adjust to everything. Then the reorganization occurred and another adjustment had to be made.

She appreciated her honesty because she knew it was not easy. The announcement of her pregnancy only heightened the sense of urgency for her. She didn't want her to lose hope and quit. That would have been a setback for her team. After the Board's announcement, the team leaders met with their groups and made the announcement to all of them. They thanked everyone on behalf of the board and they expressed their thanks on their own behalf. Some of the leaders cried. They did not think they would have made it and with such success. It was a very emotional but rewarding day for everyone.

The company dinner was being planned and each team had to select a member to serve on the planning committee. Crystal was chosen to represent their team. That made Jaleen proudest of all. The team leaders were asked to identify someone who had made great strides from the start of the turnaround to present. Hands down, it was Crystal. They had worked well together and they had worked hard, too.

As Jaleen prayed softly, she included all the successes of her colleagues and that of her family. She also thanked God for friendships that never ended in divorce. Pulling into the complex, she included Aaron and Jasmine in her prayers. They were her friends. They didn't stand in judgment of her. They just hung in with her despite her inabilities to socialize with them regularly. She affirmed, once again, to make a conscious effort to be more neighborly. That's how friendships grew. It's also how she would be able to meet a future husband. That brought a smile to her face that matched the one in her heart. ✿

❀❀ *Chapter Thirteen* ❀❀

When she got inside, she heard Aaron's music playing softly. She decided to call on him first. He was usually quiet, but outgoing. He was also hard working, from his appearance when she ran into him the first time. She wanted to share the good news with someone. At that point, she wished she could have shared it with Brad. Not having a telephone and telephone service on the island was truly a bummer. Her grandparents would also appreciate hearing her good news, too.

Even though she had no idea what the bonus would look like, she made a few mental notes on what she wanted to do with hers. The past two years, she had received a bonus check for eight hundred seventy-five dollars and twelve hundred dollars, respectively, she decided to go with the high end amount and build her plans around that.

She was definitely going to bank half of it and use the other half to pay off her credit card bills. A zero balance is something she aspired to maintain. The longest she allowed her balance to run, depending on the amount, was two months. She was on course to purchasing a small home or condo and she did not want anything to stand in the way of that goal. The investments she had made in the store would be treated as monthly utility bills. That way, they would be paid off within the same time frame—in two months, if necessary. Brad's tuition contribution was a part of her savings and it was a bill she took care of by setting aside additional money to cover it.

She allowed her mind to stray a little further and decided that if the bonus was at least two thousand dollars, she would, again, bank half of the amount and pay off any outstanding balances on her credit cards. Her gas card was not a problem. That was considered a utility. But it would be paid off just the same. She would send some money for her grandparents to help them with whatever they wanted and she would include some money for Selecia and Alaine. She was really glad she had taken the time to go home and meet them. They added another dimension to her world and helped her to see that what she feared was truly possible.

A prayer was said on their behalf and all the residents of the island. This is the year for rebuilding. They will rebuild their homes, their lives and the island's infrastructure. She will rebuild her life as she sought to include others in her personal circle of friends. She wasn't going to try and fall in love with the first man she met but she was definitely leaving the door open a little wider.

She tapped lightly on Aaron's door. It was the first time she was at his door, uninvited. He had said often enough that she could drop by anytime, but this was the first time she had taken him up on the offer. A level of shyness came over her and as she was about to leave, the door opened. Aaron was as surprised to see her standing there as she was that it opened.

"Are you busy?" Jaleen asked. "No, come in." Aaron said. She'd been here before but always with others. Aaron loved to cook and he would invite a few friends over every now and again. "Is something wrong?" he inquired as she came in and he closed the door behind her. "No, not at all," she responded gaily. "How was your day," she asked in return. Aaron sighed deeply and Jaleen looked at him concerned. "Is something wrong? Is everyone in your family okay?" She asked him quickly.

Motioning them to sit down, he agonized over what he was about to share. Then he began. "Today, I saw someone I knew from high school days in the park where I was working. She was sitting and staring out into the blue. When I realized who she was I approached her. But she did not recognize me. It was obvious that she was in some kind of situation and needed someone to at least talk to. As I continued working, I saw her crying. I knew she needed help but felt powerless to assist her. You see, she had dismissed me many years ago and I didn't want to risk that feeling of rejection again. So when she indicated she did not recognize me, I decided to walk away. I asked if there was anyone she wanted me to call and when she declined my offer, I wished her well and walked away," Aaron finished sadly. "I'm sorry to hear that," Jaleen replied softly. "Is there anything that can be done to assist her?" she inquired. "I called one of my sisters who knew her family pretty well," he continued. "She indicated that she would get in touch with them to alert them of her distress. So someone is being contacted about her I'm sure."

"I hope everything works out," Jaleen told him. "I'm sorry to hear that about your friend," she offered. "Truth be told," Aaron said, "she's not really my friend. I had a crush on her in ninth grade. When I gathered up the courage to speak to her, she dismissed me like I was some pesky fly. She felt she was too good for me and I never spoke to her again, until today."

"Sorry to hear that," Jaleen murmured again. "How did you recognize her? It's been a while since ninth grade, I'm sure" Jaleen said smiling. She wanted him to feel comfortable talking to her.

She hoped he didn't think she was prying. "It's been a while," Aaron agreed. "Would you like something to drink?" he asked as he went towards his refrigerator. "Yes, thank you." Jaleen responded, wondering if he was trying to change the subject. If he was, it was fine with her. She really didn't want him to think she was prying.

Aaron returned with a soft drink for them both. She accepted it and waited for him to begin the next topic. But he surprised her and continued on. "K'Leah," he said, "was a very pretty girl. She was also fairly popular. When I first saw her, I developed a serious crush. I wanted her to notice me. But I was too shy to say or do anything to capture her attention. Then one day, when I had built up the courage to say something to her, she simply dismissed me. She spoke as though I was beneath her and not worth the time of day. She never looked in my direction nor made an effort to speak to me again. My world crumbled and I felt as low as the dirt. I avoided her and anything that involved her. It hurt too much. By tenth grade she was getting involved with someone and by eleventh grade through twelfth grade they had been a couple. I believe they went to the same college, after we graduated. I just moved over here, enrolled in A & M and graduated with a degree in agricultural science. I've been in and out of relationships, nothing serious. And like you," he said, "I've also been cautious with my heart."

Jaleen wasn't sure what to say. She smiled weakly and agreed that love was challenging enough as it is. "I didn't mean to pry or make you feel uncomfortable," she confessed. "You didn't," Aaron admitted. As they sipped their drinks, Jaleen reflected quietly on what he had shared.

"Men also experienced rejection. It hurt them as much as it hurt us," she thought. "Life is hard for everyone," she concluded. "So what brought you to my corner of the world?" Aaron asked, breaking into her thoughts. He didn't want her to feel that she needed to go. She did not make him feel uncomfortable at all. It was good to talk about the past. It gave perspective to the present and focus for the future. She smiled again brightly as she recalled her good news that she wanted to share.

"Our company did some restructuring last year." Aaron nodded acknowledging her words. "A lot of money was invested in this move and we were all placed in teams," she continued. "Each year in January, the company would announce whether a profit was made or not. Bonuses were paid based on this level of success," Jaleen explained. "Today, the Board met with the managers and gave their report. We had turned a profit and it exceeded what they had expected, given the investments that were made in the new managerial and operating procedures. They are planning a special dinner to celebrate this success. The bonuses will be paid at that time." Aaron reached across the table and gave her a hug. "Congratulations! I know you've worked hard and if everyone worked as hard as you did, then the only thing to do is make a profit. I'm happy for you," he said. "Congratulations!" They hugged and then tipped their drinks in a mock toast.

"Did the tier one teams get their reports or was it done as a general announcement?" Aaron continued. He really didn't want her to leave just yet. "They made a general announcement," Jaleen supplied. "Everyone was so happy to hear that. We knew the Board was going to meet. We knew they would have been discussing the company's performance. We just didn't expect to hear that a profit had been made that exceeded their expectations. And you're right," she continued, "the performance of each team was not disclosed. I wonder why not," she pondered out loud.

"But then again, we had a managerial shift from competitiveness to collaborative efforts to ensure achievement of the quarterly goals. This meant improvements in customer service, billing, receiving and shipping, delivery and pricing. Monthly, we shared performance objectives, goals and strategies that supported achievement of them. We even had teams within our teams to ensure success individually and collectively. So maybe they didn't announce the individual team earnings in order to promote a more collaborative environment," Jaleen concluded. "But that's a good observation, though," she added. "How would you know where to strengthen as far as the efforts of the team, if data wasn't being kept on team performance?" Aaron queried. "It's nice to have everyone working on goals and achieving them. But you still need to know where your potential trouble spots are so that you could continue to invest in them and strengthen them and the team." "I agree," Jaleen said. "Maybe that information will be revealed at the dinner," she said. "And if it isn't," Aaron said, "don't let me find you sitting in your car crying. Life's too short to invest in sadness. Continue doing your best and let God do the rest."

They spent a few more minutes talking and laughing together and then bid each other good night. Jaleen was glad she had chosen to speak with him. She learned something about him and men that she did not think about before. Additionally, he threw something at her that none of them had considered after the announcement was made. It was true that the individual team reports had not been shared. They were all caught up in the fact that they had done well. All the hours of training, coaching each other, working together on all aspects of the work their team members produced had been worth it. This certainly proved that competition wasn't for everything or everyone. The collaborative model had proven that they could do better and they did. ✿

❀❀ *Chapter Fourteen* ❀❀

Jaleen and Aaron spoke for a few hours that evening, sharing little tidbits about their day and time with the companies they worked for. Aaron wanted to ask her out but felt the opening to do so was not evident. He enjoyed listening to her speak and didn't mind what the topic was as long as she was with him, he was fine just being in her presence.

"So, besides working all the time, what do you do for fun?" Aaron finally asked. He wanted to invite her out and he knew he needed to create the opening for that to happen. Jaleen thought for a few seconds and realized that she hadn't gone out and done anything for fun since her break up with Clay. Jaleen looked him in the eye and answered softly, "I haven't been out much really since my break up. I placed all my energy into working in order to not think about him and the hurt associated with that relationship."

Taking a deep breath, Aaron took the plunge. "Would like to go to a movie with me this Friday after work? We could go to the eight o'clock showing. You get to pick the movie." Jaleen admitted, "I don't even know what's playing. Do you have today's paper? We could look it over and make a selection. I'd love to go to see a movie with you," she finished smiling.

Moving from the couch to the rack with the magazines and Sunday newspaper, Aaron retrieved the movie listing from the paper and sat next to Jaleen to peruse the movie listing and descriptions. He was smiling so brightly on the inside that he was certain, if he spoke the light would shine straight out of his mouth. She had accepted an invitation to go out with him. He gave her the listing and allowed her some time to review the listings and their descriptions.

While Jaleen read the titles and the description, Aaron got up and decided to make something for them to eat. They had been talking and enjoying each other's company and he had practically forgotten his manners, the ones his mother had made sure she instilled in all of her children.

He extracted the romaine lettuce, red onions and peppers from his refrigerator. He placed a large skillet on the stove and set it to a medium flame. The burger buns were extracted from the lower shelf and the garden burgers were taken from the freezer. After lightly buttering the buns, Aaron, set the temperature in the oven to warm so that the buns could be kept warm while the burgers fried. He sprinkled a little bit of salt and cayenne and white pepper on the two sides of the burgers and set them on the counter in a sandwich bag. This allowed the seasonings to work into the meat a little. It also added a little kick to the flavor of burgers when they're eaten. He sliced up the onions and peppers to brown them lightly in the warm frying pan. Then he separated a few leaves of the romaine lettuce along with four slices of tomato to place on the burger prior to covering it with the other bun.

"Can I help with anything?" Jaleen asked entering the kitchen. "I hadn't noticed when you left me and came in here," she finished. Smiling at her, Aaron replied, "I've got this. Have you decided on a movie for us to see?" "It's been a while for me and I don't have a clue what good or great," she stated. "I don't know what to pick." "Okay," Aaron said as he began to lower the burgers onto the skillet. "Read the descriptions out loud and let's see what we can agree on."

After disagreeing over several selections, they finally selected an action thriller involving a family and their need to locate the family's secret treasure that was left by a great grandfather who was once a pirate. The sunny, warm setting would do much to dispel the cold weather that was facing them this time of year.

Jaleen offered to set the table and Aaron told where things were located. As he finished the burgers, complete with a sprinkling of grated cheese, he whipped out a few pieces of pineapples from a jar and some cherries and promised her an ice cream surprise for dessert. While she was busy with the table setting, Aaron placed a can of whipped cream in the freezer along with the two small bowls of fruits.

As they sat to enjoy their meal of garden cheeseburgers and tall glasses of Cranberry Ale (ginger ale and cranberry juice mixed half and half), Aaron held Jaleen's hand and said grace. "*Gracious Lord, we are thankful for this moment that we are sharing at your table. We give you thanks and praise for bringing us home safely and also bringing us together at the end of another work day. Bless this meal and the friendship that is also being nurtured, in Jesus' name, we pray. Amen.*" "Amen." Jaleen echoed.

As she bit into the warm sandwich, Jaleen was pleased with the preparation and taste of something so simple. It didn't take long and she was able to add yet another selection of Aaron's specials to her list of food items she liked. She knew he liked to cook and both she and Jasmine had sampled many of his recipes in the past. They are usually mouthwatering delicious and leave you wanting more. The warming of the buns allowed the cheese to continue melting but also gave the feeling that you were eating a warm and hearty meal. The browning of the onions and peppers did not detract from the flavor but really added to the overall impact of the taste of the burger. She was used to onions on burgers not being browned. This little touch was an added bonus and she would be sure to try it the next time she prepared one for herself.

"How is it?" Aaron asked. He wasn't fishing for a compliment but her silence was beginning to cause him a bit of discomfort. "Too spicy?" he inquired. "I did use two sets of peppers on the burgers." "No, no, it's delicious," Jaleen answered. "I was just mulling over in mind how wonderful it tasted. I've always had the onions raw but cooked a little is okay, too." She supplied. "It's good and the spiciness is just right. I'm enjoying it," she added.

"So what are some of the things you like to do when relaxing and having fun, you never gave me anything back there," he resumed. Jaleen shared some of her interests with him and he was amazed to learn that she enjoyed reading, indoors or outdoors; she like to roller skate, though she hadn't done it in years and she enjoyed bicycle riding though she no longer owned a bicycle. At her previous residence, she used to go bike riding on weekends and that's how she got in her exercise each week. She would do it for at least two hours on Saturdays and she also enjoyed swimming but not during the winter season unless it's an indoor pool and she didn't know of any public indoor swimming pools.

She shared some of her experiences when she visited her grandparents in the islands and how close they lived to a beach. She would swim just about everyday when she was there for the summer. Aaron asked if she had done any swimming on her visit this time and she indicated that she hadn't. The water is usually cold during the winter season, and though some people still swim during this time of year, she hadn't been one of them. They talked about her grandparents and the disruption caused by the recent hurricane.

Because she was not as sociable as she has pledged to be more of this year, she had not told them much about the destruction to her second home and its impact on her family members back there. Aaron listened with keen interest and was able to learn about her family and her love for them as she spoke about them and their day to day events, since the hurricane.

"I'd like to visit the islands at least once in my lifetime," he said. "The ability to walk in sand, swim at the beach and simply enjoy a slower cadence to life must be exhilarating." "Consider that everyone works, some for the local government, some in stores and others in the hospitality industry since the economy is dependent on visitors, doesn't give those who live there the opportunity to enjoy the sunshine, sand and nor the sea," Jaleen shared warmly. Remember, as a visitor, you get to enjoy those things. But as a resident, you simply live and try to make a decent living as you raise your family. That's what my grandparents did. My grandfather was a builder. He and their closest neighbor, Mr. Samuel, worked together for years, building homes and other buildings for a living. When he was able to, they both bought a piece of land near the sea. That's where they live to this day. The damage done by the storm hasn't changed their minds about living there, though."

Glad that they had shared the meal and some good conversation, Aaron began to clear the table. When Jaleen started to get up to help, he said, "sit tight. I've got this. I'm just going to bring the dessert to the table from the refrigerator. Thanks. But I'm cool." He brought out the two small fruit bowls and the whipped cream. He squeezed a mound of cold cream over the fruits and said, "Enjoy your ice cream surprise!" Laughing, they dug in and Jaleen complimented his creativity. "No real ice cream in the fridge, huh?" She asked teasingly. Laughing again, they soon resumed their conversation.

"I can tell you really enjoyed living there. I'm glad you had an opportunity to visit with your family over the holidays and I am also glad that you are living here, too. "Aaron said with a smile. Blushing, Jaleen smiled and agreed with him. She did enjoy living in both places; each had its advantage. But, she also knew she was responsible for herself and so she had to live and work somewhere and so this is where her home was.

Completing their dessert, Jaleen attempted to give Aaron a hand with the clean up duties. Together, they washed the few pans and plates they had used and cleaned up the table, making sure it was free of crumbs and any sweet from their dessert. Stifling a small yawn, a result of a full stomach and good company, Jaleen thanked Aaron for giving her the opportunity to share her good news with him. She also thanked him for their meal. "It was delicious," she told him as they walked toward the door.

Aaron gave her a hug and watched as she went to her door and let herself in. ✿

❀❀ *Chapter Fifteen* ❀❀

Jasmine tried calling Amber several times that night. Each time her answering machine came on her mind raced with thoughts of where she could be and what she could be doing. It really saddened her to learn that her friend had fallen on such hard times and landed on that road. "Why didn't she call me?" Jasmine kept asking herself over and over again. She could have just picked up the phone and called. If not me, then call one of the other sisters. We pledged to be here for each other. That's our pledge for life. What's the point in pledging if we are not going to believe in its creed?" Jasmine continued to herself.

She thought of sitting outside her apartment building until she came home. She then realized that she didn't want to do it alone and would have to call on Aaron for help. Immediately, another thought captured her attention. This one, more alarming than the others: Where is Amber living now? What if she had moved since losing her job? She was more distressed now than before. Telephone numbers moved with you. She could have the same number, heck; she was calling it every couple of minutes. But is it at the address she had previously?

Jasmine decided to leave extra early the next morning to pay her friend a visit. If she was at the address, she would come back and talk with her later. If she wasn't then she would have to notify her parents to get an address for Amber. They would know if anyone else didn't.

As she prepared for bed, she suddenly felt cold and alone. She had never experienced that before. She wasn't caught up in trying to get married and raise a family. She was satisfied to live, have a good time and if it happened, it happened. Now, after learning what Amber may be going through, she felt a form of loneliness that had never caused her to be concerned before. It was as though she was alone in the world, far from friends, real friends and family. It's as though she had no way of reaching out to anyone.

First, she was despondent because the new guy turned down her bold invitation to lunch. She really felt put in her place and she didn't like that feeling. She was only trying to be friendly. She wasn't mate searching. Then she decided to wallow in her misery at the Ribs and Beer and really got something to concern herself with: her friend, her sorority sister's lifestyle changed.

Before she alerted anyone else, she needed to know if it was true. She needed to know if Amber was working as a professional escort. She also needed to know where she lived. Without any further hesitation, she took out a writing pad and made a list of things she wanted to do tomorrow. All involved Amber. She needed to verify her home address. Then she needed to find out if she was, in fact, working as an escort. She needed to know why she had chosen this deadly game to play with her life and whether her parents were aware of her decisions. She also needed to find out what happened to her job. Why she didn't contact her to assist in finding another one.

As she reviewed the list, she also added the names of two sorority sisters she would contact along with the names of Amber's parents. She would call them if she was unable to locate Amber. They needed to know. Max would not have passed it along without good proof. She felt certain of that. However, she didn't want to believe that her sister, her friend had crossed that line.

Looking back over the years, she realized that she had never been driven to that level of distraction. She had been involved with men and it didn't work out. She did not lose her sense of balance or perspective over it. Life gives lemons you simply make lemonade. When the lemons are finished, something else would come along. She had been between relationships before. She was out of a sour relationship now for almost a year and a half.

Henry Anderson had proposed to her. They had been seeing each other for eighteen months. He was hard working, had a son from a previous relationship and they spent time alone and with his son, Trayé. As they grew closer as a couple, she was certain that their relationship could work. Then Trayés mother became pregnant and that was the end of their relationship. He wasn't over her as he had claimed. At first, he denied having anything to do with her. But when she insisted on a paternity test after the baby's birth, he was trapped and had no response.

Even when she was willing to give their relationship a try, the fact that he had slept with her was a clear sign that he would never be fully committed to Jasmine. Stealing chances with an old flame does not signal a happy marriage for any future bride. And if that wasn't enough, Mr. Anderson was not a divorcée. He was still very much married to his wife.

After three crushing strikes—sleeping with his ex; his ex turning up pregnant and claiming it was his and his ex not officially his ex, Jasmine had thrown in the towel on that relationship and on future relationships for now. There was a point in her life when she didn't feel she was going to be able to get up and face each new day. But she did; one day at a time; one hour at a time; one breath at a time. She had regained her balance and was able to look life in the eyes again, standing on her two feet and not laying down weeping and feeling sorry for herself. She was also super cautious around her heart. She did not give it away easily and did not let anyone near it as easily either.

There were the usual teenage boyfriends. They lasted an average of four months. When they realized that Jasmine was not going to have sex with them, the relationship was usually over. With her big sister and brother for guidance, she knew that she did not have to let anyone have control of her mind or her body in order to be loved. With Henry, it was different. They were introduced by one of her friends. They met occasionally for drinks and a movie. The relationship developed slowly and when she decided to enter the romance arena with him, she believed it was forever. He made her feel special. He never spoke negatively of his ex and he simply introduced his son to her and they did things together. She had no idea what he had told his son and looking back, Trayé probably thought she was a cousin or some other relative. He never said or did anything that indicated his mother and father were in a relationship. But then again, what did five year olds know about adult relationships?

Jasmine closed that chapter in her life as easily as it had opened. She hadn't given Henry a second thought in more than eight months. A mutual friend told her recently that she saw Henry and his wife. They had another son. She allowed the news to remain on the surface and never allowed it to filter into her heart. She also refused to allow herself to cry over that spilled milk. Obviously, it was sour and the only person who didn't smell it early enough before drinking it was her.

When others seek the comfort of loving arms for the holidays, she simply spent her time with friends and their families. Sometimes she visited relatives and other times she just spent the time alone, hanging out with friends at the Floaters. She enjoyed teasing Aaron and her co-workers. They were closer to her than other people. She spent time with them. They shared information about their families, their lives and their ups and downs.

As Jasmine moved on, mentally, she returned to Amber. She had to find her. She had to know if she was okay and if not, what she could do to assist her. That was a dangerous life she had chosen. Venereal diseases aside, people get hurt when they interact with others from the wrong side of the spectrum. Sometimes, association breathes contempt. Not because you are with the person, it means they know all about you and you know all about them. Based on what she had seen on television, she really didn't want her friend involved in this kind of lifestyle.

First thing tomorrow, she concluded, she was going over to where she knew Amber lived. After placing her writing pad in her purse, Jasmine made plans to take her wired mind and body to bed. She hoped to fall asleep as soon as her head touched her pillow. Her trip down memory lane had opened many doors and now she was unable to keep all of them closed. She remembered the first time she had met Amber. They were in a freshman level course together. Then she remembered when they decided to pledge. Both were nervous about that decision and they tried to keep each other's spirits up. Later on, when they'd learned who the other girls were, they all talked about feeling nervous, too. They had formed a bond that carried them through their twelve weeks of pledging that spring semester. Seven girls pledged and all seven made it together. After that, they stayed in touch and tried to share photos of what was happening in their lives. "What happened?" Jasmine asked herself for the one hundredth time.

Jasmine got up and added the other three names. Though they lived in different states, they needed to know that one of their sisters may be in trouble. Perhaps they could help her regain her self confidence and assist in relocating and finding a new job. Sometimes a change of scenery was all it took to improve one's outlook on life. Whatever it took, she was going to locate Amber and try to help her bring some perspective and stability back into her life. That's what friends did and it's what sisters did for each other, too.

Tears began to build up in her eyes as she remembered her friend and the good times they'd shared. She wasn't a whiner or complainer. She was one who stuck things out, even if it meant that she had to do everything to ensure success on the assignment. She had pushed on, often alone, with many group projects, completing many aspects of the project when others failed to do their part. Her annoyance would be expressed after the project had been completed and submitted. Amber still maintained her poise and friendship with the individuals. That's just the way she was. If it had to get done, then it got done. She was goal oriented; driven; conscious of her performance and focused on the desired outcome. "What happened, Amber? What happened?" Jasmine asked herself again. When she returned to bed, she wept quietly until she fell asleep. ❁

❀❀ *Chapter Sixteen* ❀❀

As Aaron was about to step out the door, his phone rang. His sister was on the line. She had passed his concern along and she was giving him the update. "Morning, A. K'Leah's parents were unaware of any problems she might be having and they would get in touch with her," she stated. "Did you tell them I was the one who passed on the information?" Aaron asked concerned. After a few chuckles, his sister reassured him that she did not mention his name. She reiterated what she had said. "I told them that I had gotten a call from someone who had seen her and was concerned about her." She told K'Leah's parents that their daughter appeared distraught and didn't look herself.

Aaron exhaled. His sister knew the anguish he had suffered. She was a senior in high school when K'Leah had stepped on him like he was a bug. She was the one who tried to make him feel better as he tried hiding, avoiding being seen in the same corridor as K'Leah and even when he avoided going to some of the popular after school activities, she went with him to help him move beyond that incident. He just didn't want anyone to think that he was still in-love with her, after all these years. He wasn't.

He had found the one who was the light of his world; his port in a storm; the heart and soul of his being. She was created just for him and he was meant for her. All he wanted was a chance to rule as her King of Spades and she would be his Queen of Heart. So he didn't want anyone mistaking his act of kindness for anything else. Life went on after K'Leah's rejection. It hurt deeper than a third degree burn. But he got over it and had continued moving forward since then with several other short lived relationships that left him with no regrets.

As he hung up, he felt a sense of relief knowing that he had done his part. Turning on the engine, he breathed a sigh of relief. A support team had been activated to assist her through her crisis, whatever it may have been. He wasn't one to turn his back on someone in trouble. He wasn't one to stick his nose where it wasn't invited and he certainly wasn't one to go in search of trouble either. He had no problem helping others. But he was above being used and using others for his convenience, as well. "Do Unto Others" was a meaningful creed he tried to live by.

As he made his way to the entrance, he wondered if he would see K'Leah again. He had no idea she lived in his neck of the woods. He didn't mind seeing her again, but he was not going to approach her if he saw her again, either. As he collected his work assignment for the day, he quickly looked for the name of the park he'd worked in yesterday. It wasn't there and he was relieved. He didn't have to brace himself for a second run-in with his past. Loading up the truck, he placed his orders on the seat and made his way to the hospital. He was excited to be returning. It was his favorite place to work. In that garden, he always felt at peace.

Despite its purpose, he enjoyed the beauty and the secret world it created. He loved the way the flowers and other plants were arranged and maintained. The sense of peace and harmony that it evoked made him happy to be a part of its general upkeep. The individuals he met along the way, who took the time to appreciate the natural beauty around them made him feel good about the contributions he made to keep it looking first-rate for everyone to enjoy. When Aaron finished unpacking the tools he had planned to use for this assignment, he locked up the truck and whistled softly as he made his way down the path that took him to the heart of the garden.

His heart was light with thoughts of the one he wanted to share his life with. He wanted her to come to this place. He wanted to see her reactions as they walked through the garden. "This is the place I might propose you, Jaleen," he thought with a smile. It was a beautiful place day or night. Then mentally he raced ahead to the commercial park that had the holiday party for their staff. "That would also be a wonderful place to propose," he assured himself.

At the end of the maze, he could have her ring waiting, illuminated by one of the flood lights. As she wound her way through the park, they would be looking for something he had misplaced earlier. Then, together, they would make the discovery and he would watch her face as he presented her with the greatest expression of his love and affection for her while on bended knee. Aaron liked that idea even better. Whistling softly, he continued to embellish his plan, all the while hoping that his energies were not being misguided down the wrong path.

Jaleen spent the morning going over the reports and invoices her team had been working on. She was conscious of what she had shared with Aaron and what he had shared with her. Her heart ached to imagine him being rejected by anyone. He was sweet, kind, helpful and thoughtful. Then her mind revisited their conversation regarding the young woman he had seen in the park.

She was hesitant to label her as his friend. Friends may forget each other but they always remember, especially after chance meetings like the one he experienced yesterday. Then again, she reflected, the young woman's life had also moved on and since she had never considered Aaron as one of her friends then she really wouldn't be able to connect with him on any level, chance meeting or not.

The level of distress he expressed caused her to feel concerned about her. "What would make someone sit and cry? Many things," she concluded. The loss of a loved one, bad news about the health of a loved one, bad news about your own health; all these things could cause you to feel extreme pain that cannot be touched or sometimes shared. Then she added, most acutely, the loss of a loved one, your spouse to divorce. That, she admitted, would cause anyone to sit and cry, especially if you still loved them and they no longer shared the same feelings for you.

As she pondered what the situation could have been, she was moved, once again to reflect on her brother's relationship. She really hoped and prayed that their marriage could withstand the pressures of life. People seemed to be able to fall in and out of love at will. Something happens and they are no longer feeling the magic or free flowing, warm emotions associated with love that was able to embody everything they once thought essential to their relationship and their very existence. She also reflected on her grandparents' marriage and prayed to have something as true and long–lasting as theirs. "What makes some relationships last and others fail? What is the ingredient that must be in the relationship to make a marriage last as long as her grandparents' and beyond?" Jaleen knew that the answers to these questions were not easily surrendered to her or anyone else.

Living revealed life's secrets and she hoped to be attentive enough to learn as many of them as possible so that she could make them a part of her life. As she reflected on her grandparents' relationship, she knew that what they shared was truly a blessing. It was available to everyone. She just didn't know which secrets they had unearthed over the years that kept them going, feeling as strongly about each other as they still do, even today. "That," she reasoned, "is what she will endeavor to find out as she focused on finding someone willing to love, honor and cherish her for the rest of her life while she worked hard to continue to improve on the performance of her team."

Returning to the invoices, work orders and other buzz of communication around her, she, once again, gave her undivided attention to the work at hand. Crystal had made improvements in her abilities to read and produce comprehensive work orders. Her attention to details had shown much improvement and Jaleen was happy to be able to see these changes and note the continuous growth in her performance.

Again, the performance of the tier one teams crossed her mind and she was keen on finding out just how each team had done. She wanted some answers and knew whom to ask in order to get them. The middle managers were not always privy to what decisions and reports were shared with the upper level managers, prior to the meeting with the Board members. So she knew she could not discuss this with the team leader. She needed one of the upper level managers who were in charge of their team to get answers to that question. As she reviewed her conversation with Aaron, she knew he had thrown it out there, not to create any confusion. But once her mind had been pricked, it was difficult to let it go. The team approach, centered on collaboration: sharing and coaching had worked. This query might impede progress and give the wrong impression. She was beginning to squash the idea of asking about the tier one team performance. If it was revealed, fine and if not, fine. As a company, they had done well. They had exceeded their projections for the year. The heavy investments that had been made in training and coaching strategies to build strong, cohesive teams that focused on the bottom line had paid off. They were trained to work as a team in order to be productive individually and collectively. They had been trained in skills and strategies which promoted intergroup dynamics that were not tinged on competition but success based on consistent, efficient team work.

The good news feeling was back again and she was able to regain her sense of balance and comfort in knowing they had done well as a company. When she took her lunch break, she decided to go in search of the balloons and other little knick knacks that Selecia could use to decorate the showcase window. She also decided to write her Grandparents and let them know, once again, how much she appreciated her visit with them and to find out if they needed anything to help them with their contributions to the store. Teamwork, she smiled.

That's the one thing Brad and Selecia had going for the little store. Everyone was already focused on making it work and they were all working together to ensure its success.

As she browsed in the nearby shopping center, she came across several items she felt would be excellent for the children's clothing store. After making some inquiries, she made a note of the items and their cost. They would be her last purchase before going home for the opening. Next, she wandered into a few more stores and allowed her eyes to browse and be filled with new ideas for redecorating her apartment. She had some pictures she wanted to purchase and add to her collection. She also saw a few new frames that could be used to house her upcoming photos of her little niece and her parents.

The camera she seldom used was going to be put to good use soon, she acknowledged. She was going to take photos of everyone at Brad's graduation and that would fill up her living room, hallway and bedroom walls. With the rotation she already had in place, some photos remained on display all year long. Others were seasonal and then they were stored in plastic bins in her linen closet. There were a few new artificial floral arrangements that simply begged to go home with her. They echoed the promise of spring and she appreciated the new look. After the whimsical purchase, complete with vase and linen-look doilies, Jaleen made her way back to her car and to work. She had treated herself and she felt good.

With the promise of a bonus, she was sure the little purchase would balance out just fine. She intended to save most of it anyway. So a little treat every now and then was certainly something she could live with. As she re-entered the building, she felt the hum of excitement that had been created the day before. It felt good! She felt good knowing what it meant and she was glad everyone else was sharing in the good feeling, too. Now the challenge before them was to duplicate their efforts and yield the same results by the same time next year. With the kind of start this year was off to, she felt certain everyone would be able to rise to the challenge and make it happen. ✿

❀❀ *Chapter Seventeen* ❀❀

Jasmine was the first person out the complex the next morning. She wanted to see if Amber was at home and if she could talk with her briefly. When she arrived at the complex she knew her friend lived at, she was extremely disappointed to learn that she no longer lived there. A sick feeling came over her. The level of nausea and vomit followed by dizziness and the inability to breathe almost caused her to faint. The gentleman who answered the door assured her that he had been living there alone for the past five months and that he did not know who the previous tenant was.

As he saw her reaction, he asked her if she was okay and if he needed to call someone. For a little while, Jasmine could neither move nor respond to his question. Her feet felt cemented to the floor. She was unable to process what he had said in real time and she was unable to walk away, feeling in full control of her mental and emotional faculties. At one point, Jasmine wanted to scream. She couldn't believe this was happening. She didn't want to believe what she was hearing. Again, she asked the same question that had been plaguing her ever since Max gave her the news. "What happened? How did this happen? Why didn't Amber come to her before things had gotten so far off course?" "Ma'am, are you alright?" the voice repeated again. "Is there someone I can call to come and assist you?" he asked again. Jasmine tried, one more time, to shake her head and give him a response. She wanted to walk away, no run away to her car.

In what appeared to be in slow motion, Jasmine began to faint. The lights and everything around her slowly went out. Mentally, she kept asking for the lights to be turned on. She felt as though she was walking along in a tunnel that had no lights at the end of it. She was straining to see as her eyes tried to adjust to the darkness. Slowly, she began to process the sounds that seemed to be getting louder and closer as she walked in the darkness. There was a sense of urgency around her and she was unable to see or understand what was going on. Still, she kept walking. She wanted to get to the end of the long, dark path and walk in the sunlight once more. Consumed by the darkness, Jasmine was unable to maintain her focus and she felt herself falling. There seemed no end to the darkness or her sensation of falling. It was swallowing her up and she was unable to see or stop.

The ambulance raced through the streets as the attendants tried to assist Jasmine. They wanted her to regain consciousness. Her blood pressure was normal, her pulse was strong and still they were unable to awaken her. As the door opened at Mercy Presbyterian Hospital, Jasmine was rushed into an examining room. Because he was neither family nor friend, Al was unable to go any further with her. Out of concern, however, he waited and hoped that her prognosis would be a favorable one. He had no idea who she was or where she lived or worked. All he knew and was able to convey to the attendant and now the nurse at the station was that she came in search of someone who no longer lived at his address. When he informed her, she appeared to lose her sense of balance and focus. She appeared to be having difficulty breathing and then she collapsed.

He couldn't tell them anything and he felt helpless to assist her at a time when she needed help the most. One of the nurses escorted him to the waiting area. Facing an exit, he wondered if it would matter if he just walked away. He didn't know her, she didn't know him and he wasn't able to provide any information to assist them in identifying her or contacting anyone on her status. As he sat quietly wondering what to do, he remembered that she had a purse with her. He asked the ambulance attendant if he had possession of it still. He indicated that everything was turned over to the nurse at the time they checked her in.

Al returned to the front desk and asked about her purse. The nurse said someone from social services was contacted and they would take care of that. Feeling dismissed, Al decided to leave. He had nothing more to offer. He knew she didn't know him and he didn't know her and perhaps if she awakened and saw him, she just might react negatively again and he wouldn't want that to happen either. Walking towards the exit area, he walked down a long corridor to the elevators.

While waiting for the doors to open, he noticed the little garden on the far side. Walking towards the window, he looked out and saw the neat and well manicured topiary garden. There were a few people walking about but for the most part, it was empty. Then he noticed the guy who was trimming some of the leaves and removing the dried leaves that clung to some of the lower areas of the small trees and plants.

He noticed the level of care that the caretaker had given a small patch of shrubbery near a double set of benches. He wasn't in a hurry. He appeared to be trying to give each plant and tree his undivided attention. Obviously, he loved what he was doing. The growth and care of the plants and the garden were important to him. Al's mind went back to Jasmine, the lady who collapsed at his door. Who was providing her that kind of care?" "What is the reason for her reaction to his answer?" He knew he did not know the person she had inquired about and he had no answers that could assist her. Still, she was on his mind. He decided to return to the emergency room. He didn't know why but he did.

Al decided to wait until someone could tell him how Jasmine was doing. He needed to know that she was alright and would be able to notify her own family to come for her. If she needed help with that task, then he would assist her. But if she was able to he would leave, knowing she was safe and in good hands. One of the attendants noticed he had returned and he apprised him of her condition. She had regained consciousness and was stable. "She asked for Amber, does that name mean anything to you?" the attendant inquired. Shaking his head indicating no, the attendant sighed and touched him on the arm. Then he remembered he had received the names and numbers of the last set of people she had called. He gave Al the names and numbers and hoped he would be able to connect the dots and contact someone on her behalf. They shook hands, Al thanked him for the information and as he turned to leave, he inquired if he could see her. The attendant saw no harm in the request and he escorted him to her bed.

He was concerned that he had become involved in something that was not his fault. He also knew that he really could not see her nor receive any real information on her progress. But because they had ridden in the ambulance together and he had told him what happened, he decided to give him some information that should be able to put his mind at ease and maybe help them locate someone who was in a position to identify her and sit by her side.

Jasmine did not look derelict and her manner of dress did not suggest otherwise. It's just her reaction to the news that her friend was not there and that he was there for several months and did not know the person she was trying to locate which triggered the reaction that landed her in the hospital.

Al sat quietly and watched as her breathing lifted her chest cavity up and down. She was breathing at a steady pace and her eyes were closed. The intravenous tube was dripping liquid slowly into the tube that led into her wrist area. "What happened?" he wondered. "What's going on in your life that would have you panic stricken and land you in a hospital? Who is Amber? Too many questions and not enough clues to produce answers," he exhaled loudly.

He leaned over and touched her hand and softly, Alvin Kamaal Burley began to pray. "*Gracious Lord and merciful Savior. I do not know her but I know you do. Continue to strengthen her even now, Lord, in her hour of need. Grant her clarity of mind to focus on living again. Help her to find her friend and allow her friend, most merciful Father, to be safe and secure under your protection. Lift her up precious Lord and God and return her to us. Her life's journey must have an ending greater than this and because you are the author and finisher of all our fates, I ask forgiveness on her behalf in no other name but your holy, precious name. Redirect her path and find favor in her once more. As our Burden Bearer, Lord, relieve her of the one she is carrying in no other name but your holy son, Jesus' precious name I humbly pray. Amen.*"

When Al walked away, he walked away determined to find out what he could about this young lady. According to the information on her chart, her name was Jasmine and he made a quick note of her address before he left her bedside. He was also determined to find out who Amber was and to connect them because Amber was very important to her. He thought about their friendship and hoped they could patch things up. It was obvious that Amber moved and didn't let her know. Somehow they fell out of touch. But, he agreed inwardly, it's always good to have someone care about you. It's even better to have them care enough to come in search of you, especially when they haven't seen or heard from you for a while. It reflected the depth of their caring and that is so lacking today, he concluded derisively. "Caring," he uttered softly shaking his head.

Caring is becoming obsolete. Everyone's just concerned about self and not others. At least that's the way he felt since his divorce. "It's getting better," he said to himself. Al loved his wife and would have given her the world but he wasn't enough and his efforts were insufficient. She needed constant attention twenty-four, seven and there was no way he could be at her beck and call and still make a living. As the bitter taste began to reclaim his mouth, he decided to change the subject.

The ride in the elevator refocused his energies on something else. He was in the elevator because someone collapsed at his door. Now he had to find out who she really was, who her friends and family were so that they could know where she is. He also had to find Amber. She was an important piece of the puzzle. With nothing else but her first name and the fact that she once lived in the apartment he now occupied, he wasn't sure how it would end.

As he exited the elevator, he stopped by the gift shop and ordered some flowers for Jasmine. If there was no one there when she awakened, then the flowers would be there to greet her. Writing briefly on the card, he wished her well and signed it: Al, Apartment 120. When he asked for it to be delivered, he was unable to give a room number. He asked that it be taken to the emergency room. She was there up to when he'd left.

Leaving the hospital, he felt the coldness of the late morning breeze on his skin and face. At that moment he became acutely aware that he was not dressed to be outside in the cold January air. His mind returned to the gardener and the thermal jacket he was wearing as he diligently went about his duties with the plants. "That garden," he had observed, "was well manicured."

"I could use that jacket right about now," he thought as he tried to flag down a cab. He was a long way from home, getting hungry and feeling tired, too. After getting in late from his evening classes, he was overdue for some rest. ❀

✿✿ *Chapter Eighteen* ✿✿

Aaron called Jaleen the minute he hung up his phone. Jasmine had been hospitalized and they were trying to locate someone who knew her and would be able to provide her with some assistance. She wasn't physically hurt and had been brought in accompanied by a stranger who could not provide any information about her.

He had just left Mercy Presbyterian and was on his way to his second assignment when he received the call. Aaron pulled into the nearest lot and made a u-turn back on the highway. His mind was having difficulty processing what he had heard. Where was she and what happened? Because of the numbers in her cell phone, they were able to call him. She was among the first group of people he had given his number to. He seldom used his phone and he merely kept it for convenience and, he had to admit, moments like these. It also allowed his supervisor to call him when there were requests that came in from the area he was closest to. He didn't have to come in to the Nursery and then go right back out to provide assistance or repair to any of their plants or trees. Someone would meet him and provide mulching or other materials needed to service the additional site.

Jaleen was shocked to hear that Jasmine was hospitalized. Even more baffling was that she was unhurt and had been brought in by a stranger. "Where was she and how did this happen?" she asked herself as she prepared to leave. Moving quickly, she asked Crystal to complete the reviews she had been working on and to forward them to the team manager. With the last sentence, she was out the door and into the main foyer leading to the parking lot.

At the hospital, she was glad to see Aaron. He was talking with one of the station attendants. She had given him a brief update and he had indicated that they all lived on the same floor in the complex. He did not know how to get in touch with her parents but he knew someone who could. He would inform her supervisor and hopefully she would be able to get in touch with them.

As Jaleen approached them, the nurse concluded with the fact that she had been brought in by someone who indicated that she came there looking for a friend and when he informed her that he didn't know the person and that he was the new occupant, she simply collapsed. "Can we see her?" Jaleen asked. "She is an adult and I don't see why not. We called you so you must know her," she said looking straight at Aaron. "Please keep the conversation down. While we'd like her to wake up, we don't want her to be frightened and then develop other conditions that will require additional services," she smiled courteously, as she led them to Jasmine.

When they entered her little cubicle, Jaleen noticed that her clothes indicated that she was dressed for work. What she wondered immediately was where she went if she was on her way to work. They both stood on either side of her bed and watched as she lay sleeping. Then Jaleen touched her hand that was on the outside of the sheet. She felt cold. Had it not been for her steady breathing, she would have thought Jasmine was dead. "She feels very cold," she murmured to Aaron. He then felt her hand with the back of his hand. She felt cold to the touch to him, too.

Aaron went in search of someone to provide her with an extra layer of covering. Maybe the warmth would generate a gentler awakening. He just wanted her to feel warm and to awaken. They wanted to know what had happened to her. She couldn't tell them unless she was awake. Aaron and Jaleen sat and kept Jasmine's company. Pulling their chairs as close to the bed as possible, they spoke softly to her, hoping she would awaken. Jaleen asked her where she was headed and what happened to her. She asked her why she did not tell them where she was going, especially since she had not been involved in an accident. Aaron asked her where she had parked her car. Who's going to get it for her if its whereabouts was unknown.

Who was the stranger that called for the medical assistance on her behalf? What was he to Jasmine? These questions were repeated in several sequences, hoping to impact the part of her brain that would trigger her to awaken and respond to them. Aaron wanted to know who Amber was. The nurse had shared that she asked or called out for Amber. He didn't remember her ever talking about someone named Amber. But he decided to wait until she was awake to get that answer. He wondered if she had witnessed a crime taking place. He wondered if perhaps someone named Amber had gotten hurt.

With the anxiety that erupted after receiving the phone call, he was acutely aware of his own desire to protect Jaleen from occurrences such as this. He wasn't happy that Jasmine was in the hospital but he was certainly glad it wasn't Jaleen. He didn't know how he would have responded if the call had been about her. At that point, Aaron decided to inquire about Jaleen's possession of a cell phone. He called her job after getting an operator to give him the number. He wanted direct access to her in the event of an emergency or anything. He wanted direct access to her and he wanted her to be able to contact him if she ever needed to in a hurry.

"Why don't you have a cell phone," he asked Jaleen politely. "I know this is not the time or place but I had to get the operator to give me the number for your job. That's how I was able to contact you." A cell phone was not on Jaleen's list of priorities. She had a telephone at home and access to one at work. Whenever she spoke to her brother, she called him in the evenings when she got in from work. Her grandparents did not have a phone and she was never in a hurry to call either parent. She spoke to Claudia and Maurice at least twice per month. She just worked and allowed it to consume her time and energies.

Looking at Aaron, she responded, "I just never felt the need for one. It's the newest thing since flavored ice-cream and I don't think I need one," she replied candidly. "I hope you re-think that," he said. "After what happened today, someone should be able to contact you without thinking twice or going through channels. Jasmine's cell phone, which she seldom uses, had my number in it. We exchanged numbers when we got the phones. Now, I don't know who else has been contacted. But you see who's here," he concluded.

"I'll reconsider getting one," Jaleen stated. Looking back at Jasmine, Jaleen was glad she had someone at her bedside. She tried to imagine what it would be like to awaken with no one to greet her. The loneliness she felt those days after her break up with Clay, swept over her and she was really glad that Aaron had been notified and that he had called her. They were her neighbors and her friends. They had dinner together just a few days ago. Jasmine was going to host their next get-together. "What happened?" Jaleen wondered again.

She wished she would get up. She was getting tired of waiting and was contemplating doing something drastic. She just couldn't figure out what that meant. Jasmine was lying there very still and they were worried about her. She didn't want to shake her but she wanted her to awaken and acknowledge them. She wanted her to get up and tell them what happened and let them know how they could help her.

Aaron reached over and touched Jaleen's hand. She's going to be alright. We just need to be patient. Accepting his touch, she entwined her fingers in his and looked at him. She wanted his words to be true and she wanted her friend to awaken and make their worlds and hers right again. As their held hands rested on Jasmine, they sat and waited quietly.

Aaron was satisfied to be making progress, personally. He felt a little shamefaced that it was Jasmine's malaise that allowed them to touch in this intimate way. Nevertheless, he was happy that she was content to hold his hand, even though it may be due to trauma and not necessarily the first steps towards love on a more personal level. His mind returned to the little scenario he had created outside earlier in the garden. "This is amazing," he thought, "I had her on my mind and had plotted how I would propose to her and here I am sitting beside her, holding hands in the hospital—a few yards away from where I had allowed my imagination to run wild." Sitting quietly, he hoped that Jasmine would awaken. Then again, he reflected, he would have to release Jaleen's hand. What a bittersweet situation if there ever was one, he thought. Jasmine's demise brought them here, to his favorite job site and now he was sitting holding hands with the very individual he had been daydreaming about earlier and enjoying it. Still, he sighed, he wanted his friend to wake up and give them some answers. He also wanted to know what happened and why she didn't call him before going into the area where this situation occurred, especially if she was uncertain of the outcome. Had she suffered a heart attack? Was it a panic attack? What happened? That was the million dollar question sitting in his lap, Jaleen's and perhaps the lap of the stranger that accompanied her to the hospital. Who was he and why wasn't he here to let them know what happened? As anxiety rose within him, he squeezed Jaleen's hand. She responded with a gentle squeeze of her own.

Jasmine was asleep and unaware of the progress being made, right under her nose. At least the progress that was significant to Aaron, if not Jaleen. Her state of unconsciousness had brought them together and she was unable to witness it for herself, even though it was as she suspected: Aaron was in love with Jaleen. ✿

❀❀ *Chapter Nineteen* ❀❀

Upon entering his apartment, Al felt the experience of meeting Jasmine return. On the ride home, he relived it as he tried to discern what Amber meant to Jasmine and why she had come in search of her so early that morning. Was she trying to protect her from someone? If so, who? Was she trying to apologize for past sins and hence she had decided to end their stalemate? A knock at seven o'clock in the morning is kind of early for settling grudges unless the individual was a relative or very close friend. In either case, why wasn't she aware of Amber's new address? How long have they been out of touch? He'd been at the address for more than three months.

Looking around the apartment, he reflected on the day he moved in. It was clean and it had been vacant a week when he saw and responded to the ad. The secretary at the management office had given him the opportunity to look around and after doing so, he decided to take it. It was a one bedroom apartment with a small kitchen and dining area. The living room area faced the balcony and he sat and ate his meals looking out at the morning commuters before going to bed.

When he had looked around, everything was either high priced or run down in appearance. This complex was off the main road. The trees and other city-implemented barriers kept the main highway from appearing to intrude. It was reasonably quiet and the noise from the traffic was miniscule at best. The noise from the motoring public was also a deciding factor in his decision to take the apartment. When he had stepped onto the little balcony, it was private, quiet and the noise from the trucks were not as he thought it would have been, especially after witnessing a convoy of truckers moving on with their loads, going God knows where. The wall and trees did a good job buffeting the sounds and he was satisfied with that.

When he moved in, the neighbors were polite, friendly and not intrusive. He was welcomed and left alone. He wanted to ensure a clean and full separation by the time his divorce papers were delivered. The situation was bearable and unbearable at the same time. He still loved his wife but he was unwilling to compromise his sanity for hers. He worked two jobs to ensure that their bills were paid on time and she had the time to pursue her personal goals. She had decided to return to school, after working for a few years as a personal fitness trainer. They had met when Al returned home from playing in one of the overseas leagues. He had hurt himself and had been doing some rehab work when they met at the gym.

VaNessa had been what he was searching for; at least that's how he felt when they had begun seeing each other. She was sweet, easy to talk to, outgoing and she made him feel comfortable and free to be himself. He didn't have to impress her and he didn't feel like he was going to be jumping through hoops to earn her affection or love. Within six months of meeting and just talking, they began dating in earnest. They attended various events that gave him the confidence to give up sports and try to make it at home.

Al started working at the local YMCA as a coach. He wanted to encourage the youngsters to be their best and to invest in what they wanted to be from young. He also worked part time at the community college, teaching fitness and sports in the evening program. He had graduated from college and decided to work oversees to pursue a professional sports career. After five years, and several injuries to both his hand and foot, Kamaal, as he was known, returned home to rest and rehabilitate. He also took the time to revisit his plans for an athletic career.

Now, at twenty-nine, he was now divorced and living in an apartment that was less than half the size of his first apartment overseas. But, he wasn't going to cry over spilled milk. He gave up on sports, as a player for love. At least that's what he had tried to convince himself after he and VaNessa got married. They talked about starting a family one day. They both agreed that she would finish school so that she would be able to pursue her professional goals, as well.

So working two jobs became the way he supported them as she tried to complete her degree and get her professional priorities in order. Al knew the first time she had began to stray in their marriage. He tried to cover it up by telling himself that she was testing them. She wanted to know how far and how much their love could take them. He tried sealing his heart for the day she would leave and not return to the confines of their marriage. Somehow, he let his guard down and VaNessa crashed right through his heart and burned it. After six months of living apart, she came home to him "and like a fool," he reprimanded himself, "I took her back." The second time was even harder to bear than the first and that's when he knew he could not remain in a marriage with her.

When she announced she was pregnant, he demanded a paternity test and she hit the roof. Al knew he was not going to accept her infidelities anymore and neither was he going to accept responsibility for a child that may not be his. Without another word between them, he filed for divorce. The papers were served on her job and she was too embarrassed to face him after work. She had spent the time away with one of her friends and when she returned, she was no longer pregnant and Al was no longer interested.

As he tried to eat the light breakfast he had made, his mind reliving the scenes of his past, he took one bite, wrapped up the sandwich and took it on the porch with his late morning coffee. There was a young lady, lying in the hospital after learning her friend was no longer at this residence. "I don't know who she is but I know where she lives and I will be touching base with someone over there to have her vehicle moved and hopefully, help her locate her friend. My past is nothing, compared to what happened earlier this morning," he surmised. He sat and watched the vehicles go by as he finished his sandwich and his now cold coffee in the cold morning air.

His time at the Y began at two o'clock today and he needed to get some rest. The first class of swimmers arrived at three and he needed to be ready to work with them. It was a junior swimming class he had organized and this group gave him more fun as he watched and helped them learn to swim than anything else he had done for a while. They were all under the age of ten and their curiosity and courage surprised and satisfied him. They were eager to begin and reluctant to exit the pool when their time was up. He had even promised they could come on Saturdays and he would work with them—as a group, no new members, to give them some more time in the water.

He remembered when he had first brought it up. The director didn't think it would fly. Most kids who came to the Y just wanted to hang out and have fun with their friends. Their attention spans were so short that organized activities did nothing in terms of interest to them. When the go-ahead was given, Al advertised the class and got a few parents interested enough to secure the fifteen member minimum that was required to have the class in the first place. When he saw the little faces, ranging from six to nine years old, he wondered what he had gotten himself into.

As the lessons began to show progress, he knew exactly what he had gotten himself into. He was developing the next set of Olympic champions. He was developing a group of swimmers who would be able to safely enjoy their time around the water and their parents wouldn't have to worry as much, knowing that they had the basics under their belt to survive in the water, without any other life-threatening injuries such as a blow to the head or injury to a leg or torso which would hinder their abilities to save themselves if the accident occurred near water.

He grew up in the city and swimming was not something they learned. They horsed around at the Y just as the director had said, but he had a tough time getting it when he had to in college. All he saw was the time he could've learned it during his summers at the Y and didn't. As he pursued his degree in physical fitness, he had made a personal commitment to providing classes to students who lived within the city limits and frequented the Y. He wanted them to be able to swim, float, dive and do all the other cool stuff he had learned and admired others for in college.

The class kept him going as he worked with them three days per week. The other small groups he had were not as stimulating as this one. Board games and fitness routines were a part of his preparation routine before and after games, now he does it as a part of the program at the Y. The little swimmers were his delight. They made him feel alive. They gave him a sense of purpose as he tried to heal and resume the task of living. Their squeals of excitement whenever they realized they were further out in the pool than they thought possible, gave him a rush as well. The two aides who assisted him in keeping an eye on them were also terrific. They'd had a hard time believing that the students would have taken to the opportunity so faithfully. They were on time, dressed and ready to go like clockwork. They all hated when the hour and a half was up and they had to exit the pool. But, they were faithful in attendance and tried their best to improve each session.

"Faithful was the word," Al thought, as his mind returned to his personal life. The children had more faith in him than VaNessa did. They trusted him not to let them down or drown. Why didn't she have that level of faith in herself and their marriage? Sometimes he wondered what he had done wrong and what could he have done differently to keep her from feeling the need to stray. Other times he wondered what he had done to deserve someone who had no fidelity or capacity to remain faithful to him. He also wondered why he hadn't seen that side of her, prior to becoming involved with her and marrying her. Living alone makes you lonely and sometimes you grab hold of the first person who comes along, brightening up that darkened side of your world. "But one thing was certain," he concluded with a heavy sigh, "I am not getting involved with anyone else again for a long, long time." ❀

❀❀ *Chapter Twenty* ❀❀

When Jasmine finally awakened, she was surprised to see Aaron and Jaleen watching her so intently. She tried to get up and they urged her to remain lying down. They each kissed her on the cheek and waited for her to tell them what happened. Jasmine tried to recall what had happened and most importantly, she wanted to know why she was in the hospital.

Not knowing what to make of it, Aaron decided to go in search of a nurse or doctor to let them know she was awake. He also wanted some more information on the person who had accompanied her to the hospital. All he knew was what the nurse had shared with him. He was unable to fill in the real blanks. What caused her to end up there was a mystery to medical staff, too.

Jaleen encouraged her to lie still and she shared with her what Aaron had told her. Closing her eyes, once more, Jasmine tried to use that information to help her remember what had occurred earlier that day. Tears streamed down the side of her face as she remembered Amber and the rest of the story fell into place. Jaleen looked in her purse for a handkerchief or tissue. Jasmine's tears were about to cause her to shed some of her own. Unable to find tissue or kerchief, she resorted to using her hands to wipe the tears from her friend's cheeks. Then she went in search of tissue in the bathroom. Slowly, Jasmine tried to sit up. With help, she was propped up and she explained what had happened to Jaleen.

"Amber is a very dear friend of mine," she began. "We met in college. We pledged the same sorority and we've been friends and sisters ever since. When we moved here, though not together, we stayed in touch and went out together with some of our other sisters who pledged with us. Amber and two other sisters lived together. Then they got jobs elsewhere and relocated. Amber and I still stayed in touch and we hung out from time to time," Jasmine continued.

When she had gotten a job which caused her to commute much longer than she liked to she moved to the complex I went to this morning. We still kept in touch but we did not hang out nearly as much. Then I moved to the complex I know live in and our contact became even more distant. But, from time to time, we got together and shared dinner and drinks at CJ's Ribs and Beer. We would exchange photos, talk about what was happening with some of our other sisters and just have a good time together." Jasmine paused to catch her breath and her thoughts. She wanted to find her friend and had struck out on her second real attempt today.

"On Monday," she began again somewhat shakily, "I learned that Amber was working for an escort service. Naturally, I was stunned and tried to contact her. The bartender knew us and he felt I needed to know. He didn't like the news but felt I needed to know what was going on with Amber. I called her number several times last night. Each time, I got her answering machine. Then I called Aaron but hung up before the call had really gone all the way through. I had decided to go and have a talk with her and see if what was said was true. I was hoping that it wasn't."

The nurse and doctor came in with Aaron. Jasmine waited for them to check her over. She wanted to go home and she wanted to start the day all over again. She learned that she had been in the hospital for the past four and a half hours. She had drifted in and out of consciousness and that Aaron was called since his number was the last one dialed in her cell phone. The other numbers appeared to be out of town numbers and they had not continued calling anyone else, since they had gotten through to Aaron.

After checking her over and reviewing her blood pressure stats and other vital signs, it was determined that she could go home. They had completed a few tests that reflected she had not suffered a heart attack. The neurologist had concluded that she had fainted after receiving some traumatic news; her brain went on overload and had shut down. She was breathing on her own and they gave her the intravenous medication to keep her system calm and nourished.

After being discharged, Jasmine asked about her job. No one had called them. Aaron took out his cell phone, got the number from his phone book and called her job. He informed them that she had not been feeling well and would not be in for a couple of days. He gave his name and told them he was her neighbor and he was taking her home from the hospital.

"What did you tell them that part for?" Jasmine asked with a scowl. "Because your supervisor deserves to know you are not playing hooky and that you are not reporting tomorrow either. We have some things to discuss and get straight and with you that may take a while." "Don't say that to anyone else, please" she pleaded. "I don't want to be explaining this little episode beyond you two." As they began to exit the emergency room station, the nurse, brought the arrangement that Al had left for Jasmine. She received it cautiously, thanked the nurse and gave it to Jaleen to carry for her. She wasn't ready to deal with anything else, right now.

Flanking her on either side, Jasmine left the hospital surrounded by her two closest friends. They were both glad she had awakened and Jaleen was relieved to learn what had happened. She believed Jasmine was a strong individual. She was never easily rattled and she took things in stride. Whenever she revealed a personal encounter, she took her spills and pitfalls with grace and kept on moving on. So it was difficult for her to imagine something happening to her that would cause her to be hospitalized, and it wasn't a car accident.

When they approached the truck, it was the first time Jaleen learned about where Aaron was working. It was also at that moment, they decided to switch Jasmine's mode of transportation. It was almost one thirty and he needed to get back on duty. He had indicated he had an emergency and would need to be off the clock, but he didn't want to carry her home in the company truck.

Jaleen transported Jasmine home and this gave her an opportunity to finish what she had started, before Aaron returned with the nurse and doctor in tow. She knew she would have to repeat the story again, but she would have a break before doing it all over again. As they drove home together, Jaleen gave Jasmine an opportunity to rest or continue sharing what had happened to cause her to be hospitalized.

As they pulled out of the parking lot, she noticed the entrance to what appeared to be a garden for the first time. She had never had a reason to be at Presbyterian and she hoped not to have another reason to be there anytime soon. From what she had seen, though, she wanted to have a look at what it led to. It was a strange place to have something so beautiful, she thought. At a time when someone is suffering, dying or convalescing from surgery or treatment, she wondered if anyone ever took the time to notice or use it.

Jasmine's voice cut into her thoughts and she had to put them on hold. She wanted to explore that area and would, one day, she noted. "I went this morning to see if I could talk to Amber and see if I could help," she said. "I didn't sleep well and I was up before the crack of dawn to make the drive to her place. I wanted to spend some time with her and then go to work, knowing that I would have returned to continue whatever conversation we'd started. But when I knocked on the door and saw a stranger, I couldn't think straight. I couldn't process what he was doing there, in her place. I remember asking for her and him saying she wasn't there. Immediately, my mind went haywire. I thought he was lying. I thought perhaps he had even killed her. I remember him standing in the doorway looking at me. He was looking at me with a strange look on his face. I thought, 'what if he killed her and didn't expect anyone to come looking for her? What if I am now viewed as a threat—a loose end he had to tie up? I wanted to get out of there. I wanted Aaron to come and get me and I wished I had told him what I was going to do before I'd done it and that he was on his way to rescue me from the mess I had gotten me into."

Jaleen noticed that Jasmine was breathing very heavily. She quickly pulled to the farthest lane so she could get off the highway. She turned up the AC and encouraged her friend to breathe more slowly. "Relax, Jasmine. You're okay. You're with me. Breathe. Breathe, Jasmine! Breathe." Jaleen repeated this to her several times. When it didn't appear to work, she put the window down, put the car in gear and began to drive towards the nearest exit. She wanted to get her back to the hospital. As she raced towards the exit, she continued her mantra. "Come on Jasmine, breathe. Breathe slowly and relax, Jas. Breathe." Jasmine's breathing began to slow down. The cold air rushing in the window forced her to close the window and focus on her breathing. She also had to force her mind to slow down and acknowledge that she was in the company of her friend. She was in a safe place. She was no longer in danger. With trembling hands and voice, she asked Jaleen to take her home. She wanted to be in her own place where she knew she was safe. She wanted to go home. She needed to feel safe again.

Jaleen was not comfortable with that decision. They were going back to the hospital. She wanted something in place to assist her and Jasmine if it occurred again. She had never known Jasmine to have any pre-existing conditions, beside nosiness. Now, it appeared that something was wrong. She had either been traumatized or she had traumatized herself with her own thoughts and was now unable to relay the events without experiencing some form of panic attack.

When she pulled into the emergency room entrance, she immediately put the car in park, grabbed her purse from the back seat and began assisting her friend out of the car and into the setting she had left less than fifteen minutes ago. She wanted to call Aaron but couldn't. She didn't know his number and didn't want to deal with getting it from Jasmine right now.

Recognized on sight, the nurse asked what had happened. Without waiting for Jasmine to respond, Jaleen repeated the incident she had just experienced. The nurse placed Jasmine in an examining cubicle and went in search of a doctor, once again. Sitting beside her friend, she was glad she was able to be there with her this time. At least she was awake, a little shaken up but awake. When Jasmine started crying, Jaleen was able to retrieve a few sheets of paper towel from the holder in the room for her to dry her tears. Holding hands, they sat quietly and waited for the physician. They didn't know what would happen next, but Jaleen assured her that she would be with her to the end.

Doctor Glenville Morris entered the cubicle and introduced himself to the girls. Jaleen explained, once more, what had happened. He listened and then he placed his stethoscope to her chest and listened to her breathing. He also looked in her eyes, checking to see if her pupils were dilated or of the cornea was showing any other signs of distress. After several minutes of quietly listening and looking, he determined that the episode had passed and that she was medically okay. When he inquired about her private physician, Jasmine admitted she had a gynecologist she visited annually and a dentist but she did not have a regular physician. Doctor Morris indicated that she needed one who could assist her with this new phenomenon she had encountered: Panic Attack. It was one that once required medicines to effectively control it. There were some triggers she needed to be aware of and she also needed to reprogram her thinking to diffuse the onset of attacks. She needed to beat this before it got the best of her. It's more of mind over matter than medication to alleviate its onset.

Based on what Jaleen had shared and what he had heard from the gentleman and the attendant who brought her in earlier, she was in no immediate danger. In fact, Dr. Morris stated, "the young man stayed until you had been placed in the recovery unit. He even sent the flowers, wishing you well. Because he was not a family member and had no real connection to you, we were reluctant to release any information to him. We didn't notify the police because he had been the one to call for assistance on your behalf. He rode with you in the ambulance and provided what information he had. It wasn't much," Dr. Morris continued, "but based on what your friend just shared, he wasn't in a position to give any more details than he did. You really need to relax. You were, for all intents and purposes, in no real danger. If you were, you wouldn't be here right now," Dr. Morris said, as he rose to a standing position. "But, you do need to seek the assistance of a physician who specializes in panic attacks. I am also suggesting that you examine the sequences of events, slowly and calmly. Take stock and heart in knowing that you were not in danger. You may have had a lot on your mind, but you were not in danger. If this was your first attack, strive to make it your last. You don't want this to be the one road block that you have to overcome for the rest of the year. Get this in perspective. Focus on breathing slowly. You were okay earlier this morning and you will be okay as long as you remain in control of yourself, your thoughts and your responses. Seek a follow up with a doctor who specializes in this field. It's early and you can beat this."

After shaking hands, he wished her well and reminded Jaleen to assist her in getting someone to monitor her to ensure that this doesn't become a part of her lifestyle. Jasmine and Jaleen thanked him for his time and assistance. Again, they left the hospital, en route for home. This time, Jaleen called her job, using Jasmine's phone to indicate that she would not be able to return. ✿

❀❀ *Chapter Twenty One* ❀❀

When Aaron got home from work he stopped by Jasmine's apartment to see how she was doing. Knocking on the door, he half expected Jaleen to open the door. He was disappointed and hoped that Jasmine hadn't picked up on it. That was the kind of thing she was quick at. He was glad she was asleep when he had taken the chance to hold Jaleen's hand. He liked the fact that she did not pull away or sought to evade his touch or being in his presence after Jasmine woke up.

When Jasmine got up to answer the door, she had been lying on the couch, watching television but not really allowing the program to sink in. Truth be told, the television was watching her. She had dozed off after her visit with Jaleen and didn't know when Jaleen had left. When she woke up she felt rested and a little calmer. She was also feeling famished. She hadn't eaten all day. By now she was certain her stomach was wondering if her throat was cut. On the way home, Jaleen had offered to stop and get something to eat, but she just wanted to get home. She wasn't hungry just thirsty. She just wanted to get inside and experience the comfort and safety her apartment represented at that moment.

Jasmine wasn't sure she wanted to rehash the incident but she felt that if she didn't share it with Aaron, she wouldn't be able to safely put it behind her. This time, she told her story and didn't feel the high level of anxiety that she felt when she shared the panic that erupted in her when the stranger told her that Amber was not there. Somehow, she felt a sense of calm knowing that she wasn't in the danger zone that she had created in her head. After Doctor Morris told her what the gentleman had told them and the attendant, it helped her to put the events into better perspective. It brought a sense of calm to her unsteady remembrance of the earlier encounter with him.

Because she had convinced herself that Amber was in danger, she was unable to separate herself from that detail for which she had no information to fully support. All she had was that she was involved in the escort business. She still wanted to find out what had happened to her friend, but this time, she would do so with the help and support of her two friends: Aaron and Jaleen.

She had promised him she would not go on any more expeditions unless they could all do it together. Locating a friend, who may not want to be found, can be a serious matter. If together, they try to find her and experience road blocks, then it would be confirmed that she did not wish to be found and Jasmine would back off and leave her alone. She was old enough to make her own decisions and she had exercised that prerogative when she decided to become an employee of an escort service.

They ordered take out and Aaron went to change his clothes and join her before the meal arrived. They had eaten together many times before and he didn't want her to be alone tonight. He would quickly bathe, change and spend another hour or so with her before retiring for the evening.

He was about to knock on Jaleen's door when he decided to take a bath and change before greeting her. He had ordered enough for her to join them and he had hoped she wasn't eating or preparing to do so. But he couldn't be in her presence right now. He was not as clean as he had been earlier. He really needed to bathe and change his clothes. He loved his work and he wasn't about to apologize for it. He just wanted to greet her looking and feeling clean and comfortable in her presence.

When he got inside, he called and invited her to join them. He told her he had ordered take out and they could eat and spend at least an hour with Jasmine. Appreciative of the invitation and the kindness behind the gesture, she accepted the invitation and turned off her stove. She was about to sauté her onions, mushrooms, peppers and other seasonings in preparation for making gravy to serve with her smothered fish and seasoned rice. She had steamed some vegetables, fried some plantains and just needed the gravy to complete her meal. She smiled as she looked at the meal that would now be placed in the refrigerator until tomorrow. With the fan still on, her sauce pan would cool quickly and she would simply let it sit with the canola oil in it. She was planning on sharing it with them, but since Aaron had beaten her to the punch, it could be used tomorrow just as easily, too.

Dressed in her peach and off white fleece long pants set, she felt warm and casually dressed to join her friends for dinner. She cracked her sliding door to the balcony to let in some cool air to help cool down the sauce pan and extinguish the scent of fish she had fried earlier, smothered in dried seasonings, egg, bread crumbs and flour. She had seen Grandmother doing something similar and couldn't quite remember all the seasonings used. She used what she had on hand, substituted the commercially made bread crumbs for the grated homemade bread like her Grandmother used and she was satisfied with the taste. Jaleen rolled the fish in the egg and crumbs mixture and set them on the wax paper for at least fifteen minutes. This allowed the flour, crumbs and other seasonings to work their way into and throughout the flesh of the fish. The first time she did it, the fish looked smothered in flour; hence, she called it smothered fish. She had since learned to reduce the amount of flour to match the amount of bread crumbs. She didn't want the fish skin to be hardened when it was fried. The salt, cayenne, black and white peppers, along with minced, dried garlic all added flavor to the fish. Then she created her own gravy to pour over the fish and this completed her version of the fried fish she had eaten many times at her grandparents' home.

With Jasmine's episode, today, Jaleen wanted the comfort of her family as well. The little vacation came to her mind and again and she was glad that she had taken the time to visit and spend the Christmas holidays with them. Family really kept you grounded, she mused to herself. They also kept you feeling safe and loved. As she prepared her meal, those feelings brought peace and comfort to her troubled heart and soul.

Working quietly, her thoughts soon drifted to Aaron. When she didn't pull away from him, she couldn't explain why. She knew he was trying to comfort her. She didn't mind holding his hand or having him hold hers. She really didn't want to read into it what wasn't there. They held hands for a very long time and she thought it was nice to have someone express that level of concern. He was a warm, loving, genuine gentleman. He cared deeply and wasn't afraid to be there for his friends. With this conclusion, she dismissed his touch as being platonic. "When it's real," she declared to herself, I'll know."

It seemed like a few minutes ago, he had called her to share the evening meal with him and Jasmine. Now, he was back and they were walking the few feet to Jasmine's door. As they entered, she felt his hand on her back ushering her in ahead of him. Again, she decided not to read anything into it. He was, as she had noted before, a genuine gentleman. He made sure she entered ahead of him and he waited for her and Jasmine to sit before seating himself.

They talked and ate and made light conversation. They were trying not to have Jasmine worry or become upset. She had decided not to bring up the subject again for the rest of the evening. They had agreed to help her and when she was ready, they would discuss her next move. Right now, she wanted to enjoy the evening with the two people who came to make sure she was alright. She wanted to call her family but decided not to worry them. At that moment she had a revelation. Perhaps that was the decision that Amber had made. She didn't want to worry anyone so she just did what she felt she had to do. Had she felt the need to bounce her decision off of someone, she would have sought out Jasmine or someone she wanted to share her options with and she would have listened to their reasons and then made up her mind. Her friend was okay. But she would ascertain that when she was ready and not a minute sooner.

Her vivid imagination had landed her in the hospital with a medical affliction she could easily do without. As she re-lived the events during Aaron's absence, she realized that she had almost caused herself irreversible harm. She was still concerned about her friend but now, she was content to let it rest until she and her friends could arrange to help her find Amber and give her an opportunity to share her feelings without judging her or making her feel badly about the route she'd decided to take. Right now, she wanted to relax, keep her perspective and wits about her and not allow her emotions to run ahead of her, causing her another attack or any similar discomfort.

During dinner, Jaleen decided to take a chance and learn more about Aaron. She coyly inquired if anyone had noticed the entrance to what appeared to be a topiary garden at the hospital. When she did, Jasmine indicated she hadn't noticed it. Aaron asked her opinion of what she thought it looked like. It was his opportunity to see if she liked that kind of setting. Jaleen responded that "it appeared to be neat and okay but somehow out of place. She wasn't sure anyone took the time to enjoy it given its placement and what goes on there." Agreeing with her, he indicated that one day she should take a walk in the garden. "It might surprise you," he said. "Does your company specialize in that kind of work?" she asked boldly. "We do," he supplied. "I am one of the maintenance engineers," he smiled. "I majored in agriculture in college. I love plants but I'm not into hybrids. I just love nursing them; nurturing them and watching them grow. I love how people respond to them in their workspaces and in the public parks and gardens like the one at Mercy Presbyterian," he shared.

"How long have you been doing that?" Jaleen asked. She was amazed at how he lit up when he talked about the plants. He really loved what he did and she was just learning about it now. "Well, I've been working with this company for the past six years. They have given me an opportunity to decorate the city with some of their best prized blossoms and greenery."

Not wanting to sound like he was hogging the conversation, he asked Jasmine if she had any favorite parks that were a source of comfort to her eyes. After a few seconds, she realized that the city's great outdoors were all the same to her. Trying not to hurt his feelings, she indicated that she had not paid any special attention. Her work kept her indoors and the few fake Ficus and rhododendrons that adorned the office were in corners bringing a certain touch of class to the office space.

She didn't see a reason to mention the arrangements she had received from Al. She was toying with thanking him, but wasn't sure she was up to facing him, considering the impression she must have made. Her memory of his face was not a clear one and rather than increase her chances of a panic attack again, she decided she would have a thank you arrangement delivered to his apartment. "After all," she chided herself privately, "I do know his address. He didn't have to respond to her moment of panic but he did. He didn't have to accompany her in the ambulance, but he did. He certainly didn't have to send me flowers yet he did." It was settled. She was going to say thank you from afar with an arrangement from the florist.

Jaleen had learned something about Aaron and she was satisfied. Perhaps they could bring a plant home for Jasmine to take care of, she thought. That would give her something to look forward to after work. Plants needed care and that would give her something to put some of her imagination and energies into.

They continued to make small talk and teased each other until they were ready to say good night. Jasmine took two aspirins and was ready to go to sleep. Aaron promised to take her later the next day to pick up her car. They left, with the understanding that she would take the next day off, relax and get ready to return to work the day after that. There was no point in rushing back. She needed to give her mind and body an opportunity to meet in the middle and get back together as one.

Aaron and Jaleen walked home together. He was tempted to embrace her over the shoulders or hold her hand, as he had done earlier in the hospital but decided against it. He didn't want to scare her. He wanted to take it slow and give her an opportunity to catch up with him and his feelings for her. As he prepared to bid her goodnight, she invited him in and asked if she could speak with him a minute. "It won't take long, I promise." Jaleen told him. Aaron felt a hammer come down on his chest. Was she about to push him away? Is this the moment when she closes the door on any possibilities of a relationship with him. With a deep sigh and heavy heart, he entered her lair, expecting the worse.

Standing behind the door, he waited for her to begin. She wasn't sure how to say it but she wanted him to know. When she motioned him to the living room area, he was certain he was being booted to the curve. There was a sense of foreboding and he didn't like it. His heart was about to be given twelve hundred bolts of lightning he was unprepared to receive. He began to coach his heart and his mind. Walking slowly toward the chair, he said to them, "we will wait. When she is ready, we will be here."

Sitting across from her, he had full view of her face. He wanted to read her expressions, though he was afraid of what it might be saying. With a soft yet audible sigh, Jaleen revealed the incident that occurred when she was taking Jasmine home. When Aaron said nothing, she continued. Jasmine did not share that with him. She told him she had wanted him there, but since she didn't have his number or her cell phone, she didn't want to compound the situation by having Jasmine call him. She told him what the doctor had shared with them and that if she experienced another panic attack, then she would really need to seek out the assistance of a physician trained in this area.

Rubbing her arms, she told him how frightened she had felt and how relieved she was when Jasmine was able to close the window and request to be taken home. Moving quickly to sit beside her, he hugged her to him and confirmed that she had done the right thing. Rubbing her arms as she had been doing previously, he told her he was glad she had told him. Though they had spoken when he had checked in on her, Jasmine had omitted that part of her day's events.

"This is shaping up to be some year," she said softly. "After bringing her home and making sure she was alright, I came over here to fix something to eat. I had decided to prepare dinner for us and to have enough to take to work, also. I didn't want her to feel alone. But after she'd fallen asleep, I slipped out and came home. At that point, I really wanted to be surrounded by my family," she said. "I felt the need to be held, as you're doing now, and I wanted to feel safe; I felt lost, alone and afraid for Jasmine as well as for me. Does that make any sense to you?" Jaleen asked Aaron.

Rubbing her arms and holding her tightly against his chest, he whispered, "It does." He was unable to say much more. His heart was racing and he was hoping that she wasn't hearing it above the talking. He was so relieved that she had asked him to stop in and that it was *not* to put some distance between them. He sighed deeply as he continued to rub her arms. He wanted to release as much of the nervous energy he was feeling as he could. He still had a chance and for that he was extremely grateful. They sat quietly for a few more minutes and then Jaleen shifted her position in his arms and the magical moment was over. She busied herself closing the sliding door she'd left opened earlier.

Aaron stood and thanked her for sharing that episode with him. Hugging her, he confided that he was glad she was able to come to the hospital and even more appreciative that she was with Jasmine during that crisis. He didn't want to admit that they were each other's family. He didn't want her seeing him as a big brother but as a friend who could become her husband and lover. With that, he bid her good night and waited to hear her secure her door behind him. ❀

❀❀ *Chapter Twenty Two* ❀❀

Jasmine returned to work two days later. She was determined to put the incident behind her and not allow it to control her. She felt it had the potential to grow in strength and weaken her. This was not going to happen. Full control of her life must be maintained by her and not her emotions. She was going to get her car during her lunch break and let Aaron know the extra trip would not be necessary. She had left work two days ago, miffed over the refusal the new guy had given her invitation to lunch. This caused her to stop by CJ's and placed her in a position to receive the news she had about Amber. That was three days ago: one close encounter with a complete stranger and two trips to the emergency room.

She was now back with a resolve that was above entertaining that old annoyance and anything else petty. It had now been reduced to that because she realized she didn't want to put herself in a position to experience anything like she had a few days earlier. Life was filled with stress and she didn't need to add to the list. His refusal wasn't the end of the world. He wasn't someone she was pursuing and her attempts to be friendly had probably been too overt for the new employee to feel comfortable accepting. With sexual harassment constantly in the news she didn't need to be charged with that by anyone new or old on her job. She didn't need the drama or the implications that accompanied it. She enjoyed what she did and she wasn't about to jeopardize it.

During her mid-morning break, Jasmine had called and ordered a delivery of flowers for Al. She wanted him to know she had appreciated what he had done to assist her. He could have closed his door after giving his response to her inquiry about Amber but he didn't. He could've left her alone in the ambulance, unable to give any information on her own behalf but instead he rode with her. Though she was a total stranger to him, he had tried to be of assistance during her time of need. He even left her an arrangement of flowers wishing her well. This, she decided, could not go unnoticed or unappreciated. She had to show gratitude for his kindness towards her. One day, she contemplated, she would build up the courage to face him and say "Thank you." One day.

She had arranged with Meredith to pick up her car during her lunch break. This way, she just had to get it and drive off. Meredith would wait for her to get in her car and start the engine before she drove off. That way she wouldn't be alone and she should be able to return to work without another incident like that of the previous two days. Having her car would also close that chapter, she thought, and it would allow her to move about more freely as she did before. Having her car also meant that she had returned to the scene and officially closed what she had opened.

When they arrived in the parking lot, Jasmine approached her car with her keys in hand, ready to go. She opened the door, got inside and started the engine and was on her way. As she pulled out behind Meredith, she had no idea that Al was on his way in. He had been out doing some errands and trying to get in to catch up on some rest before his swimming class began.

He had been trying to be home when she came to pick up her car, but was too late as he could see from the departure of her vehicle going out the gate. As he prepared for his afternoon nap, he heard a strong knock on his door. Deciding she must have returned to say thank you, and she must have returned armed with a friend, he opened the door more cautiously than before.

The floral arrangement that greeted him was a total surprise. That, he had not expected. She had it delivered and it even had a handwritten message. After closing the door, he sat and read the card. She apologized for any distress she had caused him and thanked him for assisting her during her time of need. Al read the message several times before placing the card on the table beside the arrangement of flowers. He had never been given a delivery like that before. Women were usually the recipient of these extravagances, he smiled wryly. He appreciated the gesture and felt that it officially closed that chapter in his life. As quickly as it was opened, it was now closed.

He laid on the couch in preparation for his afternoon nap. He had less than two hours and he wanted to make the most of that time. His eager beavers would be there waiting to explore the water world he had helped to create for them. Their progress was amazing and their parents were extremely proud of what their kids had been able to do in such a short period of time. Some parents were asking him to have classes for the older age group. But he wasn't sure he wanted to tackle that right now. Teenagers were not as focused as their younger counterparts and preteens were just as fickle with their attention and participation.

He did, however, promise to give it some thought. The warmth of the indoor pool, especially during winter season would probably keep them interested since the persons at the Y were there for various reasons, unlike during the summer when they were just hanging out. Contemplating the start of a new class would mean planning, shifting around some of his scheduled activities and working around his classes at the community college. He would see. With that thought, Al drifted off to sleep.

VaNessa was surprised to hear from this caller. She had no idea whom she was speaking to, though the voice sounded familiar. When he expressed his appreciation for the floral arrangement, she knew who her caller was, though she had no clear facial image to connect with this voice. As they talked over the phone, they both shared some of their collegiate and professional work experiences. They laughed at each other's fiascos and they ended the conversation with plans to meet for Sunday brunch at The Hop. By the end of the call, VaNessa was excited and couldn't wait to meet him the next day. The caller was Al and he wanted to see her and get the opportunity to thank her in person and start over again. She was glad the incident was never mentioned. She really appreciated that. She was trying to put it behind her day by day.

As she spoke with her friends at the gym, her excitement became infectious. That's what had been missing for a while. She had not shown any keen interest in anyone, at least not that her friends could remember. That was at least two years ago. Now, here she was as excited as a teenager who was just invited to the spring dance by a member of the first string football team. They were happy for her. She was really moving forward with her life. She had not been on a date since heaven knew how long and to agree to a meeting with Al was also a blessing.

Al was smiling as he hung up the phone. He didn't believe that he would have completed the call. Let alone have a full ninety minute conversation with her. He felt certain she would not have stayed on the line long and he would have been shot down without any possibilities of a full conversation beyond his thank you message he had rehearsed several times. She seemed like someone friendly enough and he wasn't looking for a companion. He just wanted a clean friendship. She had appeared at his door and it wasn't by accident. He believed it was by design. They were to be friends. Her ability to try to find someone had made him realize that some people really had the capacity to care and love beyond measure. She was probably one of them.

When she shared the news of the call with her brother, he noticed her excitement and was intrigued by it. His sister was glowing. Perhaps she was ready to love again. He wished her well on the inside. He didn't want to upset her by bringing up anything from her past. The less said the better on that topic. He also noticed that she didn't miss a beat with his name, Al. That was also good. Perhaps she would not have any other repercussions from that first attack she'd experienced the first time meeting him. Though, admittedly, it wasn't his fault. He had simply provided her with an answer she was not prepared to hear. Nevertheless, he was happy that she was happy. Maybe he needed to invite them to dinner or lunch one weekend. That could be a way to get things going. "Patience," he warned himself. "Be patient. She's doing it on her own. Give her space and be patient," her brother told himself.

Al was ready for his date with VaNessa at The Hop. He had prepared his clothes and even washed his car. He wanted her to see him as she should for a first meeting. She was someone who was independent, kind, thoughtful and sincere. That's the kind of person she appeared to be. This is the beginning of a beautiful friendship, he smiled to himself. As he turned around to lock the door, Al turned over on the couch and his dream was over.

Sitting up slowly, a frown on his face, Al felt let down. The dream felt real and he was looking forward to meeting VaNessa. Imagine that, he said derisively. "I was actually looking forward to meeting her and having a sit down conversation over a meal." As he pulled himself up from the couch, his mind returned to the dream. "What a dream," he commented dryly.

He was actually excited to be meeting with VaNessa. Thank God it *was* a dream. Glancing at the clock on the wall, he groaned aloud. He was going to be late for his eager beavers. This was so unlike him. Again, he frowned at himself as he continued to get ready. "What a dream," he said again. He had no time for a snack. He packed it in his bag which had his change of swimsuits and jogging sweats and sneakers already in it. "I have a major project on my hands to begin organizing and I spent my time day dreaming, of all things" he chided himself.

There was a mini swim-a-thon he was putting together and he wanted his students geared up for it. It was going to be opened to the students at the nearby Y as well as those in his class and the other classes in session. He wanted to use the format and rotation of strokes as were used at the Olympics. In order to do that, he knew the participants had to know the names of the strokes and the basic moves that allowed the strokes to be executed efficiently.

The basic outline and expectations had been started. But the actual protocols were still being worked out. He was putting together a team which would assist with the implementation of this project. This and more needed to be worked on and he was busy having daydreams instead of finalizing this event. With the director on board, and the positive reviews from parents and the participation of the students, which had not wavered since its inception, he had a lot of work to do to keep this swimming class as a part of the regular program offerings.

Working with these youngsters helped him to feel alive and appreciated. He hated having to rush to get the pool ready with the ropes and other paraphernalia he used to keep his group safe. He wanted them to walk away feeling good about their accomplishments. They came focused, motivated and on time each day ready to have fun. That's how he wanted it to be and he worked diligently to ensure that they had fun each session thus far.

The mini swim-a-thon he was putting together was going to be the culminating activity for this class. However, he wanted to take them through the routines so that they would be able to exhibit their best strokes for their parents and other onlookers to enjoy. He had begun the video log on each group and was using it to show their before and after shots, which would highlight their growth and progress by the end of the eight week program. With about four weeks left, he was in full gear with them and he was already feeling the anxiety of being in uncharted waters. The swim-a-thon had never been done with younger swimmers like the ones he had. But, he was committed to seeing it through. With the constant pressure to add the second class, he was also beginning to think he might cave in to that thought as well. The swim-a-thon's success, however, would determine the initiation of the junior swimming class.

His world felt complete, for now. It had a certain amount of predictability and it gave him a sense of purpose as he worked through the pains and disappointment of his terminated marriage. The dream, on the other hand, gave him a look in another direction that he was not sure he was ready to delve into. He woke up feeling annoyed though in the dream he was excited. Right about now, Al was beginning to feel confused. With the door opened and his bag in his hand he was ready to leave.

Looking back at the floral arrangement, once more, he closed the door. Walking towards his car, he thanked God that Jasmine was fully recovered and she was okay. He then asked the question that was uppermost on his mind. "Why, Lord, did you provide my spirit with such a tormenting vision? I'm trying to move on as best I can and VaNessa is not a part of my future. So please don't tease me with her memories. She is a part of my past and though forgiveness is part of your words, I cannot forgive her anymore." ❁

❀❀ *Chapter Twenty Three* ❀❀

When they returned to the parking lot, Jasmine released an audible sigh of relief. She had regained possession of her car and she would be able to drive herself home. This symbolized a full return to normalcy for her. She had asked that the flowers be delivered to the address she knew Amber to live at. She just hoped he'd been home to receive them. She didn't want him thinking she was just another unappreciative individual. His kindness really saved her life. It also reinforced the words she had heard many times before. "Your imagination is going to get the best of you. You better rein it in." As a youngster she had heard those words from her siblings, mother, teachers and friends. She was now determined to do just that.

Sitting with her friends this weekend, they were going to work out a plan to help her locate and if possible, help Amber. She realized that Amber must be in need of assistance in order for them to help her. But she would listen and not be judgmental of her friend and sister. Her number at home had been accessible to Amber and if she had wanted her to know, she would have called her and discussed things with her. Still, she wanted to let her know that if ever she needed her, she was there. That's the most she could do right now.

The afternoon hours went by smoothly; slowly but smoothly. She saw a few of her returning clients and her database expanded with a few new ones. The new listings she downloaded had a few matches for clients that she had on file. She was able to make a few matches and complete a few job requests. With the last contact completed, she faxed a few clients the directions to their interview sites and she was ready to go home. After making a few telephone calls, confirming that she had sent the faxes, she made preparations to close down her computer and go home.

Maneuvering down the crowded lanes, she knew she was not going anywhere else but home. CJ's was a favorite hangout but she was not up to seeing Max nor hearing any other updates about Amber, if he had any. She had a plan in place to share with Aaron and Jaleen. Therefore, she would avoid CJ's until she had caught up with her friend. That way, she would be able to respond to Max accordingly and allow the situation to rest.

With music playing softly on her radio, she was able to relax and keep her attention on the drive home. Pulling into the complex, it occurred to her that she had not picked up anything to eat. She had eaten the last of the takeout from the night before and didn't want to cook. "Oh well," she said matter-of-factly, "you'll be cooking tonight." No sooner than she had muttered the words out of her mouth, she closed her car door and quickly made her way to the elevator. The cool air was not enticing enough for her to use the stairs. Jaleen, on the other hand, used them no matter what. "I bet she'll be using the elevator this evening," she mused. The January chill was biting.

Opening the door, she was glad to be home. She was ready to resume her life as she knew it before the incident. Mentally, Jasmine reviewed what she had available in her fridge and which items would prepare quickly so she would be able to relax by eight thirty. Feeling light hearted and in control, she rummaged through her cabinets to get the last remnants of the meal going. She plugged in her Christmas tree one more time. It was coming down this weekend. But right now, she just wanted the twinkling lights to keep her company as her spirit healed and her soul lifted up to match the new appreciation she felt about her life and her existence. As she moved about the kitchen, she prayed for her friend Amber and hoped that she was at peace, too.

As Al worked with his eager beavers, they were as energetic as ever. Willing to please and quick to show what they had learned and understood, their energy and excitement kept him going. Their enthusiasm was a lift to his battered soul. Going through the exercises, he wondered what Jasmine was doing. No sooner had the thought entered his mind, he chased it away. His attention was needed here and now and he wasn't about to lose it and lose a student in the process. This point in time, they were number one. No one else mattered.

With smiles and words of encouragement, his center of attention became the students once again. He had apologized to them for being late and he had promised to make it up by extending their session an extra half hour. Though he was fifteen minutes late, he just wanted them to know they mattered to him, too. The assistant wasn't as pleased but that was neither here nor there to him. They were there to serve the students and he was going to make sure that at least he did. When everything else around him was falling apart, personally, they were there waiting to be challenged, interested in learning and striving to get the strokes right each time they did their paces. Their smiles and squeals penetrated his aching heart and allowed some semblance of life to protrude. They appreciated him. They found him worthy of their attention and time and he was eternally grateful. They had actually saved his soul. It was retreating to a very dark place and he wasn't sure he wanted to be rescued from that fate.

As they wrapped up their session, they began to echo the sentiments he expressed to them at the end of each session. "You did well today and will do even better next session. Keep trying and give yourself a chance to succeed. You can and you will. Until next time, I'll see you right here," they ended pointing in the water. As they completed his mantra, he could only smile. They really were the center of his broken world and they made his world alright.

When he finished restoring the pool for the others to use, which was just a couple pairs of seniors keeping fit, he reflected on his day and on the dream he'd had. He wondered what it would have been like if his wife had kept the baby. He wondered if he had been too hasty in declaring himself unavailable as the father. The tightness in his throat and the tears that stung his eyes reminded him that what ifs caused just as much pain as letting go.

Sometimes he cursed himself for his failure as a husband. The children in his swimming class healed him but it was a child that had broken him down. What if the baby really was his? He'd never know and the path he had now chosen was not one for children or women who wanted to be loved in all sincerity. He was unwilling to take any more chances right now and didn't plan on taking any more chances for a while to come.

His wife's infidelities were more than he could have put up with. He was willing to work at making their marriage work. But he couldn't make it work alone. When they met, it was all fun and smiles. When did the smiles become frowns? Where did the fun go? What caused her to leave their vows behind as she slipped under the covers with someone she wasn't married to? There was something inside of her that needed to be repaired and he was unable to fix it. He sometimes questioned whether or not he caused her to be broken in the first place. The answer, however, usually came back the same: "She was broken before you met her and will be broken until she decides to do something about it."

Women, he contrived. They were hard to live with, hard to understand and just as hard to forget. This time, he wasn't feeling bitter. He was feeling apprehensive. He wanted to be able to relax and enjoy the company of both sexes but he wasn't ready to trust his heart to any woman just yet. In the meantime, he avoided all women and any situation that caused him to suspect RCR: Romance, Commitment or Relationship. It was okay to be friends but it was too dangerous for him to allow the friendship to become more than that.

Al made a scoffing sound within his throat, as he questioned his own sanity. Women can do that to you, too, he concluded. They can drive you insane. Looking back at previous relationships, he knew he had played a few games in his day. But when he became serious, he ended the games and gave his full respect and attention to the lady of that hour. He played by the 'committed' rules. We share, communicate, discuss and disagree but not disrespect each other or the relationship. When they broke up, he was back to playing around and that's the way he kept it. Of course, he would take some time to lick his wounds but he'd be back on par: Showtime! He recalled his time overseas. He never got serious. He didn't believe they loved him for him but for his name and what it meant to them financially. "Now," he mused,

"I'm getting older and I'm getting wiser, too. My heart and mind can't play like before and I've decided to take a break from the games and all the players," he mocked himself, jokingly. Besides all that, a divorce is even more serious stuff to deal with. When he had gotten the apartment, he walked away with the clothes on his back and the ones he had packed in his bags. He didn't want anything else but to be left alone.

The backgammon game was ready to roll and he was set to play. It gave him something different to do as his day came to an end. It was something he picked up overseas and he was glad to share with the staff and students at the center. The toughest part of the game was getting off the board. But once the rule was established, it wasn't so bad. Some players agreed to rolling doubles with the die to get down off the board. Others just played the roll of the dice to get down. If one of the sections rolled was occupied by the opponent, and you had more than one chip to come down, then you couldn't get down. You remained frozen on the board until you could roll a combination that was free of your opponent's chips. It was a good mental teaser and he enjoyed playing it with some of the staff. This helped to pass the time, especially if he didn't have a class at the college.

Taking his seat, the game began. ❀

❀❀ *Chapter Twenty Four* ❀❀

With the week coming to an end, Jaleen remembered her brother's departure. Her heart went out to Selecia. Even though she had the store to look forward to, her husband's departure was going to put a hole in her heart. He wasn't going to be there for her as he'd been the past four to five weeks. She had already sent her stuff home and hoped it would reach in time to pick up her spirits. The store had energized her and when she returned from her visit, she took care of some of the things she had committed to as her contribution to the store. She knew that with Brad being gone, it would have to fill the void for Lecia, as well. "Lecia," she repeated to herself. When her brother said it, it sounded so personal and affectionate. It must be terrific being in-love. There's always someone to share your days and concerns with. There's someone to make you feel better when things feel upside down.

Jaleen's mind went straight to Aaron. She had been avoiding thoughts of him all day. She didn't want to give herself a chance to analyze what she was feeling especially when she was in his presence. But she was feeling something. She knew he was kind and caring. She wasn't sure that he considered her as someone who could be more than just a friend or little sister to look out for. His embrace a few nights ago was just what she needed. For an instant, she thought they were going to kiss. Just an instant she reminded herself. The thumping of his heart was enough to bring hers to the same cadence. She loved how she felt in his arms. He made her feel safe. He made her feel protected.

"Was this how Selecia felt when Brad held her?" Jaleen wondered. There is something about a human being who can generate that kind of safety net that drew you in emotionally and made you feel that nothing was going to happen to you that this person wasn't going to see you through. That is a very powerful feeling and she wouldn't mind experiencing that the remaining days of her life.

Maybe the trauma with Jasmine had clouded her thinking. But somewhere inside of her she was beginning to open up and it was awakening her inner spirit as well as her passionate side. The thought of them kissing was something she had never processed in all the time she knew and spent with him. Which, she had to admit was not a whole lot of time. She spent her evenings working and the few social hours she spent with both friends was just that: a few social hours.

Pulling onto her exit, she looked ahead at what she would be doing for the evening: work, as usual, she concluded. She had packed some invoices and other key documents that had to be reviewed and prepared for signature. Their team leader was moving on and wanted to have all loose ends tied up before his departure at the end of the month. He had accepted a transfer to one of the other branches further west. Her team was plunged into turmoil after spending a year working together to achieve synergy and increase in their levels of productivity.

What's new, she asked herself. That's the way it always is. Do good, move up or move on. If he had moved up at least he would've been with them and they would still able to communicate on a daily basis. But moving on was a different game all together. It meant a new person to meet and adjust to and the team members had made so many adjustments already. So, she was going to be working harder to keep her team on top as they tried to meet their first quarter goals with a new leader coming on board. This had been announced the day before, too, but everyone was too busy feeling great about the previous year's successes to focus on the impact of that announcement.

As her mind reviewed the conversations around her for the past two days, it revolved around Dave's decision. They were surprised, stunned and at the same time happy for him. The collaborative teaming protocol established within their branch was being spread to another corporate unit and they wanted a few of the experienced team leaders to join them on the expansion. The training was really two edged. The company grew financially and the employees became more valuable as their level of performance and skills improved. It made them all more lucrative and efficient.

With the uncertainty, she felt alone. She was just making progress with her protégé and now they were going to have to blend again with another leader and produce just as much if not more than they did previously. Change was good but this time, it felt like it was too much.

Aaron's mind kept going back to the moment he embraced her. He was so relieved to learn that she wasn't placing distance between them. He heard what she had said but was unable to do much more than rejoice inwardly. He was still in the game and he was content with that. She wasn't difficult to love. The difficulty, he felt, was in her ability to see it, and recognize and accept it for what it was. She had the capacity to love but she was not one to openly love and lay her feelings out there for you to see.

"Then again," he cautioned himself, "what if she is relaying her feelings and he wasn't reading her signals clearly? What if he wasn't seeing or reading the signals because they were not the ones he wanted? Slow down," my brother. "Heartache is just a phone call or message away. She didn't call you off this time, but it doesn't mean she won't call you off if you got too close."

With the advertisement blitzes pushing towards Valentine's Day, he decided to step up to the plate and let her know how he was feeling. He planned to invite her to dinner and ask her how she felt about them as a couple. Regardless of the answer, he was going to find out if he had a chance at all. If it was something she hadn't given any thought to, then he would ask her to consider him as someone who was interested in getting to know her on a more personal level. He was also thinking of offering her a friendship ring. That's taking things slow but opening the door for a romantic relationship as well. Sitting on his couch, they could enjoy the evening looking out at the lights in the distant as they pondered their futures together.

Of course, he was also trying to shelter his heart from public humiliation. What if she didn't see any way to love and care about him as he did her? They would be at home and her refuge would just be a few feet away. There would be no need for a long drive in silence. He would be there kicking himself in the rump as he wondered what she was thinking of his silly behind. They could avoid each other and still be polite whenever they ran into each other outside. He would be able to lick his wounds and pour the salt in it at the same time as he watched her come and go, wishing for a chance to win her love.

He loved being able to hold her, even if it wasn't under the auspices of a romantic liaison. The ability to touch her from the outside had its potentials. Holding her near, gave him an opportunity to comfort her. It also gave her the chance to see what she's missing: someone to love and share her ups and downs with. He wanted to get to know her and hopefully she would get to know him, too. Then they would be able to meet in the middle after discovering that they could make it as a couple. He was hopeful and he was now becoming relentless in his thoughts to win her over. She was strong enough to love and weak enough to crumble him if she chose to put some distance between them. He was in love with her and he especially loved who she was and her ability to care deeply for others.

Pulling into the complex, he noticed that her lights were on. Jasmine's was on too, so he decided he would check in on both of them after he had showered and changed his clothes.

Finishing up the dressing for the salad, Jasmine had decided to have something light and refreshing. The chicken breast was baked, sliced and dropped into the salad. She wanted a chicken salad and was determined to make the dressing herself too. After pouring over several recipes, however, she settled on her own version of vinaigrette dressing. She had placed a medium sized bowl on her coffee table and was getting ready to watch the evening news and enjoy her meal. The peace and quiet was not a source of discomfort. Turning up the volume, she settled in for a quiet evening at home. She heard Jaleen come in and wondered if she had taken the elevator or the stairs. Smiling to herself, she admitted, "She did the stairs. She always did."

When Aaron knocked on her door, she was happy to see him. "Where you going," she asked, with her usual nosy candor. "You smell good, too. What's up with you?" Aaron ignored her questions and fired off a few of his own. "What did you do, today? I thought we agreed that we were going to pick up your car when I got in from work. What's up with that?" He asked pointedly. She offered him some of her salad but he declined. They sat down and he waited for her to respond. "I got someone to drop me there today and I picked it up and returned to work. There was no drama and, in fact, I felt good once I had gotten into it and it turned over. I felt that I had closed that chapter in this episode rather successfully, I might add." Jasmine felt rather proud of herself. She was beginning to let go and regain her perspective, her composure on life.

"Okay, that's good." Aaron replied rather slowly. But next time give me a call and when we agree to do something and you change your mind, it's okay to call and say that too. I got in, rushed to bathe and change only to realize your car was in your spot. He knew she wouldn't bother asking him where he was going again, especially if she was involved. He knew how to keep her at bay. It was one of those games they played—with neither realizing the other was on to them and ready to get it on. Some days he didn't mind and there were other times when he did. This time, he was able to diffuse her nosiness and he wasn't worried in the least.

"How was your day otherwise?" Aaron asked. "It was good," Jasmine said. "The pace was just right and when it was over, it felt good knowing I was going home and not thumbing a ride home to deal with getting the car right about now. I also had some flowers delivered to say thanks for what was done for me. I hope he got them and they were appreciated." As they watched the evening news for a brief moment, they were caught up in the lead story and sat listening intently for the outcome. After exchanging a few more pleasantries, Aaron bid her good night and left.

She was okay and that's what mattered, he reflected. She was okay. The old nosy Jasmine was back and that signaled that she was okay. Because she lived right next door, he didn't want her to hear him knocking on Jaleen's door. He went home and called her on the phone. When she answered, he held his breath because he hadn't a clue what he was going to say. He just knew he wanted to see her and that was all. "Up for some company tonight?" He asked. Jaleen was glad to hear from him and she told him that she was. After hanging up, she unlocked the door and waited for him to come in.

She had her papers spread out on the table and decided to slide them together and put them back in their folders. She would deal with them later. Company wasn't something she had all the time and this time she felt like having a conversation with someone and not just her papers.

❀❀ *Chapter Twenty Five* ❀❀

They spent the next two hours talking and getting to know each other. Aaron told her about childhood pranks he and his brothers participated in and she shared some of the things she had done when her family was whole. Then she shared some of the things she and her youngest brother did. They laughed together a lot. Jaleen didn't recall having this much fun in a long time.

With the shift in conversation to her brother, she was again, keenly aware of the yearning to experience the kind of love he and his wife had discovered. She acknowledged that if she took her time, it would be a part of her life, too. Aaron saw this as an opportunity to explore the possibilities of a relationship between them. He didn't want to rush things but he wanted to know if there was the slightest chance for her to love him.

He continued the conversation down that path by asking her to share what she was looking for in a relationship that she felt could last. After a few nervous giggles, she admitted that she wasn't quite sure. She just wanted someone who had the capacity to love her and provide her with the love and security that said 'I am in this for the long run.' She shared that she wanted the kind of love that lasted forever. It raised loving children and it nurtured grandchildren as well. She wanted a man who was able to see her flaws and still love her for them as well as her strengths. She wanted a man who was also willing to have his flaws exposed and not need to hide or cover them up while he pretended to be perfect in all things except truth and honesty. She was hoping to find someone who had a good sense of humor, was ready to settle down and share his life with someone who was willing to love him and share her life with him also. He had to be attentive, like her grandfather was to her grandmother's basic needs and be the one that picked up the broken toys and spirits when their children needed that, too.

When she flipped the script on Aaron, he simply sat and adored her for a long time. She had described what she wanted before and now she was even more detailed about the characteristics the man must possess in order to win her heart and capture her soul. He hoped he was capable. He believed he was. But it was her choice, her criteria that had to be fulfilled after all.

Slowly, almost methodically, Aaron shared some of the virtues he wanted in his wife. They mirrored some of what she had shared but he was careful not to use her terms. He wanted her to see if she fit into his description as much as he had fit hers. His wife had to be willing to make sacrifices so that the relationship could grow. He wanted someone who was considerate, patient, understanding and passionate. He wanted someone who would be able to capture his soul as well as his heart with her smile, winning attitude, strength as well as meekness. She had to be able to share her successes and her pitfalls, knowing that he was there to listen and help pick her up whenever she fell. Her appreciation of nature and its natural wonders had to be a part of her graceful nature and inner beauty because God had provided the external beauty in mankind and in the things that surrounded the earth. Because of his love for plants and its related species, she had to have an appreciation for them, too. But if she didn't, she simply needed to be able to acknowledge its usefulness in everyday life and he would be satisfied with that.

"Wow," Jaleen exclaimed softly. "Is that why you work with plants? Your affinity for them is not just superficial?" With a robust laughter, that made her laugh out loudly, too, Aaron nodded his head in agreement. His smile was irrepressible. He loved plants! He loved what they were able to do: provide oxygen, beautify the earth as well as nourish bodies. His preference, of course, was live plants but if the artificial ones were tastefully done, he could at times embrace them.

He told her about his job and the places he maintained. He even invited her to see one of them whenever she was up to it. With that invitation, she threw one back. "You arrange it and I'll be available," she said with a smile. "I've never visited a topiary garden before and if I did, I probably did not pay it as much attention as I should. Gardening is a peaceful thing," she continued. "My grandmother has an excellent touch. She has planted flowers as well as fruit and vegetable plants and they have all grown and produced. We have eaten from her garden on many occasions growing up. Even now, after the storm, she had begun replanting some of her flowering plants. The others, like peppers, tomatoes and peas will be replanted too. It's her peaceful place and she really enjoys it."

"Well, one day I hope to enjoy it on that personal level, too," Aaron said softly. "It's the one thing that keeps you feeling useful and alive. The plants depend on you for care and you depend on them for beauty and purpose to your days. The fact that some are edible is our biggest bonus."

When their conversation ended in silence, they just sat quietly looking out at the lights from the homes in the distance and the vehicles that moved by them. The music in the background was soft and comforting. He felt drawn to the rhythm and the intonations of love lurking in the chords and strains of the instruments.

Without thinking twice, Aaron placed his arm around Jaleen's shoulder. Placing his thumb under her chin, he gently turned her face to his and kissed her. It was gentle. It was slow and it was filled with the love he had been carrying around for her for the longest time. As his tongue made contact with her lips, tasting her and savoring her taste, she opened her mouth and he entered. His tongue teased the roof of her mouth and dueled with her tongue in a slow, gentle play of tag. When he released her, he looked her in the eyes, kissed her again quickly on the mouth once more and said, "Good night. I enjoyed this time with you."

As she rose to lock the door, her mind replayed what had just happened. It almost felt as though it didn't happen. But she knew it did. Aaron kissed her. He kissed her and she liked it. It wasn't over-the-top; there were no symphonies or bells and whistles. He had kissed her and she liked it.

While locking the door, Jaleen's hands trembled. "Was this it? Was this how it was or is going to be? Is this how it feels when the love is real?" The confusion she was feeling was making her nervous and excited at the same time. Turning the questions around in her mind, she reflected on one of her conversations with Brad, her brother. He knew she wanted to be in love but was not willing to take the chance on love. She hadn't told him about Clay. It was still too painful at that time. But Brad's words began to reverberate in her mind. *"There is someone out there for you.*

Just give yourself the chance to meet him and give him the chance to show you the kind of person he is. If he's the right person, you will know it. The things he will do for you and the things he will share with you will let you know just who he is and how he feels. Your heart and head will give you the go-ahead and you will be in the best relationship of your life. Know this, when you decide to give your heart, give it with caution. But give it."

"I like him as a person," she began. "I enjoy talking with him. He seems to really listen and understands what I am saying. I don't think he pretends to listen, does he? He didn't just kiss me as a set up for sex, did he?" Doubts were creeping in and they were erecting the fence that she usually built around her heart the minute anyone appeared to be getting too close. When her heart recognized what was happening, it began to cry out. It wanted to be free. It didn't want to be caged up; it didn't want to be fenced in. "I like the way he makes me feel when he holds me in his arms, though," she continued. "Is this it?" Jaleen wondered again. When he'd called and asked if she wanted company the call alone made her feel excited and pleased that he wanted to come over and spend some time with her. She thought about the kiss once more and decided that it was a start. If Aaron was the man for her she would find out. "No more running," she scolded herself. "No more running or hiding," she said again, this time to her heart. ❀

❀❀ *Chapter Twenty Six* ❀❀

When Aaron closed the door behind him, his heart was racing and he was unable to slow it down. With trembling hands, he fished his keys from his pocket and let himself into his apartment. Tossing the keys on the coffee table, he began to have a serious conversation with himself. "What have you done?" He asked himself softly out loud. "What if she decides to close the door and shut you out? What's the matter with you? I told you we were taking it slow." A part of him was happy, though. He'd taken a chance. If he had taken the time to think about it he would not have executed. Recognizing this, he said, "It's on! If she avoids me then it's over. If she acknowledges me with that beautiful smile of hers then I'm in and I'm in it to win it. We're going to move forward together. One day at a time, one week at a time, one month at a time. Just us making a go of it together," Aaron affirmed to himself.

He began to hope against all odds that he hadn't blown his opportunity to win her love. She was all that he thought about and he strongly believed that she was all that he needed. As he prepared for work the next day, he felt his soul rejoicing. "So, you think I've got a chance, huh? Well, work with me here," he said smiling. "I'm going to need all the help I can get. I think she's special and I think she's the one. I stepped out on faith and did my best to let her know how I really, really feel."

Lying in bed that night, Aaron prayed for help with this new situation. He wanted to do the right things. He wanted to win her heart and her love. He wanted to share the rest of his life with

Jaleen Cole and he needed help in order to do so. With a restless mind, captive heart and excited soul he drifted off to sleep.

Normally, he left around seven thirty each day. The next day was no different. He didn't want to see her and he wanted to see her. But she usually left ahead of him. This morning was no exception. When he opened his door, he noticed that her car and Jasmine's was already gone. "Good," he told himself. "I don't have to deal with the morning after so soon. I have all day to figure out what I am going to do tonight," he sighed nervously. "I've got all day." Stepping with a lot of pep, Aaron descended the stairs and drove away with a smile on his face and love on his mind.

Jaleen arrived extra early to work. She was unable to focus on the papers and decided to do it at work. Her mind kept drifting off to the couch and the kiss. She couldn't remain on task and working with numbers required that. "At least, here," she thought, "I could leave that behind me and get this ready for Dave before he comes in."

Crystal's arrival meant she wanted to hear what changes or corrections were needed. She was still working with Jaleen and was determined to make her proud. When Jaleen told her the work was error-free, she was ecstatic. Unconsciously, she touched her stomach and Jaleen's mind went completely off track. Now, Crystal's pregnancy was touching a chord in her. Making love with Aaron crossed her mind and she was surprised to have that topic in her thoughts. "We had just kissed, for heaven's sake," she chided herself. "Slow down. I want to get it right and jumping ahead doesn't help here," she warned her wayward thoughts.

When Crystal returned to her cubicle, Jaleen was left alone with her thoughts. She tried to keep them on the last two reports and they kept straying. "If a kiss could cause this much distraction," she muttered, "What would happen if they ever became more intimate?" Looking at the phone, she wished she had his cell number. "To do what?" her nervous mind asked. "To give him a call," her heart responded. "He's probably thinking about you as you are thinking about him," her heart informed her. "Oh, Lord," she lamented. "My nerves and heart are having a conversation. What next?"

"What have you done to me, Aaron Hammond?" "I'm falling apart and it was just a kiss. I'm not sure this is the kind of thing I had in mind when it comes to being in love," she concluded. Her heart was back on the bench and her nerves were leading this round, again.

By lunch time, she had wrestled with her nerves and heart and declared a truce. No more talking, thinking, remembering or running ahead until we get home. Without it, she didn't see how she would have made it through the day. She wanted to run a few errands during her break, but she was afraid to be caught doing nothing. She felt they were waiting for a chance to start in on her again and she couldn't have that. The morning was tough enough, before the truce. She wasn't about to test it either.

With a heavy sigh, she decided to work through lunch and leave early. That way she would be able to take care of the errands and go straight home. Truth be told, she wanted to see Aaron again. She wanted to be in his presence but she wasn't sure if he even wanted to see her. They had shared some special moments together. The details about their childhood and some of their past relationships qualified them as friends. But the kiss had thrown that and everything else into chaos. She wasn't sure where they were now. "Save it for down time on the way home," Jaleen reminded herself. The truce, between her heart and nerves was in jeopardy.

Al was on his way home when he decided to return the favor and send a thank you arrangement to Jasmine. He knew where she lived and had kept the little piece of napkin he'd written her address on. He wanted to know where she worked and that was where the challenge came in. He hoped she had found her friend and that things were okay in that department.

With his arrangement, though he had a special invitation to lunch. All she had to do was call and give the date. He would make himself available. His evening classes ended at ten and he reported to the Y at one. When he did not have an evening class, he reported to work at nine. Even his weekends were spent at the Y. He had kept busy to avoid the hurt from his marriage and his divorce. He began working two jobs to ensure that his wife finished college and that they would be able to invest in a home. Now, he just kept busy to avoid feeling anything at all including anger.

His little beavers made the difference and he felt safe with them. Now, however, ever since meeting Jasmine, he was becoming restless. His dream also made him realize that he was hiding and the rest of the world was still moving on. Everyone experienced some sort of pain. Everyone experienced some challenges but they picked themselves up, dusted themselves off and continued moving on. So why shouldn't he? Seeing someone didn't mean marrying them. He was certain that wasn't going to be him ever again. If it weren't for prayers and the ability to seek peace in the things he did, Al was sure he would have done something that would have ended his life, as he currently knew it. The death of his ex would have terminated his freedom; closed the escape hatch at the Y and disconnected him from the future with his classes at the community college.

Life was short and it held no guarantees. Jasmine's situation made that clear to him. She could have died at his doorstep had he opted to close the door after answering her question. He was glad that she had made it and that she had seen fit to say thanks. They were brought together for a reason and he decided to explore that reason, nothing else.

At the florist he was having a tough time getting them to send her an arrangement. They had no idea where she worked. It was a credit card transaction and they did not keep that kind of data on their customers. They couldn't even tell him whether they had seen her around before or not. With that dead end, he let it go and decided to head on to work.

In the middle of the parking lot, he stopped and returned to the flower shop. He ordered the arrangement he wanted and asked them to deliver it to him around five o'clock. He was going to dinner and she would be receiving them that evening. He knew where she lived. Fridays had no evening classes for him at the college and he was leaving the Y around six for an impromptu dinner date.

He wasn't a spontaneous kind of guy but he was going to go with the flow on this one. If she had company, he would present her with the flowers, invite her out and leave. If she accepted fine, if not, nothing gained or lost. They were strangers to each other and given time, they could become friends. If she hadn't located her friend, perhaps he could assist her. But one thing was certain he wanted to get to know her. His existence had become lonely and being away from his family and friends, his friends now consisted of the people with whom he worked. A few knew of his pending divorce. Still, he kept his private affairs to himself and allowed everyone to do the same. This way, he didn't feel compelled to justify to anyone or have anyone empathize with him as it related to his situation with his soon to be ex-wife.

With the weekend upon them, Meredith invited Jasmine and Beth Ann to a movie. It was the sort of thing they did at least once every other month and with the holidays, they hadn't taken the time to get together. Jasmine decided to pass on the invitation. She needed to be available if Aaron and Jaleen were willing to help her locate Amber this weekend. She had not revealed to them the episode from earlier that week. She had simply told them she had felt badly and was taken for medical treatment. She did not want to discuss it any further.

As they said their good-byes she reminded them to keep safe. Women travelling alone were always easy targets. It didn't matter time of day or night. They were less than ten minutes away from the movie theaters. So working until five thirty was never a problem for them. In fact, its proximity to their jobs was the primary reason they chose to go to the movies. They usually went to the six o'clock showing so that they were out by the time the teenaged crowd rolled into the theater, trying to be grown. They ate dinner, discussed the movie and waited for Beth Ann's husband to come and meet them before they all left for home. He was their safety net. Going to their cars in his presence, meant that they would at least get in and be able to head home without any negative incidents. He followed them to the first exit and made sure when they made that turn, he was the only one behind them for another block or two. Meredith lived in a subdivision that was ten minutes away from Beth Ann and her exit was the first one when they got to her side of town. For three to four years, they had done this and it was safe. Within a few minutes of their first exit, Jasmine's exit to her complex was on their right. This meant Beth Ann and Meredith just kept going straight for another seven or so minutes when they made the last exit together, accompanied by Beth Ann and her husband.

But right now, she wasn't up for it. She wanted to be available if she was going to get some assistance with finding Amber. As she merged with the on-coming traffic, Jasmine felt her mood improve. She never minded being alone and she was looking forward to a quiet evening. She already had the remnants of the left over salad and would just prepare something to eat with the chicken. A starch, the chicken and salad, she was set. She had also decided to give Amber's number a call and see if by chance she was home and picked up the phone. If she didn't this time she would leave a message. No more run-away thoughts. They got her in trouble and she was not about to have a repeat of that ever again. Rubbing her chest area, she declared, it was not going to happen again. She loved Amber and all her friends but she was not going to jeopardize her health like that.

Pulling into the complex, she turned her radio off and parked her car. She quickly buttoned up her jacket, grabbed her bag and prepared to face the cold air. Rushing to the elevator, she waited for the doors to open and darted inside. There was no way she was taking the steps. No way, she convinced herself again. The warmth of the incubator was preferred to walking up the two flights of steps. She understood the safety reasons behind leaving them exposed as they were, but when it was cold, safety was not the issue.

Al watched as she exited on the second floor. He decided to give her at least thirty minutes to see if she was having company. If not, then he would make his appearance and invite her to dinner. He wasn't sure he wanted to be indoors. It was her personal space and right now, he didn't want anyone in his. He wasn't ready for the level of intimacy that kind of closeness suggested. He tried to release the anger and hurt associated with his failed marriage. Going out and meeting people were never a threat to him. He always enjoyed the company of others, especially when it was clear that he was not the target. He wasn't quite ready for one night stands either and wasn't looking forward to that tonight. He just wanted to be her friend and help her if he could.

When Aaron pulled into the complex his eyes went to Jaleen's apartment. He didn't know what was going to happen; maybe nothing. But he was not going to push his luck any further. He had played his hand and he hoped she was willing to play with him. Now that the ball was in her court, he was willing to let it sit there a while and see if she was willing to play the game of love with him.

As he bounded up the steps, he decided to stop by Jasmine's and make sure she was okay. With that out of the way, his evening was wide open for anything else that may come along. He was hoping that Jaleen would come along. In any event, he would be ready. ❀

❀❀ *Chapter Twenty Seven* ❀❀

Al noticed the little interlude and wondered if he had gotten himself into a yellow jacket's nest. He wasn't about to fight for Jasmine or any other woman. He was just out for some light entertainment and diversion from his usual quiet days and dull nights. When Aaron left, he decided to end his charade. If she was having company, it's better for him to know now and then move on with his evening than to sit and watch and wonder. He had given her twenty minutes and wasn't about to sit in the cold, sightseeing any longer. If she was having company, she could be presented with the flowers and he could politely leave. They could get together some other time to her liking.

With flowers in hand, he approached her door and knocked lightly. As he waited, he felt uncertain and a bit anxious. When she opened the door, he was concerned that she'd have the same response again. Only this time, she was the one on the inside and he was on the outside. With baited breath, he offered her the flowers and said, "These are for you. If you are busy, I will just leave these with you. But I wanted to see how you were and to thank you for returning the kindness shown." When she caught her breath, she invited him in. The cool air was enough to help her maintain her composure. Placing the flowers on her book shelf near her television, she invited him to sit down.

"You're Al." Jasmine was finally able to say. Her mind was playing catch up and she was also trying hard to remember to breathe. She had no intentions or thoughts of seeing him again.

He was the last person she expected to see standing in her doorway. She was caught completely off guard by his presence.

Still standing, he watched her closely for any signs of a similar response to their first meeting. He didn't want her to require medical assistance again, this time on his behalf. It would be the talk of the ER, possibly even make the news. He thought wryly. "If I'm making you uncomfortable, I'll leave," he offered. "No, no, please," she said. "Sit. I'd like you to stay. Sit," she repeated, directing him to a chair.

When she sat on the couch he sat on the chair adjacent to her. He wanted to keep an eye on her and at the same time, keep enough distance between them to make her feel more relaxed. After a very deep breath, she began to relax and offered him something to drink. She was in the middle of fixing something to eat and was unprepared for his visit. Then she decided to include him in her meal plans. He was here, after all, she was fixing some spaghetti and it would be served with the rest of the chicken breast she had baked the night before. The chicken was warming in the oven. She could mix another salad and it would be more than enough.

When she invited him to dinner, she didn't indicate all that would be done. He was torn between accepting and going through with his plan to invite her out to dinner. But keeping her in her environment was what mattered right now. So he accepted. He did not want to shift her surroundings anymore than was necessary at this point.

"My name's Al. Alvin Burley and I am sorry you were startled when we first met. I've prayed for your safe keeping and was relieved when your flowers arrived yesterday. It was nice of you to let me know you were doing better." He never mentioned seeing her leave the complex the day before. As she finalized her preparations for their meal, she tried to do as he had done.

"I'm Jasmine," she said. "I apologize for scaring you the way I did earlier this week. It's just that I had expected my friend to answer the door and I was so caught up in what I had heard about her that I was thinking the worse." "Have you been able to catch up with her?" Al asked. "No," she replied. "But I've left a message on her phone this time. So hopefully, she will call me back."

They continued to talk about themselves and the things in life that have been funny to them. They talked about sports, books, movies and their concept of religion. Laughter, giggles and incredible encounters captivated them as they spent the evening getting to know each other. He was glad that he came. The light hearted conversation did a lot to improve his mental disposition and his trampled soul. Jasmine was glad to have him spend time with her as well. She had gained a personal friend who was like Aaron. He was easy going, just out of a relationship and not in search of commitment but a friendship. She liked that.

After cleaning up the kitchen and dining area, she invited him to sit and have some coffee or tea. He looked outside and determined that it was time to go home. He had spent an enjoyable evening with her and they had gotten off to a better start. He shared with her those things he felt comfortable revealing. They had laughed a lot and she was at ease in his company. Now, it was time to go home. He didn't want to wear out his welcome. The hours had flown by and now so must he.

"Thank you for a terrific evening," Alvin said. "I've enjoyed meeting you and I hope to see you again soon." Blushing, Jasmine thanked him once again for his kindness and she indicated that she would love to see him again, too. They made a date for the following Saturday night. He was going to pick her up from home and they were going to a movie and dinner. However, if something else crossed her mind, she could call him and they could rearrange their plans. Before leaving they exchanged telephone numbers and laughed again because they didn't need to exchange information on addresses.

He gave her a hug and left. He stood outside her door as she closed it and he listened for her to lock the door before descending the stairs. He had a wonderful time and it was the first time in a long time he felt complete as a person. He was impressed with her vibrancy and her ability to care. She appeared shaken at first but rebounded once the flowers were delivered and introductions made. He sighed with great satisfaction as he got into his car and navigated out of the parking lot. He had made a friend. She was someone who was a complete stranger to him. She was also willing to see him again and have dinner with him, too.

Al paused for a moment and thanked God for his good fortune. He was ready to move on. He wasn't looking for love or companionship. He just wanted to feel alive and connected. "*Dear Lord,*" he began softly. "*Thank you for what you have done for me. Thanks for the trauma that brought me a friend. Continue to watch over Jasmine as well as her friends and keep them safe. Maintain your ever present hedge of protection around my eager beavers. Bless and keep them safe and help them to learn and continue to improve. Without them, I am not sure where I would be right now. Heavenly Father, continue to bless those who strive to do your will and bless those who are afraid to come to you but stand in need of your assistance. Continue to lift me up every time I fall and keep me under your grace, gracious Lord and God. Amen.*

Jaleen was home earlier than usual. She completed her errands, which included stops at two additional stores for items of interest for the new business being started by Brad and Selecia. "He should be on campus by now," she thought. She couldn't wait to call him. She wanted to share some of the highlights and a part of her wanted to wait and see what developed. She didn't want him lifting her hopes as well as his and then things don't work out.

She decided to wait for his phone call and then she'd decide how much she would reveal. Putting her items away for shipping out, she continued with her musings. She really liked Aaron. That much she was able to admit. He caused her to feel excited and she wondered if this is what her brother and his wife felt at the start of their relationship. Lying across her bed, Jaleen wondered if men experienced the same level of anxiety when a relationship was moving towards unchartered waters. She wondered if they knew what they were doing at all times. "Were they always in control or did it just appear that way?"

Aaron's kiss left her feeling nervous, excited, and anxious like a kid at Christmas. She assumed it was how teenagers felt. Since she had not engaged in more than one relationship as a teenager and that was during her junior year in high school. She wasn't sure but she believed it was this feeling that made girls squeal with laughter when they got together and talked about their boyfriends.

"Many of the virtues she expressed the other night were evident in him," she surmised. He listened to her concerns and was never quick to judge or criticize. He asked questions that evoked thought and caused her to consider other views, aspects and opinions. He was compassionate and loving and he showed his love through his actions.

His kiss was one such action. She believed that it was an expression of his love for her but . . . "Stop butting," her heart cut in. "The kiss was a sign of his love. End of speculation."

As Aaron showered he tried to imagine what she was doing right now. He wanted to see her. She had occupied every nook and cranny of his mind all day. He would dress, give her a call and see if she would see him. If her answer was yes only to cut him down, then he would try again, he decided.

When he called, her phone rang several times. As he was about to hang up, he heard her answer in a low soft voice. "Did I disturb you?" Aaron asked. "I'm sorry. I'll call you tomorrow," he added quickly. He felt terrible knowing that he must have awakened her. He couldn't believe she was already asleep. "No, no, it's okay. It's okay," Jaleen said quickly. Sitting up, Jaleen asked him if he had just gotten in. Aaron indicated he had and asked if she was okay. "You sound a little down, he continued. "If I offended you last night, I apologize. It happened and I didn't stop to think and I'm . . ." "Don't apologize if you really didn't mean it," Jaleen cut in. The line went silent. He wasn't sure how to interpret her words. Finally, Aaron asked if he could come over. Still silence. Then he heard the dial tone in his ear.

What happened? He asked himself in annoyance. He was trying to let her know that he had not meant to offend her. He simply wanted her to know how he felt and he had acted like a teenager on his first real date. As he reviewed what he had said, he came to one conclusion. Somehow, something got twisted in the interpretation and he was out in the cold. He was literally and figuratively out in the cold. He felt crushed. He rushed and got crushed he surmised. That hurts. It hurts more than being dismissed all those years ago. Aaron was facing the same pain he had tried to avoid all over again. ✿

❀❀ *Chapter Twenty Eight* ❀❀

Panic had stepped in and Jaleen's nerves won. She was convinced that Aaron was apologizing for kissing her. He did kiss her and now he's trying to say what. "It wasn't as it seemed? He wasn't that interested in her?" She was crushed. She couldn't believe that he'd play her like that. What did he think? She was going to be an easy romp in bed? Get me thinking about him one way and then he's really thinking about me a next? This is why I avoid men! This is what I don't like! The games are annoying! Either we are interested in each other or we are not. Either we want to have a relationship and see where it goes or we don't. But we don't have to play games. We're adults! After hanging up the phone, she pushed herself up and went out in the living room.

The image of them sitting together and sharing that kiss ran her back in her bedroom. She wasn't ready to face that either. How could it seem so right and now be so wrong? Without warning, she burst into tears. Her heart felt like it had been stepped on by a two ton baby elephant. But instead of stepping on her heart and moving on, the baby elephant was sitting on it. She was unable to move or think clearly. A few minutes ago, her mind was consumed with happy thoughts and now it was feeling lost and confused. Shattered! "How could he do this to me?" She wailed as she stood in the hallway, tears trailing down her face.

Through her anguish and tears the truth became more easily identified. The reality was that she liked him. She really, really liked him. When did it happen? She didn't know. How did it happen? She wasn't sure. Looking into the bathroom mirror she just stood there and cried. After more than fifteen minutes of standing in the middle of her bathroom and crying, Jaleen removed her clothes and took a hot shower. As the warm water poured down her body hot tears streamed down her face. Aaron had trapped her heart and she didn't know how to get it back. "Worst yet," she thought, "he had no way of knowing what he had done." Quietly, like a thief in the night, he had entered her sanctuary—her home—and stolen her heart, the one she always tried to keep safe from predators. He scaled the walls she usually erected around her heart and had accessed the combination to the safe where she kept her heart hidden and had stolen it. The reserves, her nerves, her sentinels, who usually rescued her from fates such as this, had been trying to warn her all along and she ignored them. Now, her heart was exposed; ripped from her chest. Gone.

Again, her mind returned to the tender exchange of affection between them. It was unexpected and she did not resent the stolen kisses. So, how could he kiss her so tenderly and now call to say he was sorry he had done it? What is wrong with this picture?" she cried softly. "What is wrong with him? Didn't I share with him the kind of person I was? Was he really listening or was he looking for a moment of weakness to defile me?"

"Doesn't he know love when he feels it? A kiss like that could only come from one who is in love," she acknowledged. "Why pretend and kiss me if you don't really care about me, Aaron? And if you don't care about me, then why try to fool me into thinking that love was a part of your plan for having someone special in your life. Obviously you don't know what love is." Jaleen stated flatly as she cried even harder. "Does anyone really know what it is?"

As soon as she said it, she felt remorseful that she had expressed it that way. She had two wonderful examples: her grandparents and her brother and his wife. Their images immediately stood before her. She was wrong to assert that it didn't exist. It did. She saw it with them. She saw it when they looked at each other. She witnessed it in the things they did for each other. She heard it in the way they spoke to each other and about each other. Love existed. She felt their love around her while she was with them.

She had no idea how or when they had found their true loves but they had. She wanted to have something like that. Something that was able and capable of withstanding the daily ups and downs of life. She needed patience. The love of her life is out there. Her brother told her so. If he found it when he wasn't searching for it, then she could to. She recalled, again, what he had told her. "*There is someone out there for you. Just give yourself the chance to meet him and give him the chance to show you the kind of person he is. If he's the right person, you will know it. The things he will do for you and the things he will share with you will let you know just who he is and how he feels. Your heart and head will give you the go-ahead and you will be in the best relationship of your life. Know this, when you decide to give your heart, give it with caution. But give it.*"

Jaleen started crying all over again. Her heart and head wanted Aaron. She wanted Aaron to be that person in her life. She wanted him to love her and be the one to share his life with her. Before she had taken the time to hear and process what he was trying to say, her nerves had jumped into the conversation and she reacted like someone who wanted to get out of the relationship on the first available bus or plane. Sadly, she had no idea what to do to make it happen for them. She didn't have a clue. All she knew was that she loved Aaron and he wasn't ready to love her back.

She needed to talk this over with someone. Exactly who that person was, she decided, was her baby brother. Maurice was in and out of relationships like people changed clothes. She knew he was not the one and Claudia was in a relationship but they never really talked about things like that so candidly so she wasn't sure she wanted to discuss her broken heart with Claudia. She knew she could share it with Brad. They practically shared everything.

Turning off the shower, she decided to call and see if he had gotten in safely. She needed to hear his voice. She needed to talk with him. She needed him to bring a sense of calm to her heart and her nerves. Her soul was lost in all the turmoil. She was lonely again and it was the most pain she had felt in two years. When she had discovered Clay's little secret it hurt like hell. But she had made a decision and she was not willing to compromise her safety or happiness with someone who wanted to be happy with the assistance of drugs. If he couldn't be naturally happy with her then she had to be naturally happy without him. She felt like her world had exploded in a million pieces and she wasn't sure she was going to be able to put the pieces back together and move on. But she did.

To be rejected is the hardest part of loving, she analyzed. You can't make someone love you. You can't make them care. You can't make them do what their heart doesn't want them to. She learned that from her parents' divorce. When did she forget that lesson? When? She was supposed to wait for Aaron to commit to her before she allowed her heart and soul to be wrapped up in him. She slipped and fell in love and she didn't know when the fall occurred. All she knew now was that she was in love with someone who was unwilling to be in love with her.

As she dressed and cleaned down her shower stall, she began to hear another voice, reaching out to her. Her heart was trying to help her head to reason. She didn't want to hear it and tried to drown it out by working on the shower, the face basin and the floor. Still, her heart persisted. You can't have love if your heart's not in it. Therefore, you have love. Your heart and soul are in it. Now you've got to win his heart and soul in return. You can do it.

Slowly, she allowed the last of the tears to fall. Listening to her heart, she said, "You got me in this mess. Do you know how to get me out of it? You really think I can win his love? I don't know . . . I don't know how to win his love" and Jaleen began crying all over again. Admitting that she loved him was a start. But she didn't know where to go from there. She packed up the towels and clothes and prepared her laundry for the next day. Weeping softly, she tried to sort things out in her mind.

The phone rang and she chose to ignore it. As she looked at the handset, she thought of picking it up getting rid of the caller and calling Aaron back. Then she decided to just call her brother. If there was anyone else in the world she could talk to and who would listen to her, it was him. She needed the comfort and consolation of his voice letting her know that she would be okay and that if Aaron was the one all she needed to do was be patient and let things work themselves out.

She turned off the bathroom lights. Checked her front door to make sure it was properly locked and then she returned to her bedroom. Picking up the phone, she called her brother's number at Hoffman. If he's there she would share her heart ache with him. After ringing more than eight times, she concluded he was not in his room. She hung up the phone and decided to write down her thoughts. A letter is just as good. By the time he gets it the healing process would have began. Had she known she would have been writing him a letter she would have held the check and send them both express mail. Two for the price of one, she thought dryly.

Moving towards the living room, she saw them again. Aaron was kissing her and she was kissing him back. She did not resist or show any signs of displeasure. She had enjoyed his spontaneous response to their closeness. Her heart began pounding in her chest and she remembered watching him leave and how she felt afterwards. She watched the door the same way she did when she had watched him leave the night before. The uncertainty, the gaiety that lifted her soul was indescribable at that moment. She couldn't believe what had just happened to her a few seconds before.

Now, to be feeling so sad, discarded, trampled. With a heavy sigh, she sat at her dining table and wept some more as she tried to put on paper how she was feeling. It was a difficult task. She had begun by describing Aaron and she broke down in tears again. The more she reflected on their friendship and tried to put it on paper, the more she cried. She had really fallen in love with her next door neighbor and it was sudden, exciting and now sad.

Looking at the mess she had made, she ripped up the paper and decided to try again when she was feeling stronger and in better emotional control. All the lines were running into each other as her tears fell here and there on the paper. Jaleen blew her nose in the paper towel, threw it and her attempts at letter writing in the trash, turned off the lights and went to bed. It was going to be a long, hard, difficult three-day weekend. ❀

❀❀ *Chapter Twenty Nine* ❀❀

Aaron sat stunned. He couldn't believe what had just taken place. He tried going over what he had said and couldn't determine what specifically was stated to flip off Jaleen. He had paced back and forth towards the front door several times. A part of him wanted to knock on her door and request that they sit down and talk it over face to face. But he didn't want to create a scene. It was her home and she didn't even have to answer him.

To top that off, he didn't want Jasmine all up in his business either. That would be more salt in his freshly opened wound. But he wanted to talk to her. He needed to know what he had said wrong. He didn't regret kissing her. He just wanted to apologize to her if it offended her but he wanted her to know he loved her and was willing to take his time to win her love.

His head was pounding and he felt as though all the blood from his heart had been drained out of it and the rest that his brain was using was also seeping out all over his cranium. He was in excruciating pain. The woman he loved was angry with him and he made a mess of things somehow and he wasn't sure how he was going to make it alright.

Over and over again he went over the brief conversation. He couldn't understand what was said that ticked her off. Looking back, he couldn't recall ever seeing her angry. She was always pleasant and easy going. She had a smooth temperament and gentle nature. "Well," he said under his breath, "I stepped on her somehow and she has risen up angrier than a bee caught off guard sipping nectar."

Walking towards the door, he felt compelled to speak to her. He didn't know what else to do. He just wanted to make things right and he had to give it a try. He did not spend all this time trying to capture her heart, the essence of her being, only to lose her with a few misplaced or misunderstood words. Reflecting back on the days with his crush, he recognized that he was unskilled and unprepared for the ways girls treated boys. Confidence was not in great supply during that period in his life. If he had known then what he knew now, he would have picked a different point in time to approach K'Leah. Who knows? Maybe she still would have shot him down, but he would have given it a better shot. The outcome might have been different.

When he recognized where his mind had drifted off to, he made a derisive scoff. He was not interested in K'Leah. Right now, the woman he wanted in his life more than any other one in this world was Jaleen. They both had their ups and downs and they were trying to have faith in the concept called love. Right now, however, things weren't looking so hot. He had made a mess and wasn't quite sure how.

Sometimes, he wondered why people really had to speak at all. If it only created confusion, why couldn't there be an action for everything that needed to be communicated so that people would know immediately what was being conveyed? Misinterpretations lead to so many other complications that he knew some disagreements could have been avoided if an action had existed to replace it the actual words. "Listen to me, up and down on a tangent," he concluded.

He wanted this mess straightened out. He wanted to look forward to the weekend knowing that Jaleen would be a part of it. He wanted them to visit one of the topiaries his company maintained. He wanted her to see his world as much as she would let him see hers. He wanted them to spend some time looking for some of the items she wanted for her family's business. He just wanted to spend some quality time with her, holding her close and even kissing her again and he didn't want anything messing it up. He knew what he wanted. He had anticipated them having a lovely time together this weekend and somehow all that anticipation was for nothing. "Nothing," he said annoyed as he continued pacing back and forth.

Aaron sat down once again. His feelings were still in turmoil. He wanted Jaleen in his life. He wanted to convey that to her and somehow, he wasn't sure that she wanted to hear or understand anything he had to say right now. With a resigned sigh, he slowly took his shoes off. He wriggled his toes on the floor and tried to relax. As tightly coiled as he felt, it was amazing that he was able to think, let alone process anything clearly. Every nerve and fiber of his being was stretched to capacity. He rubbed his eyes and the area around his temples.

With a long, deep sigh, he undressed, and placed his clothes back on the hangers. Slipping into something more comfortable, he went outside on his balcony. The cold night air filled his lungs and he began to relax. Maybe he just needed to give her some time alone. Maybe he was moving too fast and she panicked. After all, it's been a while since she was in a relationship and she wasn't exactly trying to get into one as far as he could tell.

He took another deep breath and as his mind slowed down he began to feel better. He began to relax and gained a better perspective on the situation. Perhaps that was her avoidance mechanism. Maybe she felt scared and didn't know how to communicate with him after the kiss. She didn't give any signs of displeasure and he was almost certain she had begun to respond, just before he ended it. As he walked towards the door, she didn't say anything to stop him and she didn't say anything to indicate she was unsure of herself either.

He remembered leaving; walking slowly enough to give her a chance to either delay his departure or indicate her displeasure. He waited for her to lock the door and she did, a few seconds after he was standing outside. She didn't open it in search of him nor did she open it to indicate she didn't want to see him again. Either way he would have been right outside waiting for her if she had a response. But she didn't.

The kiss could not be the object of disdain, he concluded. She must have experienced a delayed response and what a delay it was. Not bragging, but he knew he was better than average when it came to kissing. A kiss was the sensual and most intimate act in a relationship. It communicated what was being felt between the two individuals. It opened the door to intimacy of the highest level. When he kissed Jaleen, he wanted to let her know she was special and important to him. He wanted her to know that he loved her. He didn't want to seduce her. With that thought, Aaron stopped short with his reflections. He hoped that that wasn't what was behind all of this. He never intended to do anything of the sort when he had kissed her.

For the first time, he realized that his kiss could have been misinterpreted. He hoped that it was not the case. He didn't do anything that should have suggested otherwise. He wanted her as his lady not a person for simple sexual relief. That was not in the relationship he envisioned for them. He never saw her as someone he wanted to have sex with.

Aaron knew that making love was something reserved for couples who were ready to express their love on another level. It was the consummate act that bonded true lovers together as one. He wanted that when they were sure that they were ready to move their relationship forward. That wasn't for them right now. Although, he acknowledged, that he would love to make love to her. But the kiss was not a prelude to that. Not that at all.

He had loved her secretly for some time now, almost a year. He had risked everything when he kissed her. It was impulsive and had he taken the time to think it through, it probably would not have happened. After this, why should she rush into loving him now? As impetuous as he had been the night before, he had no regrets about kissing her. The fact that she had not responded adversely to his show of affection could have meant anything.

He knew she had been caught off guard. It could also have meant that when she had caught herself he did not give her an opportunity to respond. He had bid her good night and hadn't waited for her to say anything.

Stepping back inside, Aaron had concluded one thing. He wasn't going to give up just yet. She may have stung him like a thousand bumblebees all at once. But he wasn't going to give up. He loved her and he was going to wait.

Her kind of love was worth it. He closed the door and sat mindlessly in front of the television. He needed a diversion in order to allow his mind to remain on the path it was currently on. He was more relaxed now than he had been a little over an hour ago. He had felt like he had been crushed with no means of ever rebounding. But, taking a few minutes—more like hours, to review the situation, he was able to arrive at this state of being.

Jaleen was his world. He loved her and he knew she wasn't seeing anyone else at the moment. She had been out of a relationship for a little over two years. He also knew she was afraid to love but wanted to fall in love and settle down in a good relationship with someone who loved and cherished her.

Well, he loved her and he was willing to make her the center of his world anytime she was ready to move on with him in her life. If it took more than a year, he was willing to wait and win her love. He was this close, he motioned with his index finger and thumb and he would regain the ground lost this evening. All he had to do was wait and hope. "A little prayer couldn't hurt either," he concluded with a heavy sigh. ❀

❀❀ *Chapter Thirty* ❀❀

Al was ready to work out earlier than usual that Saturday. He felt good and he felt rested. Despite his dream a few days ago, he felt ready to take on the world. He had made a new friend and she was willing to go out with him next Saturday. He wanted to move on but not fall in love or become entwined in an intimate relationship. He even admitted to himself that it felt good to have someone else to talk to beside his coworkers and students.

Life was too short to spend it on regrets and sadness. People died every day. Some were loved, some hated and some even unsure as to whether they were really loved at all. Maybe he wasn't the best provider or husband. But he could be a good friend. He had almost forgotten what that was. Overseas, he had many friends. They all hung out together and they played around. He wasn't in for making babies for babies' sake. When he had a child of his own, he wanted to be there for it and to enjoy the relationship that evolves when you are responsible for another human being—one you created.

Some children had a tough enough time growing up without the love and support of both parents. The evidence of this was everywhere. He didn't want to be a part of that negative cyclical relationship phenomenon. He wanted to enjoy the company of his children and watch them grow and learn. He wanted to see his children make something of themselves and with him there encouraging them along.

Al believed that he may experience it one day. Where there's hope there's the possibility of buried treasure—waiting to be discovered. The mother of his children would have his support, assistance and love. That he was certain. However, he knew that none of this was in his immediate future, given his current feelings and circumstances surrounding his soon to be single status once again.

Jasmine, on the other hand, was slow getting up. She had stayed up late watching the television and going over the evening's events. She was glad she had declined the girls' offer of dinner and a movie. She would have missed out on meeting Al and discovering that he wasn't a villain who had disposed of Amber's body. As she chuckled at herself, she also had to admit that what was thought about was real. It's just that it didn't happen in this instance and for that she was glad. Amber was okay for now. He even volunteered to help her locate her friend.

Aaron hibernated like a bear. He was emotionally and mentally drained from his latest fallout. He hoped to see Jaleen and to be given an opportunity to clarify the misunderstanding that had sent them both into opposite directions—for now. He was determined to regain her trust and win her love. He was going to have to be patient, though. He knew that now.

With a cursory look in his fridge, he decided against preparing anything. His heart wasn't in it. He wanted a change of scenery and he needed to pick up a few things anyway, his laundry for one. Without another thought, he decided to take a walk in his favorite park. This would afford him some distance and more time to think and regroup.

Jaleen was up and working on her laundry and clearing out her closet. She was looking for items to donate to the Goodwill in preparation for her spring additions. She was also looking for something to wear to the dinner celebration at the end of the month. With Crystal on the committee, she was kept up to date and reminded almost daily. So if she had chosen not to attend, she really could not say she had forgotten about it. Crystal was her reminder and human calendar.

She had this weekend to find something to wear or she would be faced with purchasing something and then donating that, too. She didn't want her closet over run with clothes and other items that were not being used regularly. Clutter was something she was seriously allergic to. Her cabinets in the kitchen held just the items used regularly. There were no extra pots, pans or dishes beyond the ability to feed four people.

The vanity in the bathroom held enough toilet tissue, soap, cleaning agents and shampoos without looking all disorderly and unmanageable. Her linen closet had enough towels and sheets to be used at least for a month without being washed. She had no overages. She did not believe in excessive quantities. They added to the appearance of clutter, especially when they were not folded neatly or packed away neatly.

As she tidied up her apartment, she began to tidy up her mind. She felt that she needed to speak with Aaron and resolve what had happened. If he was, indeed, sorry about kissing her then so be it. But if he had the capacity to love, then she would try her best to win his heart for hers was lost to him forever.

He wasn't one who needed to be impressed with gossip. He never shared any and she never had any. She was independent and would continue to be herself and hope that one day they could share something deeper than a superficial friendship. She had no intention of sleeping with him in order to win his love.

That would be another disaster. It would only lead to lustful satisfaction. Her heart and pride wouldn't be able to stand a relationship built on that alone. That was rejection of the worst kind, too. She couldn't live with herself if she did that. It was love or nothing at all.

Right now, she decided, she wasn't ready to see him. So she would remain indoors today and simply clean up her apartment. When she was finished wiping down the cabinets, she rinsed out the dishes, pots and pans that were stored in them and allowed them to dry in the dish drain. She replaced the shelf liners in the food cabinets after wiping them out. The bottom cabinets under the sink were next. She removed everything, wiped down the shelf, replaced the liner and repacked the items on the shelf.

As she removed the items from the refrigerator, she realized that it had been cleaned prior to her trip home. Still she moved the items off the shelves and wiped them down. The fruit and vegetable bins were wiped out and the few fresh pieces were placed in the bins once again and placed in the fridge. Jaleen was well on her way to cleaning her apartment in record time.

It kept her busy and helped her to use the nervous energy that was building up inside her. With the shower cleaned from the night before, all she had left to do was clean the windows. She decided that the outside window nearest her door would be the first she cleaned and the sliding door would be her last. Armed with the window cleaner and her damp and dry rags, she sprayed and wiped the inside and went to tackle the outside.

Despite how she was feeling, she really didn't want Aaron to step outside right now. Cleaning was something, once started had to be finished before she lost her steam. Talking would slow her down and though it would get some of the load off her mind, she wanted to finish cleaning and then deal with him. As she finished the last of the windows she could reach without the step ladder, she scooped up the cleaning solution and scurried back inside. It didn't occur to her to check the parking lot to see if his car was there. She was out and then back in without missing a beat. With her music playing softly, she cleaned the sliding glass door, with the assistance of her stepping stool. She enjoyed sitting and looking out in the distance and as things stood now, she was going to be doing that even more, alone.

With the general tasks associated with dusting and cleaning out of the way, Jaleen prepared the mopping water. She mopped from her living room to her dining and kitchen area. She even mopped her porch, left the glass door ajar and then headed down the hall. She changed the water and then mopped from the hall to her bedroom door and finally the bathroom floor. When she was finished, Jaleen showered, used her towel to make her path back to the washer and dryer. She had two more loads and the last of them were the towels. Satisfied with what she had been able to accomplish, she turned up her music and began to fold the clothes that were removed from the dryer.

Working peacefully, she tried desperately to keep her mind focused and her heart and nerves quiet. She just wanted to enjoy the calm that was needed to get her through this love storm. It had been a long time since her heart was involved in a relationship and she was trying hard to avoid shedding any more tears. She had also decided that it wasn't over until she was sure she couldn't have his love.

With the dinner celebration coming up, she decided that she would go out and look for something new to wear. They had worked hard last year and with the bonus, she was going to enjoy some of it on herself, even if her spending was premature. She knew it wasn't wise to count the chickens before they hatched. This was especially so, given the expenses on her plate right now with the store and her need to save for her down payment on her house, that she was looking forward to. However, she needed an emotional pick-me-up and shopping for something new and special would be the cure for her right now. The change of scenery would also be welcomed. The apartment held too many recent memories that she could not avoid unless she stayed in her bedroom throughout this entire weekend. Jaleen knew that that was not going to happen. ✿

❀ ❀ *Chapter Thirty One* ❀ ❀

Jasmine decided to have her neighbors over for dinner. She wanted to tell them about meeting Al and his invitation to dinner. She also wanted to find out if they were ready to help her locate Amber. Though Al had volunteered to assist, she would at least begin with them and if they faltered along the way, then she would seek him out and take him up on his offer.

But when she called, Jaleen was in the middle of her shower and missed the call. Aaron was also out. When she called him on his cell, he simply accepted her invitation. He wasn't doing anything and it would give him a chance to see Jaleen and gauge her true feelings. That was if she wanted to share their company this weekend. Groaning inwardly, Aaron wanted to know why he had even accepted the invitation. It was going to be punishment for him if she decided to ignore his presence or be civil. With that thought, he began to school his emotions in preparation for the emotional assault.

Examining the contents of her fridge once more, Jasmine decided to do a light shopping. She didn't have enough of anything to feed three people. If she were dining alone, she would be fine. But with company coming over, she had to adequately prepare. As she was walking out the door, Al crossed her mind again. She decided to invite him for dinner and to meet her friends.

With her heart racing, she dialed his number. She wanted to include him in the trio and at the moment didn't see anything wrong with the last minute invitation. As the phone rang, however, she began to have second thoughts. She was about to end the call when Al answered. "Hello." "Good morning," she said sounding out of breath. "Good morning and how are you?" Al responded cheerfully. "I'm doing fine," Jasmine admitted. "I was wondering if you'd like to join my friends and me tomorrow evening for dinner," she explained. "It's not a big thing. It would be a party of four. I'm going out to pick up some groceries and decided to include you, if you don't mind," she finished. "Well," Al responded slowly. "Is it a couple's thing?" "No, it's not," Jasmine answered quickly. "They are my neighbors and we get along fine. They're the ones who came to me when I was in the hospital." "They're not a couple?" Al asked. "They are my neighbors and they live to the left of me in their own apartments," she said smiling.

"Long as it's not a couple's thing, I'll consider joining you," he said with a hint of a smile in his voice. "I don't want to be blindsided and I don't want to give any impressions that are not so," he stated calmly. "We're friends and I'd like to introduce you to them." Jasmine waited for his final acceptance. She hoped that all his concerns were allayed and that he would agree to join them. "Okay," he said after a slight pause. "What can I bring to this dinner?" he asked. "Just you," Jasmine returned, excited about his acceptance. We'll meet tomorrow evening around 6:30," she continued. "That way we spend some time getting to know each other and by dinner's end we would all be stuffed and better acquainted." After a shared chuckle, they bid each other good-bye.

With a song in her heart and pep in her steps, Jasmine took the stairs instead of the elevator to her car. She was having company over and it was going to be nice to have someone else to focus on. She enjoyed her spars with Aaron, but this would give her something else to do. "Who knows," she said impishly, "Al may help Aaron get off his romp and say something to Jaleen." With that, she began to hum the refrain, "Let's get this party started! Let's get it started!"

Al was surprised at his acceptance to the invitation. He wasn't one to jump the gun or jump to conclusions but having an unfaithful wife had taught him many things. The wiles of women are not to be trusted. What appeared to be innocent on the surface usually had rip tides following closely underneath. He wasn't ready to play games and he didn't want to be drawn into any either. Still, the invitation intrigued him and he was happy, at least for now, that he had accepted the invitation.

Since she indicated that they were her neighbors, he steeled himself against the odds that the male caller he had seen the night before was more than likely one who was invited. He was at least two doors down from her apartment on the left hand side. It's going to be an interesting evening and he was trying to psyche himself up for it. Looking around him, he tried to think of something he wanted to carry for dinner. Even though she had indicated that he bring himself, he knew that good manners dictated that he brought something to the event. He wasn't sure if they drank as a social rule so he ruled that out. When they had been together the night before, Jasmine never offered anything stronger than a soft drink.

He spied his backgammon board and decided that he would get one for his hostess. This way, if the evening runs low on conversation, a game would be able to occupy some of the time and they would have spent the evening learning something new and challenging. He liked games that provoked thought as well as developed one's competitive nature. But, in this kind of setting, he wanted something that would bring out the best in all of them and decided to get something else in case the backgammon proved more of a challenge than was actually necessary for a night out on the town—though it would be strictly indoors.

With something new to do on a lazy Saturday, beside work at the Y, Alvin decided to go to the mall. If all else failed, he would give his hostess something to read. Not that she was short on intellect, mind you. They had spent a beautiful evening talking and making each other laugh. But he just wanted to have something as a backup if he didn't find another game beside backgammon. Four adults ought to be able do more than just talk. Having a good time is why they're coming together and have a good time they shall.

When Jaleen finished with her hair, she decided to take a nap. She had worn herself out cleaning up and was now ready for the rest of the weary to claim her mind, body and soul. She had had a restless night since her conversation with Aaron. Her head and nerves wanted to fight over who was right and who was wrong. Mentally and emotionally, she was too tired to care right now. She just wanted sleep to claim her faculties. She was physically, mentally and emotionally exhausted.

Several times she jumped out of her sleep. She thought she had heard a knock at her door. Subconsciously, she wished that Aaron would come knocking. She felt badly. She also felt broken in a million pieces, though she wasn't sure if that was what it was. She just wanted to see him. As she was drifting back to sleep, she heard a knock on her door. Hoping it was Aaron, she hurriedly went to the door.

"Hi," Jasmine said. "Hope I didn't wake or disturb you. Want to come over for dinner tomorrow evening?" She asked in one breath. With some reservations, Jaleen accepted her invitation. She remembered Jasmine's earlier promise and wished it wasn't to be executed now. But, she did promise that the next get together would have been held by her. So, she accepted.

Closing the door, she felt disappointed and even sadder. The cold breeze had done nothing but add to the numbness she was already feeling on the inside. Now she was going to have to endure an evening with Aaron and she wasn't sure how she was going to do that. It's like breaking up with someone at work and having to see them every day, sometimes multiple times per day. She wasn't sure if she really wanted to go through with the invitation after all. Facing Aaron with this stalemate between them was not something she could do. More than anything, she believed he would be able to see that she loved him and that would simply make already bad matters worse for her.

As she returned to bed, she felt even more weighed down than before. How had things gotten this complicated? One minute she was simply cruising along, excited about her visit with her family in the islands and the new business they were about to launch. Now, she was bruised from the inside out and felt uncertain about her own abilities to enjoy an evening among friends.

Pulling the covers up to her chin, Jaleen decided to sleep all the way to Monday. If she heard anyone knocking on her door, she would simply ignore it and hope her dreams were strong enough and sweet enough, to envelope her soul and keep her from hearing the intrusions to her semi-conscious world. That was the best that she could hope for at that moment.

The hospital's garden was always a source of peace to Aaron. Today was different. He was feeling low. Again, he reviewed the conversation in his head and he was still unable to determine where he went wrong. He wasn't trying to seduce her. He was trying to communicate his true feelings to her. He was making his move and it backfired somehow. As he walked around, for the first time in a long time, without any of the equipment to clean, prune or do any kind of repairs, he felt even more listless. Here is where he entertained perfect memories of him and Jaleen. Here is where he envisioned asking her out in an effort to propose. In this garden, Aaron saw them walking together; enjoying the architectural green thumb that had been created to harness the peace and comfort that nature provides. Unable to sit and simply enjoy the hues of green and other variety of colors, he decided to go home.

As he pulled into the parking lot, Aaron hoped that he would be lucky enough to get to his apartment without seeing Jaleen. He didn't really want to make a fool of himself and he didn't want the opportunity to prove more painful than it already was. He had concluded that she needed time and space and he would give it to her as much as possible. But he was still determined to let her know she meant the world to him. If she really didn't feel the same about him then he would accept it and coax his heart into moving on. It had been broken before and survived. It will survive again, though it may be in a million pieces for a while. Walking towards the stairs, Aaron looked at her apartment, trying to determine if she was up and about. At the last minute, he decided to jog up and go straight to his apartment. If they happened to meet, he'd greet her and just keep going. ✿

❀❀ *Chapter Thirty Two* ❀❀

Jaleen called Jasmine to see if she needed help with anything. She had an order of flowers delivered to Jasmine's since she didn't feel like preparing anything in particular. When Jasmine indicated that she could use some company, Jaleen joined her. She knew it was going to be a challenge being in the same room with Aaron and not being able to relax around him as she had done in the past. But she had to try. If nothing else, they were all friends. Nothing more.

As the time drew near, the knock on the door brought her heart to a full stop. She expected Aaron to walk right in behind Jasmine. To her surprise, it was someone she had never met before. He gave Jasmine a small shopping bag and then presented her with the gift wrapped box. Jasmine introduced them and told Jaleen she would save the details of meeting Al until Aaron arrived. Teasing Al, she said, "Meeting him flipped me out!" They laughed together and everyone returned to the living room. When she opened the box, she saw it was a backgammon set and Uno game.

With delight and sincerity in her voice, she asked Al to teach them to play. She had never played Uno or backgammon before. "Which game would you like to learn?" Al asked. When Jasmine selected backgammon, he proceeded to setup the game board and explain the rules as briefly as he could. He knew from experience that if you made explaining the rules a chore, then players lose interest and the game is over before it actually began. He gave both girls an opportunity to play each other. That way, they could learn the rules together and play the game whenever they got together. Somehow, he suspected it was often.

As they rolled their pair of dice and began to move their chips around the board, the squeals got louder and louder. When Jaleen was placed on the board, Al gave them two versions of the rules for getting down. Again, he wanted them to decide how they would get down. By deciding little things, ownership of game occurred. As he watched and guided them, they became immersed in the thinking that was necessary to create strategic moves and traps. None of the ladies heard the knocking at the door.

Rolling their dies, moving their chips and laughing at each other's pitfalls kept Jaleen from noticing Aaron's arrival. The men introduced themselves and the ladies continued to play. As Al refereed, he began to relax and enjoy the atmosphere he had helped to create. He really didn't want the kind of small talk that led to minding other people's business or dipping into the personal affairs of others. He had endured much when his wife had cheated on him and he did not want to participate in that level of idle chatter. Games were a neat way of getting everyone focused on learning something new and thinking strategically while having fun. With the last roll of her dies, Jasmine was able to defeat Jaleen. Both had two chips left on the first and third spot for Jaleen and two on the second spot for Jasmine. The rolling of the double deuce made Jasmine the winner. With shouts of excitement and groans of defeat, the girls laughed together.

When Al asked Aaron if he wanted to get in on the action, he was game. After listening to Al explain the rules once more, the ladies had an opportunity to watch the men play. The game lasted just as long as the girls' game had and shouts and hollers were just as hearty as when the girls had began to get the hang of it. With the movement of chips up and down the board, the shouts and clapping of the hands grew louder. Finally, Aaron won. Jasmine was almost certain that Al allowed him to win. He seemed to have shifted the plays when he rolled the ace and deuce. She was almost certain he had another roll coming. But overall, they had an exciting evening.

During the meal, they formally introduced themselves and shared something special about themselves. At that time, Jasmine chose to share that Al was the person now living in Amber's apartment. Aaron almost dropped his fork. He quickly rebounded and extended his right hand to Al. "Thanks for doing the right thing for Jasmine, man. You're alright," he complimented him. Jaleen added her gratitude to Al for what he had done as well. Al accepted their compliments and then informed them that he would do it again. He even told them that he had offered to help Jasmine look for her friend. "So, let me know if I can help," he said politely.

After dinner, they moved back to the living room area and began to play Uno. With the scoring mechanism in place, each person tried to rid their hands of their cards in an effort to win and receive the points represented by the cards in their opponents' hands. The movement of the game increased with each new twist and turn of the cards. One time Aaron was causing Jaleen grief then a next time, she was doing it to him. Al sometimes punished her along with Jasmine depending on the direction the game had been moved in due to the instructions on the cards.

They played together for more than two hours. Be it beginner's luck or simply the strategic selections that were played, the girls beat the guys. Jaleen had the most points, followed by Jasmine and Al. They all had the time of their lives and it was exhilarating for Al, too. He hadn't had so much fun since the early days of his marriage. As quickly as the thought entered his mind, he refocused on the game and dismissed it. He didn't want any comparisons that involved VaNessa.

They participated in the clean up, which was something Al admired about Jasmine's friends. Before saying good night, the dishes were cleared and cleaned. The left-overs were wrapped and placed in the refrigerator after the to-go plates had been prepared. The stove top was wiped clean. The living room and dining areas were restored to their previous condition; pillows were repositioned on the couch, chairs were back in their usual position and the items on the coffee table were back in place as well. They had opened the sliding door just a peek to let in some fresh air as they tidied up the place. Housekeeping finished, the door was closed and the aroma from the floral arrangements encircled them once again. Goodnights were now being said as they thanked Jasmine for dinner and Al for the games.

Jaleen hugged him and Jasmine and bid them both good night. Aaron followed suit and he also left. Al was last to leave and he, too, hugged Jasmine and thanked her for inviting him and including him in her circle of friends. "I had a wonderful time." Al said. "Thanks for the invitation. I will try to return it to you and your friends real soon." After another hug, Al left and Jasmine locked the door behind him. The evening was a success and she was happy about that.

On the drive home, Al reflected on his evening. He really had a wonderful time. They enjoyed the games and he was especially glad he had taken the time to select both. Leaving them with Jasmine meant that whenever they got together, they could play and continue to learn how to strategize as well. The mind games were half the fun if not the most fun of all. Anticipating what would be made and then watching them unfold only added to the excitement of the game. He was really happy, like when his eager beavers had a good session and they felt proud of their accomplishments. He enjoyed that feeling of success with and for them. That's how he was feeling now.

He sensed a level of tension between Jaleen and Aaron. He was almost willing to bet that they were lovers or in the early stages of a more personal relationship. She avoided partnering with him during Uno and he appeared unaffected. But Al believed it bothered him. Being neighbors, they were probably used to ribbing or hitting on each other. But something was amiss, of that he was certain. He was also certain that they were terrific friends.

The way they cleaned up and made sure everything was in place before leaving was a first for him. People usually had dinner, enjoyed the evening and left. The hostess was left to clean up after the guests left. He really admired that about them. It indicated that they were truly good friends and it was nothing for them to help out and minimize the work before going home. Al appreciated that gesture more than anything else he experienced that evening. Some people definitely knew how to be friends.

Jasmine was exhausted but happy. She and her friends treated Al like he was a part of their group for years. She hoped he noticed it. She told him it wasn't a couple's thing and she was glad that her words had been true. She knew Aaron was in love with Jaleen and Jaleen was oblivious of the fact. Maybe one day, she thought, one day Jaleen would slow down long enough to notice Aaron. "I hope he'll be around then, too." Smiling to herself, she also realized that she did not get a chance to rib Aaron once. But, she admitted they all had a great time with the games. "Who knew that games could be that much fun," she mused. It was definitely a first for her and it won't be the last time games made it on her get-together list of activities.

After finishing her shower, Jasmine turned off all the lights and went to bed. Tomorrow would be her lazy day and she intended to spend it resting and relaxing. She'd had an enjoyable evening with her friends and had thoroughly enjoyed herself as well. Waiting for sleep to claim her, Jasmine's mind ran on Al and she wondered if he had gotten home safely. She thought of calling him but then she decided to let him make that call. She didn't want him to think she was pursuing him. Still she wanted to be sure he had arrived home safely.

Jaleen and Aaron lived just next door. If others within the complex were ever invited, they lived within walking distance. He had at least a twenty five minute drive from her home. Jasmine lay motionless on the bed for a while. Maybe he'll call to let her know. If he didn't, she was going to give him a call and then call it a night.

Aaron was glad to be home. He felt anxious about the dinner date and even more anxious being in Jaleen's presence. She was polite towards him and she didn't give any signs of being hurt or upset. As she left ahead of him, she didn't wait for him or appear to want to talk to him. He half expected that and had decided not to push her. If she needed space, then he would provide it.

As long as she didn't want unlimited time and space he was willing to wait. Playing the games was relaxing and he did enjoy the evening, despite his personal dilemma. Al seemed like a nice guy and he hoped that they could get together again soon. They were all able to laugh and enjoy each other's jabs as they implemented tactics and strategies to improve their own chances of winning. The backgammon game was of peak interest to him. He had seen the game many times and never thought it was something he could learn to play. He decided to purchase one and to play alone so that he could learn it and be able to play Al more skillfully the next time they got together.

Jaleen took a bath and went to bed. She felt tightly wound and was deliberating whether or not to drink a cup of tea or simply take an aspirin to relax her nerves and muscles. She didn't want to hurt Aaron in any way. She tried to address him as politely as possible whenever she had to and was glad that he afforded her the same courtesy.

When his hand touched hers as they dealt the game cards, she felt a sharp pain inside. She wanted to talk with him but was unsure if he would have responded to her request at the end of the evening. So she quietly opened her door, entered and locked it. She even waited a few seconds to see if he would have knocked but he didn't.

Disappointed, she took her bath and was now deliberating whether to have the tea or an aspirin. Brad crossed her mind and she decided to give him a call. Looking at the clock, it was almost midnight. Jaleen changed her mind. It wasn't an emergency and they were taught that the only time a phone rang after nine o'clock at night was because it was an emergency. Reflecting on the calls she had made to him during the aftermath of the hurricane they were more than an emergency. He needed to know and she tried to give him whatever comfort and solace she could as they struggled to get news about their grandparents, his wife and daughter.

Her mind returned to Aaron and she wondered what he was doing. A part of her wanted to call him and invite him over and another part of her was afraid to reach out to him. She wanted to know if what she concluded was really what he had been conveying in his apology. She wanted to feel close to him, if nothing else. Feeling restless in her spirit, she went to the kitchen to prepare some tea. "You can't want someone more than they want you," she scolded herself. "If friendship is all that he wants, then that's what it will be." With those words, her heart erupted and tears began to fall once again. She was hopelessly in love with Aaron Michael Hammond and was unable to do anything about it. At least not right now. She didn't possess the nerves to call him on the phone or to knock on his door and try to make things right again. The more she thought about the situation, the more she wished she had simply listened and not said a word. As she reviewed the conversation again, for the millionth time, she realized that she jumped off and didn't really give Aaron an opportunity to complete his thought. She also realized that she didn't know where he was going with his apology. She was expecting to hear one thing and when it didn't begin that way, she just reacted without really hearing what he was saying.

After another round of mental deliberations, Jaleen concluded that she was at fault and didn't have the nerves, the same nerves that got her into this mess, to approach Aaron and try, yes, try to make things right. The fear of rejection kept her grounded in regrets with no courage for action. She wished she could just knock on his door, offer an apology and end the madness that now existed between them.

In the end, Jaleen made some tea, drank it and took her weary, confused mind and aching body to bed. She had worn herself out mentally and physically cleaning her already clean apartment. Then she had spent a pleasant evening among friends, with the object of her unhappiness just a few inches away wreaking havoc with her senses, perhaps not even realizing it. She had opened the New Year hoping for love and now, she was in turmoil over not being loved or better yet, not knowing if she was in love or simply infatuated with the idea of being in love and with someone who wasn't interested in her in the same way. ❀

❀❀ *Chapter Thirty Three* ❀❀

When he finally made it home, Al wanted to call Jasmine to let her know but decided against it several times. He wasn't sure if she was up and she may not be up to a phone call of this nature and he didn't want to send any wrong signals. He really had a great time and it wouldn't hurt to express that one more time, he contrived. Without another thought, he dialed her number. It was the courteous thing to do he finally decided.

Jasmine answered on the second ring. "Hi," Al said. "I just wanted to say thanks for a lovely evening. I enjoyed myself and meeting your friends. Thanks, again, for inviting me." Jasmine was glad to hear his voice. She was also appreciative of the call. "You're welcome," she said kindly. "I think we all had a great time. Thanks for the games," she stated appreciatively. "They were a hit and they contributed greatly to all of us having a good time. So, thank you, too," she concluded. "I know it's late and I don't want to keep you any longer, so, good night and thanks again." Jasmine smiled and said, "I'm glad you had a terrific time. Thanks for calling and letting me know. Good night."

Al felt the need for a swim. He had a lot of restless energy romping through his body. Sitting on the couch and looking out in the darkened sky, he opted to crack the sliding door and allow the cool night air to soothe and settle him down. He hadn't envisioned having a friend so soon. He had made up his mind to avoid all women, at least those who were interested in relationships. While he wasn't keen on one-night stands, he was cool with one-nighters now but he wasn't interested in that right now either.

At the age of thirty, many of his friends were either settled or in steady relationships. The few who were free, single and disengaged were not in his close circle because he was married and didn't want to be running with them. He wasn't interested in anyone else except his wife. Now that he was free to prowl, he just hadn't developed a sexual appetite that needed to be fed. He was cool living alone and working. But after tonight, he recognized that a solitary existence, though it has its privileges, wasn't the best thing for everyone, all the time.

He had a good time and he wanted to be able to look forward to more evenings like this one. "Then," he interrupted, "you have to become more sociable. It doesn't mean that everyone is out for a husband; some people just enjoy life and don't need to have someone attached to them to feel alive. Tonight was a perfect example." Speaking realistically, he was not a loner. He could be one if he had to but he enjoyed the company of friends and family and he missed that very much.

He was looking forward to having a family of his own. He had planned to visit his family and his wife's family every other year for Thanksgiving and Christmas. He wanted his children to know both sides of their family and the Thanksgiving and Christmas holidays would have allowed that to happen. His children would have been good with board games and using their minds. He wanted them to be able to think and strategize mentally. That, he felt, promoted critical thinking and problem solving skills; skills that all children need in order to navigate through life successfully as adults.

Leaning back on the couch, Al closed his eyes. The memories he had just visited, for the first time in a while, gnawed at his soul creating an indescribable pain. Where did he go wrong? What did he fail to do that caused VaNessa to step out on him? Standing and walking towards the glass door, he stepped outside hoping that the cold night air would numb the pain he was feeling inside again. As hard as he tried, he could not escape that pain that threatened to destroy him.

Love was something real to him. It was the one thing that made living worthwhile. "When you lose your partner to death, it must really and truly feel like death has taken you, too," he reasoned. Because to lose them to infidelity was a gut wrenching pain that was simply intolerable at best. He didn't want to experience it again, and so he had made up his mind to avoid relationships, at least for now. He had lost faith in women and their ability to love from the heart. If his wife was any indicator of what was out there, he didn't want to look any further.

Anger began to fill his heart again. He had tried hard to block out the feelings associated with being played and feeling betrayed. Some days he wanted to lash out and physically hurt VaNessa. During those dark moments he relied on prayer. Trouble was never his best friend. He couldn't let it get that close to him right now. It never discriminated. In the end, it always left you facing the problem it helped to create. At that moment, when Mr. Trouble was around, it was on the prowl for its next victim. He used you, fueled, tooled and fooled you and when he had satisfied himself, at your expense, he distances himself from you, leaving you in the midst of sorrow and despair, his other two partners. They love the misery you're now facing. Mr. Trouble gets you in all kinds of situations and leaves you there wondering how you got into it in the first place. Getting out of it is now your primary concern, your worry, not his; no sir, not Mr. Trouble's.

Since Al resented feeling sorry for himself, he knew he had to avoid being caught off guard by this number one enemy. He came from a family who prayed and he had relied on it, especially during these times, to pull him out of the darkness his moods allowed him to enter. The darkness zapped his energy, compromised his sanity and caused him to be resentful and mean to those around him. It opened the door for Mr. Trouble to walk right in and take over. During these foul moods, Al ignored questions asked of him, robotically executed his responsibilities in literal silence and looked at you as though you were in his private space. His eyes literally yelled, "Get away and STAY away!"

These shifts in his personality lasted longer than he would like to admit. Climbing out of those darkened places took more effort and energy than going in. Prayer helped him to balance out his feelings and kept him on even keel. It helped him to avoid stepping into the darkness and losing his mind, heart, freedom and soul. Some days he prayed and fasted to ensure he wasn't losing his mind. That occurred during the toughest battles with the darkness and he knew that it helped to cleanse him and renew his faith in the one Supreme Being over us all. Whenever anger threatened him like it was doing now, he knew he had to fight back. He knew *how* to fight it and he was eternally grateful for the weapon of prayer.

Stepping back inside, Al closed the sliding door and decided to take a hot shower. As he prepared for his bath, he stopped for a moment and prayed. Not because he was slipping away but because he was able to recognize it and head it off before it consumed him again. He was in a good place mentally and emotionally and he would do his best to remain there.

"Almighty Creator, I am before you once again. I am and will always be in need of you. I need you right now, Lord. I need you to keep me safe. I need you to keep me pure in mind and actions. I know you are not the God of accidents. You are the God of purpose. I know you did not bring me this far to abandon me. You are just a prayer away and you hear me whenever I call. Thank you for this evening. Thank you for placing Jasmine Murphy at my doorstep. Thank you for also delivering her during her moment of peril. Her presence in my life has helped to re-open doors I have chosen to close. I know, Lord, that you want them opened though I would prefer them closed. I know you are guiding me, though I sometimes resist walking the path you have placed before me. Thank you for the friendship that has been established. Thank you for this evening. I really enjoyed myself and believe that they did too. Continue, most merciful Father, to bless and keep her and her friends. Continue to strengthen the bonds they share and allow them to be there for each other in good and bad times. For we know you are always there and you have also placed others in our paths to provide the safe haven needed to shelter us from life's blistering storms. Though I am weak and have often lost my way, thank you for having the faith in me that I must have in you if I am to continue on this journey. You have lifted me up and placed me upon solid ground and I will seek you, Lord, and only you when I am feeling tossed and unsettled in my spirit as a result of one of life's storms. Whenever I question my role in my marriage, Lord, please remind me always that you are still here, working with me and not

against me. For it is during those times, during those reflections I am aware of the devil's presence. He is always nearby, lurking in the dark places, trying to steal my joy. It's times like now that I must show him that I know you are even closer to me than he will ever be. It is times like now, I must call on you to show him that you are my strong tower, my refuge and he cannot enter in and reign. Continue to work with me, O Lord, as I try to move forward, trusting in you for my hope, my joys, my strength and my happiness. I know that all things are possible to those who trust in you and I will continue to hold onto you for as long as I have breath. Reinforce my hedge of protection, Lord. Preserve and protect me and all those whose life my life touches so that we may enjoy this New Year you have given us. Deliver me always in your son's holy, precious name I pray. Amen."

Al thanked God for everything. He had prayed for as long as it took to eradicate the feelings of anger, wrath, disappointment and resentment from his countenance. He had sought comfort in the one who had delivered him from the darkness that threatened to consume him a few minutes ago. He didn't mean to go there, especially not after such a wonderful evening. He prayed until a sense of calm and completeness had filled his mind as well as his soul.

Sometimes, being alone did more harm than good. But he had learned to utilize the quiet time to rescue his soul. There was no special time for prayer and there was no special place. As he concluded his prayer, he asked for the physical, emotional and physiological strength necessary to face all that the New Year had in store. If this evening's dinner was any indicator, he was going to have a wonderful and blessed year. His soul began rejoicing as he took his bath.

Jasmine was happy that Al had called. She knew he had arrived home safely and he really had a good time with her and her friends. Though he wasn't looking for anyone to love, she sensed that he was more getting out of a relationship than trying to get into one. The little talk they'd had previously made that clear. Nevertheless, she was happy that he made it home safely. The two games he had given to her were going to be used often. She could play alone and learn to make the kinds of moves she saw him make without physically counting the stops for the chips. "That's called knowing the game board for yourself as well as your opponent," Al had told them. With practice, she would develop the skills necessary to play well. That was her pledge as she drifted off to sleep. Her world was finally back in order and she was determined to keep it that way. ✿

❀ ❀ Chapter Thirty Four ❀ ❀

With the celebration one week away, everyone was excited and couldn't wait to receive their bonuses. Crystal was hoping to use hers to pay down on her wedding or their new home. She was excited and undecided. Serving on the committee also gave her the opportunity to observe some of the skills and strategies that were covered in their training. Despite the fact that they were planning meetings, they were conducted with the same principles and decorum as their team meetings.

As she shared her observations with Jaleen she sounded even more committed to excelling in her current position, thus enabling her to be promoted once the opportunity presented itself. She knew she had learned a lot and being paired with Jaleen had certainly helped her along immensely. She was beginning to take some of her work home, striving to submit more accurate and precise quotes that embodied all the components of a good sales agent. She was trying to do what she had seen Jaleen doing. She noted that Jaleen never mentioned that she took work home. She never lamented over the amount of time she put in after hours to ensure that the level and quality of work was as expected.

Crystal wanted to move up. The planning meetings had established that desire within her. The committee had members from all levels and she was truly happy that she had been chosen to represent their team. She had also taken the time to review the manuals they had received during their training sessions, and she even copied specific sections that she was implementing with greater consistency. Key phrases that were copied could be seen posted around her work station. They were reminders of the goals and attributes she wanted to adopt as part of her own professional practices.

Some days she wondered if her drive was from becoming pregnant or from the success that was reported a few weeks ago. Whatever it was, she was glad to have it. She was glad to have this new attitude. She felt valued as a team member and was doing her best to ensure that her team continued to generate the level and quality of work that was expected. Their goal setting and review meetings were also a plus. Because no one was excluded, all members of their respective teams got an opportunity to listen, learn, ask questions, and understand their role as it came to the goal that was decided on for the team. Everyone was respected and regarded as having value and worth to the team and the company.

During her lunch break, Jaleen decided to step out for a while. She felt like she was going to explode and she knew it had nothing to do with the work. She needed some fresh air and an opportunity to calm her nerves. They were beginning to affect her ability to focus and she had to settle them down. As she looked across the street, she was reminded of the items for Selecia. That, she decided, was the distraction she needed. She knew her mind and heart were set on Aaron and her nerves were not giving up. The knots she was feeling in her stomach were now proving to be a distraction at work. Working with numbers, she did not want to endanger her performance evaluation so early in the year.

As she began to exit the parking lot, she saw a truck with the logo that represented Aaron's place of employment. Her palms instantly moistened. What if Aaron was the driver? What if? . . . It was someone else. Jaleen breathed a sigh of relief and let her windows down a crack. She needed the cool breeze to sooth her rattled nerves. "This is ridiculous!" she exclaimed aloud to herself. Pulling into a parking space next to the store, Spaces, she turned off the engine and took a few minutes to gather herself.

"This was harder than breaking up with Clay." She concluded. "At least I knew it was over because I ended it. I didn't want to ever see him again. Now, look at me, all nervous if I think I'm going to run into Aaron. What's wrong with me?" she asked. "You're in love with him," her mind answered, "and you don't want to confront him and get that issue off the table. That's what's wrong with you." With a weak smile, she agreed. The area in her chest thudded in agreement as well.

Stepping out of the car, she grabbed her purse and walked briskly to the store. She was going to look around and see what else she could get for Selecia and Brad's store. This should do it for a few minutes, at least, she thought. As she entered and began browsing in earnest, she felt a sense of calm and focus. She just hoped it would last long enough to get her through the rest of the day when she returned to work.

There were a few Ficus trees she thought would add to the store front window. They were not too tall and they could be used to provide extra trimmings as the holidays rolled around. There were other cut outs that could be painted and used from time to time to change the look of the window as she changed the clothes she had planned to display. As she made her notes on a receipt she found in her purse, she decided to purchase a small writing tablet she could keep in her purse for moments like these. That purchase helped to reconnect her to something less stressful and more productive.

The ideas, once they began flowing, became an endless listing of materials that could be used to dress up the window of the new store. Fall could be represented with leaves that were available in three different shades and strung like garlands. They could be hung from the Ficus plants and made to appear like they were falling from the plant. Red, white and blue streamers could be used to celebrate famous American holidays like the fourth of July and Memorial Day. She even made a note of some turkeys and similar decorations used to announce the Thanksgiving holidays and of course, Christmas trimmings were included without saying. Jaleen's eyes helped her mind to refocus on things she had some control over. She found some hats in varying sizes and colors, beach balls in primary colors and assorted sizes and a few sand pails. These, she thought, could represent summer. She found curtain rods, also of varying sizes and decided that one could be placed across the store front, signaling the change of window decorations and giving a slight peek into the unveiling of something new. Some prints celebrated summer, while others could be used to generate specific holidays and themes. Flowery curtains were indicative of spring, and curtains with fruits and vegetables could be used to reinforce the Thanksgiving ideals of sharing from one's bounty. Those with leaves and soft panels depicting gardening, winter and other picturesque ideas could simply add color and background to the clothes that would be feature for the month. Walking around Spaces, Jaleen felt the excitement about the store return.

With her list in hand, though, she made a bee line towards the exit. She had been there longer than she expected. Feeling pleased with the ideas she had for the store window, she returned to work and decided to allow that to occupy her mind whenever it strayed to Aaron. She really needed a distraction and this would have to do. At least until she had built up the courage to approach him and get this situation resolved. She would write to Selecia and share some of her thoughts and wait for her responses before she proceeded. But she had something to occupy her mind, whenever it roamed towards Aaron and not on her work.

Jasmine was in the middle of an interview with a client when the delivery came. She was not expecting it and was caught completely off guard. As she wrapped up the interview with the directions for the new client's job interview, she ripped into the envelope. She couldn't wait to find out who had sent the arrangement of fruits. It was Al. The card stated, *"Thanks for a wonderful evening. Best regards, Al"* Jasmine was really surprised. She was also pleased that he felt moved to do something like this.

Meredith was on her frame about the new admirer. Jasmine debated sharing the details with her and then she finally caved in. She gave her the annotated version. She left out her hospital visit and the fact that when she took her to pick up her car it was at his complex. She told Meredith he was among the friends who had been invited to an impromptu dinner and about the games he had brought and how much she and her friends had enjoyed them. "Maybe there's something more than you anticipated," Meredith said smiling.

"He's not looking for someone to share his life with. He's coming out of a relationship," she repeated. She didn't want Meredith going in circles and taking her there too. She was content to have Al as one of her friends. As they sat chatting, they were interrupted by the new guy. Jasmine returned to her duties and Meredith went to see about his needs. She wasn't about to butt in with him again. That was certain. If he addressed a question to her directly then she would respond. Otherwise she was cool. Friendships are best when people come together under their own terms. She was trying to be polite and he was simply maintaining a safe distance from her and everyone else. No harm done. Perhaps when he got to know everyone and felt comfortable around them, he would better understand what was behind her initial invitation to lunch. For now, he was free to his space and she would continue to enjoy hers.

By the end of the day, Jasmine was ready to give Al a call. She was appreciative of his gesture of thanks. But, his phone call was sufficient. Still, he sent her something to show how much the evening had meant to him. When she got home, she dialed his number. It rang more than seven times. He wasn't home. No one answered her call. Opening the cellophane wrapping, she took out an apple and bit into it. "Sweet," she thought, "just like Al."

Turning on the television, she settled down and tried listening to the evening news. From time to time she reflected on the fruit basket and the note. She hoped that her friend Amber was blessed with someone to be as nice to her, no matter what line of work she had chosen. When Aaron stopped by, she decided she would illicit his help in finding Amber this week. She just needed to know that she was okay. She wasn't going to mention what she had heard. She would allow Amber to share that with her, if she felt comfortable enough to do so.

"Life is so strange," she thought somberly. When she felt that her friend Amber needed a friend, she ended up with a new one instead: Al. "What a mixed up world this is. It's not what we want but what is needed that is provided. Here I am thinking that Amber needs help; she needs a friend. When, in fact, Amber may be just fine. Perhaps she really didn't need a friend or sister after all," she reflected thoughtfully, just a good friend to understand and not judge. "I may be the one in need of a good friend. One to help me become better grounded and settled in my thoughts and future actions." No sooner was the thought released when Jasmine sat up alert and feeling like she'd just had an epiphany. Maybe Al was the person who needed to be rescued, not Amber. Al may be the one in need of a friend. ✿

❀❀ *Chapter Thirty Five* ❀❀

With the session with his eager beavers wrapped up for the day, Al cleared away the materials, took a swim and decided to leave early to get a head start on his evening class. Many were returning students working on a degree. Some were simply upgrading their skills in hopes of being promoted. Since they had been in his class before, they knew his routines and it made it easier for them to move forward at a more rapid pace.

Because he detested the classes where you read and came in to discuss the chapter and have the new readings assigned, he tried to keep his class as active as possible. They discussed, demonstrated, examined real life situations and worked in small groups to present information on some of the situations covered in class. He also interspersed his sessions with guest speakers, videos and off site visits which gave his students an opportunity to see, up close and personal, some of the city's finest facilities and those in need of upgrades. This aspect of the class helped some of them, those who had not yet entered the world of work in their fields, an opportunity to become familiar with the kinds of working environments they will be looking at when they complete their degrees.

It also made for some of the more interesting and vibrant discussions in terms of what can be done, given the limitation of funds to those facilities, to improve them and make them the kind of places children and families, in general, would patronize. These discussions also made projects possible as they were encouraged to redesign the facilities and present their designs, for a grade, to the city planners.

Al's hope was that if this type of activity caught on then many of those facilities in need of additional funds to renovate or spruce them up would move up on the list of priorities that get funded each year. While the arts are not exactly fully patronized with public funds, its funding base could always use a boost. Awareness, on the part of city planners and other local officials, can boost the level of support and funds needed to allow these facilities to thrive, long after the children are grown and have families of their own to utilize them.

Tonight, the first class would be reporting on their first visit. This documentary was a first for him and his students and he was excited about it. They were given two weeks to photograph some of the parks, playgrounds and public sports facilities to determine if there was potential for expansion of the services currently offered. If the possibility for expansion existed, they were to indicate what it would be and how it could be implemented. His students totaled twenty four altogether and they were grouped in teams of six. Armed with their written instructions, listing of materials and equipment that could be used, listing of facilities to be included in the study and criterion for evaluating their final product, his students were on their own.

Each team would receive fifteen minutes to present and entertain questions from their peers. Using the criterion, Al would listen, ask questions if necessary, assess and record the grade for the assignment. He would make available to them the final grade for the project individually and collectively and afford them time to discuss any concerns with him after class. His students generally liked the way he operated his class and they seldom questioned his assessment of their work. Everyone knew what was expected because he always provided the grading criterion being used to assess their performance. Tonight, would be no different.

As he entered the building, he felt the buzz that usually meant they were there and ready to go. Oftentimes, when presentations were being made, they switched to the theater building. This gave the presenters the feeling of being on center stage. It also afforded them the opportunity to utilize the technology to showcase their work and gave them a sense of what their future work may entail.

He just liked being there ahead of them to provide any last minute assistance and to ensure there were no glitches with the scheduled use of the room. From the buzz, he could tell that everything was as expected. They were early and getting themselves situated to begin when called upon to do so.

From the first to the last presentation, Al felt proud of his students. He could see that they had put their all into the assignment. The quality of the photos, the interviews that some of them included in the presentations, the slide shows all helped the students support their positions as they identified specifics that could be done to improve the existing structures as well as the activities being offered. It was a terrific feeling to watch them as they worked together, assisted each other with holding up some of the poster sized photos they had enlarged to ensure full viewing by everyone.

Al was especially pleased that it wasn't a competition. Life had enough of those, he reasoned and he didn't want that particular atmosphere in his classroom. By virtue of the work they would become involved in, that's where the competition should remain—in the sporting facilities among the teams or individual competitors. He wanted his students to be able to see beyond their immediate desires to operate or provide programs at these facilities, be it public or private. He wanted them to be able to see beyond themselves so that they remember to focus on the children and adults who would be patronizing the events and facilities on a regular basis.

The Y was a good example. It was a publicly funded facility. It also relied on the generosity of benefactors who had enjoyed what it did for them as kids growing up. The facility was in good condition. It had been expanded over the years and he was blessed to have an opportunity to work there. But, he also knew that without the appropriate level of funds, the building's physical plant would become dilapidated and the level of support and use from parents and other members of the community would decline. That's why he was working on his latest pet project, the swim-a-thon. He wanted to keep the facility always in the forefront of the community's mind and that of the city planners' so they would continue to appropriate funds to support renovations as well as added programs that benefit children and adults of the community. Too many facilities needed help and not enough financial support was being generated to help them all.

By providing these students with opportunities such as this, he hoped he was also making a difference in this area, as well. Going into the field took some of the glossiness out of their eyes early. It also prepared them to face the real hurdles. Insufficient funding, revamping of programs to entice greater support and participation among community members and leaders, internal networks that liked things the way they were and therefore, were unable to see that they were not a part of the solution but the problem. These were edifices of the real world and he wanted others coming into the field to be a part of the solution. He wanted his students to hit the ground running, not with ideals but with realistic approaches to solving the problems many of the public facilities were facing, which impacted participation and the facilities' very existence.

Aaron came home mentally and physically exhausted. He wanted to simply get in, take a shower and get in bed. As he finished parking, he noted that Jaleen's lights were not on. "Probably working late, as usual, what's new?" he said disconsolately. Walking up the steps, he decided to give Jasmine a shout and make sure she was alright. Then he would go home.

Knocking on her door, he waited for her to answer him. When the door opened, she invited him in but he refused, citing the need for a bath before he could be anyone's company. He asked her how she was and after she indicated she was okay. He left. He knew she thought he was coming back. But he wasn't. He wanted to be alone. His wounds needed to be licked and he was the only person who could do a decent enough job of that, it seemed.

After locking the door, Aaron turned on the lights and decided to listen to some music. He had his favorite gospel CD out and in no time The Brooklyn Tabernacle Choir was ministering to his blistered soul. As he took his bath, he allowed the musical medleys to relieve him of the tension he was feeling. "God must really be in a mess of pain," he thought. "If loving Jaleen is hurting me this much, what is God feeling for us when we fail to live up to his standards every day?" Al wondered. "His pain is truly greater," he conceded. "He loves the world. I'm just trying to love one woman in His world."

As the winter season rolled on, he would eventually be outdoors less. The moisture in the ground would allow the plants to survive. The pruning would happen with less frequency until the first signs of spring or the call for service. He was dreading being indoors. He enjoyed the solitude of the plants. This was his toughest season. Less was required. The plants and foliages grew slowly and the pruning was reduced significantly. The fallen or broken branches and twigs were taken care of by the maintenance section of the various parks and gardens. So he would be enclosed pretty much until spring.

The only blessing he saw in that was that he had no chances of running into Jaleen. Being indoors during the hardest part of the winter season, meant he worked mostly in the greenhouse. The nurturing and monitoring that occurred there was wonderful, for those plants. But the outdoors was his thing. As he finished his bath, he paused briefly to view himself in the mirror.

It was time to begin working out and working off the holiday pounds. Though they were not noticeable, he didn't want to wait until they were. Working indoors usually left him feeling like he didn't work at all. So the gym became his place after working hours, at least for a few months, anyway. This allowed him to feel lighter on his feet and he needed that right now. Aside from the emotional tension he was experiencing, his feet simply felt heavier during winter. The work outs would do him some good, physically, if not emotionally.

Feeling refreshed, he decided to spend some time with Jasmine. He had promised to help her find her friend. In a while, that promise will be at least a week or two old and if nothing else, he was a man of his word. He allowed the choir to finish their refrain on the 'Days of Elijah' then he turned off his set and left his apartment for his neighbor's two doors down. How he wished it was the one right next door. ●

❀❀ Chapter Thirty Six ❀❀

Jasmine shared the contents of her fruit basket with Aaron and the phone call she had engaged that evening with Al. Listening intently, he sensed that there was a point to this and she was about to get to it shortly. Concluding with the phone call this evening that wasn't answered and her thoughts about how they came to be acquainted, her point was made. Her epiphany appeared to have some merit and even if he didn't agree totally, there seemed to be some credence to the way things have played out. Their meeting, hers and Al's, had a purpose.

"Well," he began, "this sounds like fate. You were thrown in his path for a reason. He has become entwined in yours for a reason, too. What we don't know is why?" he concluded. "Sounds like you are off to a good start as friends. How do you feel about him, personally?" Aaron asked. "I don't know." Jasmine replied. She appeared to be turning over his words in her mind, searching, searching. After a brief pause and deep sigh, she continued. "He's polite. He's courteous but cautious and he seems appreciative of the simpler things in life."

"He's indicated that he's coming through the throes of a divorce and that he's not interested in a relationship right now, which I can understand," she added promptly. "There's but so much your heart and soul can endure and it appears that the break up was not on his accord, though it seems he initiated the divorce proceedings. So, there's some pain there, I'm sure. Other than that, he seems like a really nice guy," she said.

"What does he do for a living?" Al probed. He was trying to get a fix or read on Al; not that he wanted anything to be wrong with him. He, too, believed him to be a nice, decent fellow. He was just trying to see if there was anything sticking out that they were not seeing that could help put a finger on him, one way or another. Jasmine wasn't sure exactly where he worked. She knew it involved children and adults and that he taught. He didn't seem like the professor type, but he could be, she presumed.

Again, she searched her mind for details about Al. They had spent a wonderful evening talking and laughing and sharing minor details about their lives. She felt comfortable and safe around him. He did not give her any qualms about her safety or her sanity, for that matter. She seldom invited strangers to her home, especially male strangers. But she knew that Aaron was just a few doors down if she ever needed him and so far in their four years living close to each other, she never did.

She trusted her instincts and she used common sense in her decisions about men and the kind of information she revealed about herself. She seldom told where she worked, though she must have to Al because he sent her the fruit basket. She never gave out her telephone number unless she felt safe with the knowledge she had of the person and their ability to respect each other fully. She hadn't survived this long on her own by being silly and throwing caution to the wind.

But, they both agreed there was something about their coming together, she and Al, which does call for some thought as it related to their newly formed friendship. They agreed to monitor the situation in the event they have a stalker on their hands. Though Aaron pointed out, her information was blatantly available at the hospital. It was on her chart at the foot of her bed. He also reminded her that if Al had meant her any harm, he had the opportunity to drag her into his apartment, tie her up and do away with her little by little and no one would have been the wiser since she had neglected to communicate her intentions to him or Jaleen.

Jasmine apologized and promised, once again, not to do anything like that again. "You're right," she admitted. "That's how people turn up missing and end up dead. No one knows where to look because the clues were missing. That won't happen again," she told him. "I promise." Seizing the moment, she returned their conversation to the topic that was uppermost in her heart: Amber.

"When are we going to try to find her?" she asked in earnest. She was no longer as worried as when she had first gotten the news. Still, she felt a need to assuage her conscience and make certain that her line sister was doing okay. "You've already visited where she used to live. Is there anyone who can give you some information as to her current address? We know who lives at the old one." They both laughed and this lightened up the mood and the atmosphere a bit.

"All I have is her telephone number. Do you suppose that she's listed? I never thought of that until now." Jasmine got up and went in search of the phone directory. The metro area one was her first pick. "If she's into something she'd rather not be known for, why would she keep her number listed?" Aaron retorted. "Seems to me she would go unpublished since that's the way her clients would be able to remain anonymous. Her number being published would establish a loose end for them if they wrote her number down and forgot to destroy it. Let's try looking under the professional escort services listings and see if the number you have matches any of the numbers. If nothing else, we could call all of them and ask to speak with her. I could pretend to be someone who misplaced her number but needed to get in touch her."

Though she didn't like having to call and ask for Amber, Jasmine had to admit it was the best back up plan they had since the number could be unpublished. Looking through the metro and outlying counties' listings, she and Aaron struck out.

They decided to try writing down the listing of escort services before calling them. That way they would be able to strike off numbers called that provided no leads. The listing was incredible. Neither of them had any idea that there were so many services operating in their area let alone the nearby counties. Jasmine began to feel apprehensive about what they were doing. Maybe her friend didn't want to be found. This was simply outrageous, she thought to herself.

"Aaron," she said quietly, "I don't want to do this. I'm beginning to feel overwhelmed. Can we continue with this maybe tomorrow?" Sensing fear and concern mingled into one, Aaron stopped writing, collected the directories and placed them on the floor beside her wall unit. He immediately opened the sliding door, remembering what Jaleen had shared with him about Jasmine's trip home from the hospital. He got her something cold to drink, turned up the TV and proceeded to get her mind on something else. He checked to see if she had eaten and if she wanted them to order take out. She declined and got up and made them something to eat. She had shopped for their get-together and she wasn't about to encourage any extra spending on her behalf.

"Thanks," Jasmine said, "for understanding. I know I asked you to assist me and I am glad you're willing to help," she stated, "but right now, everything seems so ominous and gloomy. First, she's not listed. Though her number rings and rings whenever I dial it. Her answering machine comes on and I refuse to leave a message. The one time I did leave a message, she never responded and I don't want to force her to change the numbers just to avoid me. I only hope and continue to pray that she's alright. That's what matters most," she said matter-of-factly.

Clearing his throat, Aaron agreed with her and allowed that topic to be dropped. He challenged her to a game of backgammon and when they finished their sandwiches, they settled in for a best of three games series. He wanted to make sure her mood was shifted and that her attention was on something new and different. Though, he wasn't so sure about the different part. They were able to play the game because of Al. She met Al because she was looking for Amber.

Nevertheless, they played three spirited games that lasted longer than two hours. The first game was a refresher for both of them. Several times they looked at the rules to ensure that they were playing the game accordingly. Jasmine was able to place Aaron on the board several times. The risks she took paid off and she was able to win the first game hands down.

Aaron attributed that win to the fact the he was preoccupied with the actuality that she may have really had an epiphany. The collision of her world with Al's coincided with her inability to get in touch with Amber. He prayed silently that she really was alright and that whatever she did, she was kept safe. The second and third games were wins he garnered because he became more focused and took a few risks himself. Both wins were tough and he was only able to pull out the final win when he rolled a pair of doubles twice. Her spirits had been lifted and when she lost, she challenged Aaron to another round of the best of three. He obliged her and they were more in tuned with the game than they had anticipated in such a short space of time. The first game was Jasmine's once again. She played extremely risky when he was playing very cautious. The second game was Aaron's. The third and final game was a nail biter. Each time they placed each other on the board, they were able to get down and put the other up. It came down to the final roll for each of them. Jasmine rolled a pair of doubles and that ended her game. The evening ended in a draw.

By this time, Aaron was really ready for bed. As he hugged her goodnight, he had decided to really get him a game so he could practice. It was one thing that had the capacity to engross your mind as you worked your side of the board and your opponents. He found himself doing it a lot. Whenever it was Jasmine's turn, he anticipated what she might roll and when she did roll her dies he looked to see which moves would be more to her advantage. He was certain she was doing the same when it was his turn.

As he walked by Jaleen's apartment, he noted her lights were on. He was glad to know she was finally home. He assumed she was also working. What else was new? ✾

❀❀ *Chapter Thirty Seven* ❀❀

Jasmine appreciated the time Aaron had spent with her. Tomorrow or maybe this weekend, they could begin calling the numbers. She was unable to process any more details that would leave her mind racing down a path which contributed to her experiencing an anxiety attack. Amber was a dear, dear friend. Somehow, she was getting the feeling that perhaps Amber really didn't want to be contacted or located. She had left her a message and she hoped she would give her a call.

She decided to call Al once more. This time he answered and she felt a thrill that was indescribable course through her body. He really answered and she has happy to hear his voice. "Hello," was stated just as casually. "Goodnight," she responded brightly. With the sound of her voice, Al felt his world turn upside down. "I just want to say thanks for the fruit basket. But you didn't have to do that." She said smiling into the phone. "I appreciate knowing you had a good time and that was enough. But, thanks again. The contents have been devoured considerably during the past few hours and they're delicious," she concluded.

Al smiled and responded, "You are very much welcomed. I really enjoyed myself and appreciated you thinking of inviting me to join you and your friends for dinner. I know you didn't have to and I, too, am glad that you did. I had no plans for the evening and it was spent in a rather relaxing atmosphere. So, thanks again, for including me."

Because he didn't sound chafed by her comments, she decided to press further. I called earlier and you were out. Hope you don't mind my calling you back at this hour. I wanted you to know I'd received them and that I'd also began putting them to good use." "Not at all, he responded. In fact, he was glad to hear from her. He had an excellent evening with the students and he decided to share it with her.

They spoke for at least an hour and she was more focused on every word he had shared. He did work at the community college in the evenings and was an assistant director in charge of athletic events at the Y which was about thirty to forty minutes from where she lived. It was, however, closer to where he lived. He shared his plans for the swim-a-thon and invited her to make plans to attend. Once everything was in place, he promised to let her know so she could be in attendance.

When they hung up, Jasmine felt at peace. For the first time in a long time, she felt connected to someone and it wasn't romantic. At least that was her interpretation of it. She liked hearing from him; keeping up with him. She felt a special kinship to him. Perhaps because of the experience they had shared or simply because they were both single and enjoying their own paths in life, proceeding cautiously but proceeding nevertheless.

Al was happy to hear from her. The strangeness of it all was that he was hoping to hear from her. The energy and excitement both classes generated within him, made him want to share the details with someone and he wanted it to be her. The drive home was preoccupied with the presentations and how much the students were able to glean from their site visits. He was glad he had given the opportunity to do that project this early in the term. This way, they were better prepared to showcase their solutions for the final grade. It took away the uncertainty some had previously expressed when they had to design solutions and present them to the planning board and other city officials.

He had used his professional name, to get the officials involved. He had also asked that they keep his professional name from any conversations with the students. He enjoyed the anonymity among them. It made it easier to teach and get the course descriptions fulfilled without a lot of fanfare and questions about his past as an athlete. The fact that he worked for the Y also made it possible for him to garner the cooperation of some of the more lucrative benefactors whom he simply introduced as judges and not persons of interest who supported the local sports facilities in their respective counties or districts.

The students' zeal and excitement as they shared what they had discovered made his evening classes worthwhile. To have someone to share it with was a beautiful ending to a most wonderful and productive day. He couldn't have asked for anyone better. With those words, he realized that he really liked Jasmine. Her free spirit was much like his own. However, he threw up a yellow flag of caution. He did not want to become involved with anyone, at least not right now.

He was not up for the woes and throes of a relationship and he was going to steer clear from any entanglements of this nature if he saw it coming. Right now, they're just friends and he liked that. He liked that very much.

As he reflected on his spur of the moment invitation to the swim-a-thon, he chuckled to himself. "You were just rattling off at the mouth there, Kamal. Slow it down before you become the hunted. You know you cannot afford to be caged again." The smile remained on his face until he had eaten, showered and went to bed. He had a friend. And he knew she was the caring kind of person because of how they met. He, too, had a friend in Jasmine.

Jaleen had been greeted with a letter from Selecia. She was happy to hear from her. It meant she had received the samples she had mailed earlier. She had also made some selections and was hoping that the cost would not be great or place any kind of financial strain on her. Smiling, she sat down to respond to Selecia. She had a little sister and she was happy to hear from her.

In her response, she told her about the list of things she had made after visiting some stores. She had outlined her ideas so that Selecia would be able to conceptualize them and see if they could work for her store front window. She also reminded her that the tissue paper and boxes and shopping bags should be there before or by the end of February. They were ordered and were being made as they 'spoke'.

She tried to allay her fears concerning the cost. She was also thinking of asking her sister, Claudia, to join her with some of the items anyway. They were family and that's what families did. They helped out. When they were not preoccupied with work, that is, she reminded herself.

She inquired about her favorite niece and told her she had seen some shoes she wanted to get for her but she needed to know her size. She would purchase them a little bigger than her foot so she would be able to grow into them and have them for a while. Jaleen closed down her letter by telling Selecia to expect a surprise package. She had visited the sewing store and there were some handy little items she felt Selecia and Grandmother would enjoy using as they worked to build up the inventory for the store.

When she had sealed her letter, she dropped it in her purse near the door and called her sister. She had brought home some invoices to review and other correspondence to compose. But tonight, she decided, was family night. She would call Claudia then Maurice and last would be Brad. This way, everyone would be in the circle for the New Year. "Everyone except Aaron," her heart reminded her.

Choosing to ignore that dig, she called her sister. They spoke for almost an hour. She found out that Claudia suspected that she might be pregnant. The excitement of that news really picked her spirits up even higher. "Another niece or perhaps a nephew," she responded excitedly. "Wow, what did mom say," she asked. Claudia hadn't mentioned it to anyone else yet. Not even Will. She was waiting for the month to end before going to the doctor for a confirmation of her suspicions.

Jaleen told her about meeting Selecia. Since none of them had been able to attend the wedding, they had not met their sister-in-law. She told Claudia about their niece and that she was a peach. Her mother did an excellent job taking care of her and she also talked about her little outfits. "Her mom is very talented," she stated excitedly. They talked about the store and how it came about. Claudia was surprised to learn about it. "Neither Brad nor Grandfather hadn't mentioned it in their letters," she said. "Perhaps because it was a surprise and it wasn't unveiled until Christmas," she informed her. "Grandmother, her mother and aunts will be busy making pieces to help her build up her inventory for the store's opening," Jaleen continued. "That's not happening before Brad's graduation, is it?" Claudia asked. "No. It's going to happen the first Monday in June. Brad would be home and he would be able to help out until he gets himself a job," Jaleen confirmed.

"I've already ordered the tissue paper, the gift bags and boxes and I even have some labels with the name of the store being imprinted on them," she added happily. "What's the name of the store?" Claudia asked. "Are you ready for this?" Jaleen responded gaily. "Guess! I'll give you three guesses," she said. Thinking aloud, Claudia said, "Tots Town?" "No," replied Jaleen, giggling. "What about Selecia's Children's Creations?" Claudia suggested after a long pause. "Guess again," Jaleen responded giggling louder. "I don't have a clue. Tell me," Claudia said.

Jaleen baited her sister for one more guess. When she couldn't think of any more names, Jaleen finally said, "Handle-Cole Children's Clothing." Claudia repeated it. "Handle-Cole Children's Clothing." Then she repeated it again. "Sounds good," she said finally, after tossing it about out aloud. "Well, let me know how I can help," Claudia said. "Sounds like there's something coming into the family that could last for a long, long time," she surmised happily.

"This is a very large undertaking. Are they able to handle this financially?" Claudia continued. "Well, everyone there is helping out by contributing to the inventory. Her mother and aunts sew professionally, too and Selecia had a little savings from the work she did while she was pregnant. Her mother and her aunts have provided the sewing machines and the store. We just need to keep her supplied with fabric and other accessories so that the store opens with a sufficient quantity to last at least two to three months. She is talented, Claudia." "Alaine's little outfits can attest to that," Jaleen reminded her. "They had the store bought look and quality. But they were made by Selecia. She even accessorized her clothes with matching hats and bibs. A few outfits have a little purse to match that she tote over her little shoulders." As they talked about the store, Claudia reminded Jaleen that perhaps she would have to be the first customer if her suspicions were confirmed.

Promising to keep that news quiet, they affirmed their love for each other and hung up. Jaleen loved that about speaking with Claudia. She never ended their conversation without telling her she loved her. Now she had shared a special secret with her. She might be pregnant. That was a first for them. They never shared secrets, not that she could recall. But she was happy for Claudia. Another member might be joining the Cole family. "Alaine, you may have your playmate sooner than your dad thought," she whispered smiling again.

With a smile in her heart, she called Maurice. They spoke for about thirty to forty minutes and he was seeing someone. She was happy to hear it. They met around Thanksgiving and they attended a New Year's Eve party together. He was going slow and still checking things out, he said with a hearty laugh. She was really glad to hear *that*. She wished she could tell him about Claudia but since she promised she would have to keep that tidbit to herself. She also wanted to share about Aaron but knew it would be wrong to do so. There was nothing going on in her personal life that she could share. After speaking with Maurice, she called Brad. His roommate indicated that he was at work and that he would let him know she called. She really wanted to speak with him. ✸

❀❀ *Chapter Thirty Eight* ❀❀

The news from Claudia and the letter from Selecia were the highlights of her evening. One day she would be able to share something as fantastic as Claudia's or Maurice's news, she promised. One day she would be able to have them feel the joy and excitement for her that she was feeling for them now. Everything just takes time and faith and prayers she acknowledged.

With her declaration of family night, she recognized that she had an estranged relationship with her parents. She called them to wish them happy birthday and things like that but she didn't practice calling them to share news about her day or her feelings. But since this was family night, she decided to include them in her calls.

First call went to her mother. It was brief and there was nothing special there. She had a friend in her life and Jaleen and Brad were the only two who hadn't met him. It's not that she resented him or anything. She just wasn't interested or excited about meeting him. Period. That call lasted less than ten minutes and she was glad when it ended. There wasn't much to share and she didn't want her mother thinking that anything she said needed to be shared with her friend. His feedback wasn't something she wanted either.

When she called her dad, it was pretty much the same thing. Out of duty, she called and expressed her best wishes for a good year and that was it. He, too, had someone in his life and she hadn't met her and didn't plan on doing that either. When her parents broke up they really broke her heart. She simply felt connected because of birth issues but that was it. "Next time," she declared, "I will call them first so that my family night ended on a high note and not on a low one."

Because it was still early, she decided to put in an hour on the invoices. They were the first order of business the company needed to ensure profit or loss. After an hour, she had made a few corrections and had begun working on composing the letters and memos that needed her manager's signature.

Jaleen always felt independent. She remembered applying to the business college after high school and enrolling herself. She remembered working in the evenings to ensure payment of her tuition and related fees. When she finished, she had invited Brad to her little commencement ceremony. The two of them went to dinner at a nearby restaurant and celebrated her accomplishment. She had waited until the last minute to invite the others because she really didn't want to see them. Now, she wished she had at least invited her sister and brother earlier. They would have been able to make arrangements to be there to support her.

"When you are in pain," she reflected, "you make decisions that reflect it." Her parents were no longer together, she was not especially close to her older siblings and she was most comfortable with Brad. It was her commencement ceremony that got him interested in college. So, if nothing else good came of her decision, it was that. Now he was in his final year and she knew, with God's help, she was going to be in attendance. College opened doors that otherwise appeared closed.

She was glad that she had gone to college. This was her second job since her commencement exercises and she enjoyed what she did. The numbers and the sales end of the job were intriguing and she enjoyed communicating with the customers; even the ones who were not sure whether they would be able to afford what they were viewing. She had a knack for making them feel at ease and then working out payment schedules that allowed them to make the purchases they really wanted. Of course the items were delivered when payment was rendered in full, but affordability was the angle she used when working with her customers.

When she was promoted from the sales representative position to an administrative assistant, she felt she had been moved away from the action. But now, she realized that she still had the ability to work with the clients who were the big spenders. Her role required her to monitor their accounts and satisfy their needs. The company had moved to an on-line virtual catalog and based on the rooms created, selections were made without coming into the store.

This was a new way of operating and it required someone with knowledge of the merchandise and its cost to be able to keep up with the customer care as well as supply and demand side that the virtual world was beginning to actualize. Now she was working more closely with the team leader who was leaving for another assignment. Many things were being consolidated and she had to make sure all of his accounts were up to date before he left. This way, his replacement would be able to begin with a portfolio of clients and their history of purchases, the team members who handled which aspects of the sale and the level of reciprocity that occurred within each account.

She wanted the turn over to be a smooth one and she and her team had begun the task of putting that portfolio together. The announcements about bonuses were still in the air but added to it was the names of the new replacements. With the celebration dinner just about a week away, everything had to be in order. So tonight, she was going to complete both tasks so that they could present it to Dave Taylor, their outgoing team leader and manager.

With one last review of the documents, she placed them in their folders, and situated them in her attaché case and turned off the lights. She had no idea that Aaron had just passed by, lingering outside her door. It was almost eleven o'clock. She was emotionally charged from her telephone conversations with her sister and brother but mentally exhausted from her work and ready for bed.

The upcoming dinner celebration was shaping up to be something worthy of their accomplishments, despite the challenges and changes they had encountered the past year and would be experiencing again this year. She needed to focus on what she was going to wear. Last minute decisions never sat well with her and she could see one was coming with regards to what she was going to wear. She decided that when she got up in the morning, she would make a note of it and place it in her bag. During her lunch break she would look for something before it got any later. Sleepily, Jaleen drifted off to sleep.

As before, her mind was on Aaron. She hoped she would develop the courage to call him and explain that she had jumped the gun and didn't give him a chance to fully explain what he was saying. With the passing of each day, she was made more and more aware of her shortcoming. Now, she was also hoping for a way to correct the wrong she had actually created.

She was very much aware of him as she entered and exited her apartment. If she saw a truck like the one he used at work, he became uppermost on her mind and if she looked out onto the porch and allowed her mind to run free, she was able to see them embraced as she shared her painful experience with him and she was also able to remember the kiss they had shared. Again, she wondered, when it had happened. When did she really fall in love with him? Brad was right. There was someone out there for her and she really needed to give herself the opportunity to meet that person and get to know him. Hiding wasn't the solution if she wanted to meet someone special.

This time, she wasn't hiding. She wasn't looking for someone to love either and what happened? Her next door neighbor had her heart and didn't know it. Maybe he really liked her. Maybe he wanted to get to know her too; maybe he was . . . Jaleen drifted off to sleep. ❀

❀ ❀ *Chapter Thirty Nine* ❀ ❀

Once again, Jasmine felt a sense of urgency with regards to contacting Amber. She wanted to get it over with and sometimes she wanted to avoid it. But she knew one thing: she wanted her friend to be okay and she needed to know this in order to move on. With what she and Aaron had begun, she decided that she had to see it through. She wasn't about to go on any wild goose chases alone, but, she was ready to begin the chase.

One must end so that another could begin. Her friendship with Al was a beginning and her relationship with Amber was coming to an end. Somehow she felt that it was the course of events that was unfolding in front of her. Either way, she wanted some closure to Amber's situation and she couldn't get it with inactivity.

When she finished working that afternoon, she decided to leave a message inviting Amber to a get-together at her place. If she responded, it would be an opportunity for them to talk and for her to meet with her and bring this saga to an end, emotionally, anyway. Without an address, she was unable to track her down and have a heart to heart and so she had to risk what she feared would happen: the changing of her phone number.

Aaron's visit was expected. She told him what she had decided; that she would like a little get-together so that everyone could meet Amber and she would be able to learn how her friend was doing. He liked the idea and gave her his full support. He even suggested they get together the following Sunday afternoon. That way, it would give them an opportunity to come together, have a relaxed afternoon together and meet Amber at the same time. If it appeared that they needed some time alone, he and Jaleen could leave early enough for that to happen. Jasmine decided to include Al. Had it not been for Amber they really would not have met.

With a date in place, Jasmine put her plan into motion. She called and left a detailed message inviting Amber to her place. With Aaron making noise in the background about playing Uno or Backgammon, it really sounded like a casual invitation and not an inquisition in the making. She decided to call Al later and invite him as well. She enjoyed talking to him but wanted to do so without Aaron distracting her.

They settled for a fiercely competitive game of Backgammon and spent the evening trashing and ribbing each other with every play. When she asked him to invite Jaleen, she noticed his hesitation and then she plunged in head first. "Look, when are you going to make the first move? Are you waiting for someone else to step in and then you get bumped to the curve because you were afraid to step up?" Jasmine teased. "Use the opportunity to invite her and also begin something you know you want to explore. If it works out that's great. Terrific! But if it doesn't it wouldn't be because you didn't try."

Aaron listened to her and remained silent on the matter. He heard what she had said as a friend, but he knew he was knee deep in something with Jaleen and wasn't ready to let Jasmine in as yet. For the moment, he decided that the game was more than enough for him to concentrate on. Then he ribbed her about her own relationships and they moved on, keeping the atmosphere light and lively between them but fiercely competitive. Jasmine knew he never talked about that topic. His silence confirmed her suspicions and she allowed him to have the time to make his own move. She had shared what was on her mind with regards to that relationship. Aaron knew that Jasmine meant him no harm. They played until Aaron had beaten her two out of three matches twice.

With an early evening to himself, Al debated calling his folks or calling Jasmine. He felt up to some company. Tonight he didn't want to be alone. Jasmine's friendship had reopened a new world to him. Spending time with her and her friends gave him another opportunity to view the world without jaded eyes. Some friendships were as they seemed. He was glad he had taken the time to do a little scouting of his own. It also helped him to feel comfortable with what she had told him. Her neighbors were her friends. They looked out for each other. It wasn't a sexual relationship but a friendship based on mutual respect and genuine caring. It was something his heart, mind and soul needed to get him beyond the shadows of darkness and doubt, despair and depression.

Now that it was within his grasp, he didn't want to seem intrusive of their newly formed friendships but he didn't feel like being alone either. He hoped they were taking some time to play the games, especially Backgammon. It was a wonderful game that gave you a chance to think for yourself and your opponent. Only when the final move was made are you certain of your opponent's decision and its impact on your next move. He really liked the game. From the way they played the other evening, he was certain Jasmine's friends enjoyed it too.

Restlessly, he turned on the television and decided to listen to the evening news. As they moved from one incident to the next, Al compared their news reels to the occurrence in life. Various scenes are played out each day in the lives of everyone. It's just not a part of the morning or evening news for the viewing audience. But it occurs. Someone's heart had been lifted up with the right words right now while someone else's heart was crushed, much like his. Neither occurrences made the evening news but they happened in someone's life today.

A child experienced a devastating defeat today at the hands of a classmate or supposed friend. It could be at the hands of an adult as well. That's news for that person. Nothing else being broadcasted has any impact on the level of pain and disappointment being experienced now by those individuals who have been made to feel hurt, sad, dejected, happy or defeated. But only the receiver and the giver know about it. The rest of the world was not aware because it didn't make the morning or evening news for all to see or hear.

With his mental reverie over, Al began to focus on the classes he had coming up. His eager beavers were where he would like most of them to be. The pressure was still on for the intermediate group and he was working on putting that together. The swim-a-thon was also shaping up. He had invited some of his students to help referee and monitor the day's events. This, he felt would give them the up close and personal experience they needed to prepare them for their roles as sports directors or facility managers.

He made a few notes on his pad that was near him whenever he planned for both activities. He knew it not only kept him straight but it also helped him to iron out those smaller details that were sometimes lost when the big picture remained the focus. As he finalized some of those minor details and contacts that would be utilized to work them out, he decided to call Jasmine.

VaNessa's betrayal didn't spell betrayal in all things. Because she didn't want to be committed to him and him alone wasn't a problem. Cutting off his relationships with everyone else wasn't going to change or make her any better for him or anyone else. It only allowed him to crawl into a place that he would much rather avoid.

Speaking with Jasmine didn't mean they were involved. It just meant he had a life line that could be instrumental in keeping him grounded, feeling worthy and appreciated as a human being. He had a long road ahead of him and he knew it was not going to get any tougher. He had a friend in Jesus to accompany him all along the way. When the heart is wounded, it is the most difficult organ to heal. It is expected to work as though nothing has happened to it; much like a car involved in car accident. It is expected to operate though it just got rear ended by another vehicle. The car is in terrible condition but the owner is expected to get to work on time and perform as though nothing terrible has happened. The heart endures much and is expected to perform as though nothing has happened either.

Isolation is the first order of business. It is also the worst when it comes to the heart. It becomes hardened and unwilling to give each part of it a chance to heal, work and receive the care and love that it was meant to absorb. Well, Al decided, not me. I will not be a part of that. After putting away his notes, he turned down the volume on the television and gave Jasmine a call. ✸

❀❀ *Chapter Forty* ❀❀

After seven days of emotional dodge ball, Aaron decided to call Jaleen. He wanted to iron out this misunderstanding. The silence between them was something he was unwilling to endure any longer. He really wasn't sure what had led to their great misunderstanding. If she felt he was trying to play her, well that wasn't so. The kiss was a genuine expression of his love for her and he wanted her to know that. Not speaking to each other was not getting him or her any clarity on the matter. He really wasn't looking forward to passing her like they were just mere acquaintances. That's not how he felt about her at all. He wanted to share his life with her and it wasn't going to happen if they were unable to communicate. He listened to the phone ringing in his ear. He knew she was at home and probably working.

When Jaleen finally answered Aaron asked if he could come over for a few minutes. After a moment's hesitation, she indicated that he could. Aaron was at her door within seconds. He didn't remember if he had even hung up the phone. He waited for a while before actually knocking on the door. He inhaled deeply in order to allow the cold air to calm him down as he prepared to enter his lioness' den. "Tonight," he reconciled to himself, "was all or nothing at all." He was putting all of the cards on the table; all of his marbles were going into the ring. This was going to be it. Either they were going to get on board with this relationship thing or they would straighten out the misunderstanding and continue with their lopsided, platonic relationship.

Knocking softly, Jaleen opened the door. Entering her apartment, Aaron greeted her with a kiss that was equal to the first one he had given her before. Without so much as a second thought, Jaleen accepted it and kissed him back in return. Hugging her tightly against his chest, he closed the door with his foot and proceeded to kiss her again. His heart was beating faster than a lion's who was about to spring his trap and capture his first meal of the day. A few minutes later, much later they stood looking at each other before walking hand in hand to her couch. Though she was unsure of its true implications, she was willing to go with the flow at this point. If his actions were as just demonstrated, then she had someone who was interested in her, too. With that assumption and the memory of what had just happened, Jaleen tried hard to breathe normally. Her heart was beating so fast she was almost certain that Aaron could hear it. There was no reason to kiss her like that if he was not emotionally involved or willing to become emotionally involved with her, too.

Sitting on the couch, Aaron sat facing her. He missed being able to see her without the tension and negative energy that had passed between them. He missed being able to look at her, feeling excited, knowing he was secretly in love with her. He wanted to disperse the anxious and uncertain feelings that now surrounded him every time he thought of her lately. He had loved her from a distance. He wanted to love her, straight up and out in the open.

He had decided to take it from the top and explain to her what he was trying to convey that fateful evening when things seemed to go all wrong. He wanted the air between them to be fresh and free of irritants. He wanted his life to be free of complications and uncertainties. He wanted to be able to relax and enjoy her presence, her company, her friendship. He wanted to be able to communicate with her and know that they are on speaking terms, focused on the same thing: building a lifelong relationship together. He wanted the complete package: fiancé, marriage, wife, kids, home and the whole nine yards. After organizing his thoughts as best he could, under the circumstances, he exhaled deeply and began.

"J, I am not sorry I kissed you," he said. "But," placing his index finger across her lips ensuring her silence and that she heard him out this time, he continued, "if it offended you or made you feel uncomfortable, I apologize for that. I want to be more than your friend, Jaleen. I want to get to know you and I want you to get to know me. I want to be that special person in your life. I want to share my life with you and I know that I'm moving kind of fast right now, when you would probably like me to go a little slower, and I will," he smiled uneasily. "But I just want you to know that I love you and I care about you and I want to share my life with you.

I want to be a part of your days and your nights. I want to be there when you are experiencing your ups and your downs. I want to be the one to listen when you need to talk. I want to be the one to comfort you and help make things right. I want to make you laugh and enjoy the sound of your laughter as we share and build memories together. I want to marry you and share in the joys of raising a family together. I want you, as the mother of my children to be their comfort as well as their confidant. I want them to reflect your grace, your steadfastness, persistence and willingness to help, to share, to love. I want my life to be complete with you as the center of my world, my life, my existence. I've been admiring you secretly for a little more than a year now and I'd like you to give me a chance to make you happy; to be the smile you wear just because you love me. I want to wear that same smile when you grace me with your presence. I just love you, Jaleen and I hope you can love me, too," he said from the depths of his heart and soul.

As she stared into the eyes of the man who had just boldly, profoundly confessed his love for her and whom she knew she loved, slowly, ever so slowly, warm tears sprang into her eyes and ran down her face. She felt her nerves trying their best to erect the fences around her heart. But she also felt her heart fighting back. It knew the names of the picket fence gang: scares, fears, misgivings, the worries—they were all beginning to quietly walk away. She wanted to have someone special in her life. She wanted someone she could love and she wanted it to be someone thoughtful, hard working, honest, respectful and kind. She wanted someone who cared about the little things in her life as well as those things that seemed insurmountable. She wanted someone who was willing to be faithful to her. Her heart was willing to accept him and give him a chance to love her, unconditionally. Her nerves were still a bit timid but convinced he was the one. Her head remembered her brother's words and she was determined to proceed with caution. But proceed she would. With her nerves unable to intervene with an escape plan, she could not retreat and allow the picket fence and wall of silence to be her defense against this man who had just professed his love for her.

Looking at Aaron, she wasn't sure where to begin. She wanted to apologize to him for misunderstanding what he was trying to tell her. Her nerves wanted to play it differently; they wanted her to blow off the incident from that ill-fated night. But her heart encouraged her to do what's right. "Apologize! Clear the air! Start anew. This is the time to get it right," her heart coaxed her. "Let's get it right! You can do this. We can do this."

After finally calming her nerves and getting them in check, Jaleen took a deep breath and holding his hands she began, "I've enjoyed the times we've shared alone together." Speaking softly she continued, "I've thought about that kiss a lot, too. I'm not sure where this is leading but I am willing to give us a try," she concluded. "I am willing to try. I think I've fallen in love with you, Aaron," Jaleen admitted. "I'm not quite sure when it happened and I am sorry I didn't take the time to listen and understand fully what you were trying to say. I thought you were apologizing for kissing me because you knew you didn't mean it; you didn't mean for it to happen. I thought you were backing out and I couldn't take that. I wasn't ready to be rejected not after you kissed me like that. I'm . . . I'm sorry, I didn't listen; I didn't stop to think . . . I . . ." Slowly, Aaron wiped away her tears. His heart was soaring. She was in love with him! Then he lowered his head to hers and they kissed again.

He was so happy to hear her admit what she felt for him. She felt for him something that was more than simple friendship. He was even happier to hear her admit it. She cared about him. Holding her closer to him, he hugged her as though he was never going to let her go or let her out of his sight. Sitting quietly together, he slowly rubbed her shoulders and arms as they held each other tight.

Enveloped in the silence, lost in the words they had both expressed, they sat reflecting and rejoicing in the knowledge that they had finally found each other and in doing so, they had both discovered love. As the tail lights and head light reflected in the sliding glass door, Aaron and Jaleen looked out into the darkness and at their reflections in the glass. Then, they kissed each other again, this time as an acknowledgment of what they had both discovered: their true feelings for each other. Resting her head against his chest, Jaleen listened, assured by the beating of his heart. His heart was happily beating with love for her. Had he listened to hers he would've heard the same: her heart beating happily in the knowledge of his love for her. She wasn't sure how long it would last but she was going to work hard with him to make this relationship work. She hoped it was what her grandparents had. She hoped it would be like what her brother and Selecia had. But for now, she was happy. She was going to face the challenges and surprises ahead, with Aaron by her side. There was finally someone to love and that special someone loved her, too. ❀❀❀

ABOUT THE AUTHOR

D'Sarah Daniel lives in the U.S. Virgin Islands where she was born and raised. She is looking forward to retiring and spending more time writing, promoting her work and enjoying the company of her three grandchildren. A romantic at heart, D'Sarah enjoys a good novel with an ending that is often not mirrored in many of the relationships today. Married to her high school sweetheart, who has also been her source of inspiration and strength, they have raised one child who has blessed them with three beautiful grandchildren and a wonderful in law. She believes that good story endings make reading more enjoyable. While challenges are a part of life and await us all, D'Sarah writes about relationships with love, support and lots of it, to overcome every situation, challenge or crisis faced. These situations give meaning to life and also strengthen one's resolve to be better than was believed possible. Her stories focus on characters that must come to terms with the force and impact of love, trust and commitment. Therefore, as long as we live, there will be challenges and how we address them will ultimately determine our own destiny; our happiness. D'Sarah believes that with love as your compass, your destination will always be forever.

Other Books by D'Sarah Daniel include

- Summer: Season for Storms and Love
- Family: Another Word for Love
- Handle Cole: Moving Forward

Feel free to share your thoughts with D'Sarah at her website:
dsarahdaniel@hotmail.com

Coming Soon!

Jaleen, With Love
Handle-Cole: Embracing the Future